FIDDLER'S DOOM

FIDDLER'S DOOM

by

ALLAN FRASER

AUTHOR OF
'HERD OF THE HILLS,' 'HANSEL CRAIG,' 'SHEEP FARMING'

W. & R. CHAMBERS, LTD.
38 SOHO SQUARE, LONDON, W.1; AND EDINBURGH

First published . . *September 1939*

Printed in Great Britain by T. and A. CONSTABLE LTD.
at the University Press, Edinburgh

INTRODUCTION

SOMETIMES on a winter's night a parade of ghosts comes stealing through the Druid's glen—or so folks say.

First a cry—nothing but a cry in winter's darkness. It starts as a whisper from the slit in the rocks at the head of the glen, comes down through the glen, a wind out of nowhere stirring the tops of the trees new-planted there. It grows louder like the stag's roar echoing in the hill passes. It sweeps on through the glen to the arms of the sea.

There is silence when the cry has gone. Then, beating up over the strip of turf by the river's edge—the muffled thunder of galloping horses. Starting faintly at the mouth of the glen, it grows stronger where the glen narrows, then dies away far up at the feet of the high mountains. Hundreds have heard the galloping horses, but none have seen them—or so folks say.

Again there is silence when the galloping horses are gone. Then comes the sound of strange old bagpipes playing a strange old tune—a strange old tune the like of which is never heard played to-day—this strange old tune and the shuffling of many thousands of brogued feet on heather and grass. Some say there is a whispering, too, of many tongues talking in Gaelic—but in a dialect that none have ever heard. The piping, the shuffling feet, the whispering pass on, and there is silence in Glendruid, until . . .

The wailing of women and the crying of children, the crackle of flames, the lamentations of the homeless are heard in the glen, and something like the Devil leaps out of the darkness, sneers 'Progress,' and is gone. And there is silence in Glendruid, until . . .

The sound of fiddling comes from the ruins of a cottage in the glen and a light, lit by no hand, shines from its paneless window. And all the wild things come silently from beneath the growing trees, turning their soft noses and mild eyes towards the ruin where the fiddle plays. They are listening to the ghostly playing of old Alicky Mag—the shepherd who talked Latin in his cups and made more music than money.—Or so folks say!

And this is his story.

PART I

MAKING

I

THE woman sat before the fire thinking of the boy she hoped would be with her when spring came. When the lambs were born on the hillside, when the snows were melting in the corries, sending liquid laughter singing down the valleys, when the birds came sailing back over Ben Cruachan from the Western seas, sailing with stilled wings over the peaks of Ben Cruachan, when hazels and willows by the Druid's stream grew golden, then in the spring-time her boy would be with her. It could not prove to be a girl, or there was nothing in prayer.

She would call the boy Sandy after the finest man the world had ever seen. She would rear him up to fear God and to be gentle with all helpless things. She would have him with her on the summer days, when the quiet waters trickled round the feet of the big stones in the river-bed, when the glen was all flowers and the singing of birds, when the *gobhlan-gaoithe*, the bird that oars the breeze with its forked tail, gathered sand in its beak at the river's edge to build its nest against the byre wall. She would

have her son, her first-born, and she would call
him Sandy after his father, after the finest man
that ever lived between the Western Isles and the
Eastern Sea.

Janet Fraser the woman was called, and she
had come first to the West country as a maid
from the Aird of Inverness, where the fields
smile and all the people are kindly, and the
Gaelic is the best in all Scotland. The Gaelic
was the tongue of her home and of her people;
the English she had learnt from the Bible and
Josephus, and she spoke the English that Milton
wrote. She had the auburn hair and the green
eyes and the delicate thin skin you find among
women in the Aird of Inverness, and she was just
twenty years old and married one year. Married
to Sandy Macdonald who had come as a boy
from the island of Islay, an island which grows
good stock and fine men, to the herdings of
Argyllshire, a namely county for hill sheep. He
was a boy when he left Islay and no more than
a boy when he met Janet Fraser, and the blue of
the sky grew a finer blue and the clouds in the
sky seemed to laugh as they ran because he
loved her so. He had been married one year,
and the old women who lived at the bottom of
the glen said that ill luck would surely come to
Sandy Macdonald because he allowed the happiness in his soul to shine out of his eyes.

And the snow began to fall. Janet heard the

wind—the cold, cold wind that had blown all day—die down. Surely there would never be snow falling so early in the year, four weeks and more before Christmas! Yet the cold wind had suddenly died down as though a great hand had stretched out over the hills, bidding the wind be still. There was a great silence as though all the living things in the world had paused in whatever they were doing—to listen. There was silence —and waiting in Glendruid; silence and waiting.

Janet pushed back her chair, and the scraping of the chair's legs across the stone-flagged floor seemed an irreverence to the still world. She threw a fresh peat on the hearth and the fine white ashes flew up in the air and came floating ever so slowly down, like *loineagan*, the little white fleeces, the finest of little white fleeces that were falling outside, down from a cold sky. She noticed how early darkness was closing in on that day of late November, how the room was in shadow when her eyes left the glow of the fire. She lit the lamp on the kitchen table, and when its flickering stilled to a warm glow, she saw all the familiar things come back to life— the table and chairs, the black sheepskin rugs before the fire, the white plates arrayed in rows above the dresser, the silver tea-pot given her as a wedding present, the grandfather-clock half-sleeping in the corner by the door. As the flame of the lamp gathered strength and the light in the room increased, so much darker grew the view of the hills through the small window.

Janet crossed to the window, pressing her face against the cold pane, wiping away the moisture of her breath from it so that she could see. The white flakes fell in endless monotony. When she looked upwards they seemed to be grey specks regretfully leaving the grey clouds. As the flakes fell they gathered speed and whiteness. Through the lace curtain of drifting snow-flakes she could see the dimmed outline of the byre's gable, the blackness of the stacked peats, the hay-rick like a collapsed giantess tramping off to market, the speckled brown and white of the high hills opposite shutting in the glen. Even as she looked the hills opposite became less speckled, the giantess tramping to market drew a white mutch over her head. Janet left the window to pile peats on the fire. Sandy would be cold and wet when he came home, she thought. He had been out on the hills since mid-day arranging the bridal of sheep in unseasonable weather. He would be cold and wet when he came home. And the grandfather-clock, half-sleeping in the corner, chimed out the hour. Before the hour struck, the mechanism of the clock ground harshly to a climax behind the polished wood. When the hour had struck, it grumbled back to rest, and its loud tick continued—time passing —time passing, and Sandy not home.

It was late for him to be out, Janet thought. The year was wearing on to the shortest day. It grows dark by five o'clock in an open plain in a Scottish November. In Glendruid, in November, shadows fell deep by four, and that in clear weather. But when the grey clouds came creeping down the hillsides, throwing long fingers of mist into the depths of the glen, or when the heavy grey snow-clouds sank to rest on the brows of the mountain, then a stranger, hurrying to friendly shelter through the unhealed scar in the hills they called Glendruid in ancient times, might lose his way in the dusk at three o'clock of a late November afternoon. Losing his way he might wander from the path that was sometimes a sheep-track and sometimes a shingle bed left by spate waters, until he found the peat quaking under his feet and felt the down-sucking pull of death on the heels of his hill-boots. There, where the moss might quiver beneath the weight of a bolting hare, a man missing his way could sink from sight, and only the hoodie crows flapping like crêpe rags across the valley, would know his grave. There, where turf grew slippery towards the river's edge, a man in the gathering darkness might stumble and fall, and the Druid river, that coiled like a snake through the cleft in the hills, would carry its freight of death down to where white gulls moaned above sea tangle at Lochend. And the man's dogs, lifting strained throats upwards towards the moon, would howl like wolves in their fear and in their sorrow.

Janet sat down before the fire again. It would be the bairn that was coming that made her anxious and afraid, thinking of all the terrible things that never happened to one's own. No, it was only other women's men that might die before the first year of their marriage was gone. Such sorrow would never come to her. It could not, but if not, why did the darkness deepen, the snow still fall, the grandfather-clock tick the hours away and Sandy not home?

Sandy was a strong man and a young man in all the pride of his strength and of his youth. Sandy knew the hills and the ways of the hills as few men knew them. He could leave the house in the morning and be over the tops of the hills to the Western sea by afternoon. He had done that once soon after they were married and had brought her back shells, in which, when she held them close to her ear, she could hear the laughter of the sea-waves for herself. Sandy thought nothing of wild weather; nothing of the winds that met a man at the high march fences with giant blows, nothing of the blinding mist that sped downwards with the secrecy of twilight and the speed of deer. He thought nothing of the cold that froze and the snow that stifled. Sandy was so strong, so brave. There was nothing could come over Sandy. But if not, why did the darkness grow and the snow persist, and the grandfather-clock continue ticking?

Janet grew afraid. She tried to still her fears, telling herself that the snow would pass, that Sandy would soon be home, that spring would bring the sunshine and her boy to her. But if anything had come to Sandy, were he lying hurt or sick on an out-by heft, had he lost his way in the stupefying snow, what could she do? She was alone in the glen save for the half-dozen of *cailleachs* that still lived in the half-ruined clachan at its mouth, the old *cailleachs* who could only mumble with toothless jaws tied together with the strings of their white mutches and who could do nothing. All the youth of the valley had drifted away. It was said that on a dark night in the glen one might hear the laughter of unborn children seeking for their homes. But the youth of the valley had drifted or withered away. Only the *cailleachs* were left, and what were *they* fit for save the talking of old times, old women living on tea and memories until death should claim them. Why think of death when she and Sandy were both young? It was the old people that died. Then why was Sandy so late from home on a night of snow?

Janet bent down to draw on her shoes. She would go out, just a little way up the glen, calling to Sandy in case he were hurt. She felt a fluttering within her as though young birds turned round to settle warmly in their nest. She thought that she must not give way to her fears, her panic, or harm might come to the little one within her and he be born afraid. Sandy would never be proud as she wished him to be proud, were his son craven. She must be brave.

She pulled a shawl over her auburn hair, holding the ends of the shawl together on her breast with her hand that was thin and worn with work. She unsnecked the door and paused on the threshold to steel her shrinking body to face the cold. She looked upwards where the last of the evening's light glowed faintly yellow through thick grey clouds, and between her and the grey sky the air lived with flakes of falling snow. Everything was so still—no motion, no sound. Even the river Druid, that coiled its way like a living snake through the sunless depths of the valley, roaring dully in autumn spate, whispering to the alders and the willows on a summer's afternoon, even the Druid had fallen asleep under the soft snow.

Janet walked a little way up the glen, the fallen snow pulling her feet back so that she kept slipping. She tried to look ahead but the wet flakes falling on her eyelashes blinded her. She shouted twice, 'Sandy! Sandy!', but her voice sounded strange to her, like that of a lost soul calling out over a dead world. She looked back to make quite sure that she did not lose her way and she could still see the light of the fire and lamp shining through the window of the house. She thought that she would go farther up the glen and call again. Perhaps Sandy's dogs would hear her call and bark in answer. She walked farther on, and when she looked back now she could not see the reassuring light of lamp and fire. The last glow of sunlight in the grey sky had faded too. Soon it would be altogether dark, and Sandy not home yet. She ran up the glen in haste, calling out his name in desperation, but no answer came.

Then somewhere out of the darkness ahead, away up at the glen head where it narrowed to a black slit in the black rock, there sounded a cry such as Janet had never heard. It grew louder, coming towards her out of the darkness, a crying as of one who had seen all the misery and knew all the sorrow of the world since its beginning, and before it came the wind, with the sough of a breeze in the branches of trees, and behind the wind, the voice crying and coming towards her.

Janet knew not and cared not where she fled. She cared not supposing the black river lay in her path, or the bog which shook beneath the weight of a harried hare. All that was in her mind was escape from the crying of the world's sorrows coming down upon her behind the wind. And why should the wind have the sough of its passing through the branches of trees when no trees were in Glendruid? And why should all the sorrow of the world come crying through Glendruid? Why should the wind and the crying come down the glen, as the *cailleachs* had told her that some day that winter they would surely come, when she had left the cottage and was out alone in the darkness and the snow. She ran on, crying 'Sandy! Sandy!', forgetting he was lost and late, seeking the comfort of his strength in her fear. She ran on until the snow tugged the shoes from her feet and cut the skin so that they bled. She ran on and on until she fell. She bit the shawl between her teeth in an agony of fear when the wind and the crying passed over her head. Then she lay still, wondering dully whether the child had died within her. She lay still for a long time until she felt arms about her—the arms of the strongest, bravest man in all the world.

II

AT first the doctor couldn't understand it at all.

He had ridden from Lochend that April
morning, taking the longer road by the sea-loch
because the day was fine, his mare fresh, and
because a woman having her first-born was
seldom in a hurry. He had found much pleasure
in his riding that morning, and for two good
reasons additional to the comfort of fine weather
and an easy mount. He was pleased with the
repair Willie John Maciver, the saddler, had
made to his pommel. It was as neat a piece of
work as ever Willie John had done, and the
man could do good work given encouragement
and his own time. Willie John Maciver always
said he could easily finish a job by the week-
end, but he never said which week-end he
meant. The doctor was pleased likewise with
the sight of a ship under full sail coming up the
loch. Sail above white sail blew out in the
wind, with the blue sky behind them. That
was a rare sight, also, to greet a man on his
morning ride. For Dr. Thomas Reith, liking
most sensible things in life, found pleasure in
sound harness and good ships.

He liked his work, too, if it lay among the right sort of people. He liked the glen folks, the men and their wives, provided they had enough English to say whether the pain they complained of lay in their head or in their toes. When he first left his medical school of Marischal College in the Broad Street of Aberdeen to practise his art or profession (or the queer combination of sorcery and sham he sometimes thought it) among the hills by the Western sea, he had found the competition of the Gaelic-speaking Dr. Macinlay difficult to combat. But now he himself knew some Gaelic and all but his oldest patients knew some English. Moreover, Dr. Macinlay had never recovered the reputation he lost when he packed his howdie bag and left a cottar's house before the second of twins had arrived. Indeed, Glendruid, towards which Dr. Thomas Reith was riding on that early May morning, had once been a monopoly of Dr. Macinlay. Now it was all Reith practice, but the way folks had been leaving it lately there would soon be no one to practise on, once the last of the *cailleachs* had passed to her rest. Of course, the sheep would always be there, for the four-year-old blackface wethers were namely at Falkirk tryst, and where there were sheep there must always be a shepherd with his wife and weans. And there would never be a finer couple than Sandy Macdonald of Islay and his bonnie wife Janet from the Aird of Inverness, to herd the sheep in Glendruid and to rear a family there—good luck to them both.

Thinking of the Macdonalds made the doctor press his unspurred heels against his mare's flanks, loosen rein and lean farther forwards in the saddle. The good beast broke into an easy canter towards the glen road and the cluster of thatched cottages the road ran through. At the sound of horses' hoofs the old women hirpled out to their cottage doors to make sure it was the doctor right enough; that Sandy Macdonald had found him sober and at home, and that, maybe, in passing through, the doctor would give a word of advice without asking a fee for it. An awfully hard man Dr. Reith was in that way, lifting a kebbuck of cheese or a setting of eggs if he couldn't get cash! They watched him come up the road from the lochside, a squat black figure on his brown mare, a tall black hat stuck on the back of his head, his red face like a moon above his white stock, his nose stuck well forwards, as though to prove his contention that he could diagnose all the youthful ailments, mumps, measles, chicken-pox, whooping-cough, body and head vermin, by his sense of smell and that alone. Grey side-whiskers came well down over his cheek-bones. Otherwise his face was bare and clean, save for the gashes on his chin where he had cut himself shaving, and for a bunch of grey bristles sprouting out of his left nostril. As he passed through the clachan he sort of girned at the *cailleachs*, pursing out thick lips at them while they mumbled beneath their white mutches blessing him in Gaelic. He gave them no word of greeting or advice, but he marked down in his mind, the only note-book he ever kept, that Bella Campbell had the jaundice and old Grannie Macpherson a tumour, and that both would require his last ministrations before the year was out. Then he rode out of the clachan into Glendruid itself.

A lonely, bleak, desolate place it was, with the high hills on either side of it shutting out the sun from the South, the West, and North, with the black, coiling Druid river on the right-hand side of the track he rode. It was almost a year since Dr. Reith had visited Glendruid. He wondered at the daft stories the *cailleachs* told of what happened in the night-time there, of the unearthly cry, and the sound of horses galloping in the darkness, and of the pipes and the shuffling feet and the muttered Gaelic, and all the other imaginative nonsense the Highlanders made out of the noise of river water and the wind in ravines. Now, in the plain country of Buchan where Thomas Reith had been reared to broad manhood and a face wind-reddened, in Buchan a noise in the night was a noise in the night, nothing more than that. Of course, if

Buchan men had nerves, which praise God they hadn't, they might rave of bogles and kelpies in the rain outside when it was only the orra loon chucking up stanes at the kitchen-deemie's window or a horse rubbing its itchy back against the low branch of a creaking tree. Still, Buchan was a plain open country, good arable land most of it, where ghosts were reserved for fisher folk living in hidden hamlets at the feet of cliffs. 'Perhaps,' thought Dr. Thomas Reith, 'if men have cliffs or mountains ready to fall on top of their heads by day or by night, such men's heads will grow soft in the end.'

A cock grouse rising from the heather in the splendour of its mating plumage and a whirr of blunt wings made the doctor's mare shy perilously close to the river. He cursed the bird in honest Doric, and at some distance it sat on a boulder shaped like a patella bone and called on Dr. Thomas Reith to 'Go-back! Go-back!' 'Now, if my name was Macalpine or McSporran,' thought Dr. Reith, 'I'd take that as an ill omen and ging hame.' But, having told the bird to warm itself and the mare to mind her manners, the doctor stuck out his lips and rode on to the white-washed, heather-thatched cottage where his aid was required.

When he got there he couldn't understand what he found. The babe was born and in swaddling clothes, held by old howdie Campbell from the clachan, the tears running down the furrows of her worn cheeks, dislodging the dirt and leaving white lines. In the box-bed in the wall the babe's mother lay dead.

Dr. Reith took half an hour to get the truth out of old howdie Campbell, and even when he got the truth from her he scarcely believed her, or if he did believe he couldn't understand. For she told him this story—

Sandy Macdonald, the bonnie man, had come down the glen in the grey hours of early morning. The sweat was on him, because he had been running. He had battered at her door until she came out to him and he had told her to hurry up the glen, as his wife Janet had taken to her bed and he must away in to Lochend to fetch the doctor. He had set off at once for Lochend, running all the way. She, herself, had made the best speed she could up the glen, for her rheumatics were none the better for the bottle she had been taking as she had been told to take it, and there she had found Janet lying down but happy and brave. 'Janet wouldn't be done talking of the fine boy she was going to have shortly and how proud Sandy himself would be when he would come home to her and she would give him the babe to hold in his arms, and me saying to her—"Wheesht, lassie, wheesht, are you wanting to bring ill luck upon us all?"

'And it was easy on her, doctor, fine and easy,

poor lassie, and the babe soon born. But, eh! God save us, doctor, what a babe was in it! You'll be taking a look at it, doctor?'

Thomas Reith took the writhing bundle of clothes. He pulled the shawl down to look at this mite of a thing which had caused so fine a woman's death. In his four years of medical training and ten years of practice, he had never seen a child like this. He hoped he would never see such another.

It was under-sized, a mere rat of a thing, which made it all the more strange that its mother should have died in the bearing of it. A miserable, stunted boy-child, with a yellow skin and the tired face of an old, old man, no single hair on its head and a birth-mark like a fiery red claw across its back. There was life in it, a strange amount of life for such a withered babe to hold. It squirmed and cried in the doctor's arms like a sick kitten, a strange creature indeed to be the child of Sandy Macdonald and of Janet his wife!

The doctor pulled the clothes over the baby, then handed it back to howdie Campbell. He nodded towards the bed, 'Now, tell me, grannie, how this happened.'

'And it was this way, doctor. When the babe was born, she that's gone, God rest her soul, she turned herself round saying to me, "Is it a boy, grannie, is it a boy?" And I says to her, says

I, "Aye, it's a boy, my dear." And she says to me, says she, "Let me look on it, grannie; let me be seeing Sandy's fine boy!" And I says to her, says I, "Not till the doctor's here, my dear, wait you till the doctor's here. Rest yourself, my dear, rest yourself," says I, not wishing her to see what a like creature was in it.—"But let me see him, grannie, let me see him, grannie," she kept crying, until to quieten her, I shows her *this*!—Eh! doctor, I'll hear the *screat* she gave till the day of judgement. She gave the one shriek, doctor, and she goes into some kind of a fit, and before I could be doing anything to help the poor dear, she was away with it. Aye, she was gone.'

'And sma' wonder, ye daft old woman,' said Dr. Reith. 'What was the sense in showing a bairn like yon to the poor woman before her strength came back? Ye as good as killed her, ye gowk!'

'Eh, doctor, and never in my life before would a body be speaking to me like thon! I've been at many a case with Dr. Macinlay in my time and never would he be saying words like thon to me. Dr. Macinlay was always a gentleman at a case.'

'If he'd been less o' a gentleman he'd hae told you your business and your place long before this, Nurse Campbell.'—The doctor stuck out his red face at the woman, his look freezing the half-formed words on her lips. Then he crossed the room to seek a natural cause of death for Janet Macdonald. He was determined in his mind that there must be some natural cause of death, a stroke, a failure of the heart, something a medical man might put a finger or a label on. Women never died of disappointment or of fear, not, at any rate, in text-books or in Buchan.—But as he looked on the dead woman's face he thought that perhaps a woman in the Western hills might, after all, have died of fear.

As he left the bedside his face was more fierce than ever, but not so red. He said to the howdie again, 'Woman, how could ye hae been sic a gowk!'

But Grannie Campbell was pointing through the window down the glen road and muttering, 'Here he is coming, Sandy Macdonald himself; he must have been running all the way. He'll go clean daft when he hears of what's been doing while he was away. You tell him, doctor, *you* tell him—bless you for a good soul, doctor!'

And Dr. Thomas Reith prepared himself to tell. In a way he blamed himself for this tragedy. He should have stretched his mare to a gallop coming up the lochside instead of taking his time, enjoying the fresh morning and the sight of a ship in full sail coming down the water with an easy wind behind her. But in his experience women having their first-born were seldom in a hurry, and if he himself had not been in a hurry at least he had wasted no unusual amount of time. He could not gallop to every confinement, else where would his mare be at a winter's end? But now he had to break the news to Sandy Macdonald. How would the man take it?

A fine handsome man was Sandy Macdonald of Islay, broad in the shoulder, long in the thigh, with the hill-man's easy way of walking, a fine straight sculptured nose above his black beard, his eyes brown and full of expression, now blazing with laughter or passion, now heavy with despair.—Dr. Reith went slowly down the road to meet him. The shepherd was panting like a hunted deer,—

'Well, doctor, and will it be all over now?'

'Aye, Sandy, a'thing's over. There's nae mair to do. The bairn's gey wee and no bonnie yet——'

'Never heed the bairn, doctor! How's Janet?'

'Well, Sandy boy——' The doctor hung his head. Almost immediately he felt the vice grip on his left arm and heard Sandy Macdonald hissing in his ear: 'Ye needna be telling me, doctor. I know. I *know*. I heard her death-scream an hour back, coming up the road. And me telling mysel' it was only the river or the wind or a hare caught in a snare, and knowing fine that what was to be was come on us. Aye, doctor, you'll no' be believing me, but I saw it all coming on us six months back. Ye needna be telling me what like bairn is born to us, doctor. Aye, I saw it all coming on us six months back, doctor, on a night of snow, aye, a wee dried-up thing wi' a mark of fire on its back and the face of an old, old man. And me telling mysel' it was just the glen putting them daft-like ideas in my head, and when Janet would be speaking of the summer coming and of the boy, I would say to mysel', "Sandy Macdonald, put those daft-like ideas out of your head!" But all the time I knew what was coming on us, doctor. I'd seen it all coming on us, doctor.'

Dr. Thomas Reith planned a strong sedative prescription in his mind. This man would need something strong to put an end to his raving and his pretence to second-sight. There must have been some spying through the window before Sandy Macdonald could so describe his new-born child. Some of these Western people would practise any deception to lay claim to the madness they called second-sight.

'Come awa' into the hoose to rest yourself, Sandy,' the doctor said. 'I'll gie ye a drink of something that will pit you right. Come awa', Sandy! There's mony a man had to go through this afore you.'

'I couldna bear to look on it again, doctor. I couldna bear to look on the thing that's no

31

bairn of mine or of her that's gone. It's the
evil that's in this glen that wished that on us,
doctor. I must away to the hills to seek for the
bonnie bairn that was hidden away from us
when the cry passed over her that's gone on
thon night of snow. I must away.'

Now, Dr. Thomas Reith in the prime of his
life was reckoned a strong man. In the days of
his youth on his father's Buchan farm he had
followed the ploughmen to the grass park at
lousing time to throw the hammer and putt a
stone. His bones were thick and strong from
the breeding of a hardy people, sea-winds, and
the oatmeal, herring, and milk he had been
reared on. On any ordinary day and occasion
he could have mastered the supple hill strength
of Sandy Macdonald by the very weight of his
body and the indomitable strength of his will.
But on the April day that Janet Macdonald
died of her fear so far from home, her husband
had more than normal strength. He slipped like
an eel from the doctor's grip, and when Dr.
Thomas Reith recovered from a stunning blow
on the roof of the left orbit—when he had recovered from the shock and the stabbing pain
of it, he saw Sandy Macdonald, running, running, half doubled like a wounded beast, running to the glen-head and the Western hills.

The doctor watched until the shepherd's figure
was a moving dot among the heather and fern.

Then he shook his head, trying to drive pain out and reason in. He thought that ten years of sitting at bedsides must have sapped his strength. He gripped the biceps muscle of his right arm and, contracting it, felt the doughy mass writhe and quiver into knots and cords of steel. There was nothing wrong with his strength! Then how had the shepherd, well built and all though he was, escaped so easily from his grasp? Was there, then, truth in these mad stories of a glen bewitched? 'Nonsense! Daft nonsense,' thought Dr. Thomas Reith. But a whaup passed over his head crying to the hills like a wailing child. Although the day, considering the direction of the wind and the early season, was a mild one, the doctor shivered. He shivered, pretending the onset of an ague, and went in.

He said, 'Weel, weel, Howdie Campbell, the mither's deid, the faither's gane daft, and the bairn's aye wi' us. What'll we do with the babe, Nurse Campbell?'

'Where's Sandy away to, doctor?'

'To the Tir nan Og or the Banshees' Battlefield or maybe to the island of Islay to cry in his mither's lap. With the strength that's in him this day maybe he'll leap the Atlantic and land himself in America.'

'And where was it that he himself, the bonnie man, said that he would be going to, doctor?'

'*Him!* Oh, he said *this* thing here was no

bairn of his or of his poor wife's. He must have taken a keek through the window at it. He wasna pleased wi' the look of it, and small blame to him. But instead of facing his troubles and responsibilities like a man, he's shamming madness and gone chasing awa' into the hills to search for some handsome bairn he swears his wife dropped, poor woman, when she heard the whine of the wind at the back of a shower of snow.'

'And it's searching to the end of time he'll be, doctor, before he'll come on the bairn that's lost. He'll maybe come on the rainbow's feet, or the fawn's bed, or on the otter's track, but he'll never come on his bonnie, bonnie bairn that's been taken from him.'

Dr. Thomas Reith watched the old woman huddled in a chair before the fire, the babe on her wide-spread lap, her peat-coloured, lined face under her white mutch bent over the child, her lips mumbling, '*Moolie mathaitl, moolie mathaitl*, my darling, my dear one,' and making the sign of the cross beneath the shelter of her shawl, secretively, so that he would not see.

The doctor said angrily, 'Awa' wi' your Popish tricks, woman, and tell me what we're tae dae wi' this orra wee beastie that ca's itself a bairn.'

The old woman looked, timid and ashamed, half lost in remembrance of old legend yet

34

thinking shrewdly of her job. 'Indeed, doctor, and how would the likes of me be telling the likes of you what to do? We've got to think of what's right to be done, doctor. Maybe Sandy Macdonald, himself, will be back by night. Maybe no. Maybe it would be kindness to put the wee creature on thon wee green mound at the back of the house beside the wishing well. Maybe them that put it here would have pity on it and take it away. But maybe, doctor, you'd be thinking it best to take it to the poor-house. But it'll be for you to say what you would think best, doctor.'

Dr. Reith spread out his legs and thrust his red face forwards. He bent towards the child, pulling the shawl gently down from over its face. He looked at it for a moment, and the bald, wrinkled face of the miniature man seemed to smile. Dr. Reith whispered, 'Poor bairnie, poor bairnie—puir wee lambie, and is yer mither deid and yer faither awa'?'

The doctor turned to Nurse Campbell. He asked questions no longer, giving orders which she would obey. He shouted at her, 'I'll swear that man Macdonald is only shamming madness. I swear he'll be home by night. When he comes home he'll mind his own bairn or I'll break his neck till him. In the meantime I ken of a coo that's new calved in a byre at Lochend, and I'll take the brat home with me and feed it.'

35

'And if Sandy Macdonald would never be coming, doctor?'

'He'll come hame sometime.'

'Maybe, maybe no. But if he never did, doctor?'

He looked at the bairn, and laughed for the first time that morning. 'Sandy Macdonald will come hame right enough when he's tired playing at bogles and fairies. But if he doesna come hame? I'll tell ye what I'll dae, Howdie Campbell. I'll rear the brat on white fish and education, Howdie Campbell. *White fish!* And send him to Aberdeen to come out for a doctor there. I have my theory that white fish will mak' brains oot of onything. It was yellow fish my landlady gave me in the last week of my finals that kept me from Harley Street and sent me to practise in these glens. Aye, yellow fish, not usquebaugh! And *that's* what I'll do, Howdie Campbell. I'll rear up this full-time abortion on white fish and make a medical genius o' him. That will be *proof.* And that's what I'll dae—*if* Sandy Macdonald should never come hame.'

And Sandy Macdonald never *did* come home.

III

'GOT ye! Got ye! Ye can search yer Concordance frae end to end but ye'll niver find a text will win ye oot o' yon snorl!'

So said Dr. Thomas Reith as he watched the Reverend Jock McFadyean attempting to seek a way out for his black king from the host of white bishops, knights, castles, and pawns.

'You are certainly in excellent fettle to-night, Thomas. Shall we have one more?'

Now, it was the custom of Dr. Reith and Mr. McFadyean to meet each Monday night for a weekly game or rather games of chess. The battlefield was the Manse or the doctor's house on alternate Mondays. The campaigning season extended from the first day of October until the last day of April of each year, and over a series of two hundred and eighty evenings and over a thousand games neither had achieved any marked superiority. The contests were fought at a sharp pace without too much regard for the profundities of the game. As Dr. Reith expressed it, 'If a body thought too long he aye made mistakes.' Win or lose, the doctor enjoyed his contests, but on the rough night of the second Monday of April in the year 1871, five games, two to himself, one to the minister and two drawn, satisfied his zest for play. He wanted an hour's talk before the accustomed breaking-up time of twenty-five minutes past ten o'clock. He wanted to talk. Moreover, he wanted an old friend's advice. So he answered the minister.

'That'll dae fine the nicht, Jock. Pull your chair in about to the fire. Stick on a peat or twa and gie us a bleeze. I'm awa' ben for the glesses.'

Jock McFadyean thrust one heavy foot in the fire, stirring the slumbering peats to glowing life. He stooped down to throw on two peats of generous size, then stretched himself on his accustomed leather arm-chair on the left-hand side of the doctor's ingle-neuk opposite the door. He pulled out his pipe, filling it with golden Virginian flake tobacco, meanwhile watching the doctor's broad back at the entrance to the lobby cupboard, and listening to the pleasurable click of glass against glass.

McFadyean was a noted preacher and sufficiently stern in the pulpit. But seated beside the doctor's fire on a rain-splattering blowsy night of early April, he seemed a mild and contented man. Indeed, his round boyish face, made still more boyish by the fluffy black side-whiskers and the fringe of black beard confined to the oval of his chin, proclaimed a gentle soul who in very pity strove with his eloquence to conquer sin. His black and worn clericals did not disguise the bodily strength he possessed and retained without special effort. Like Thomas Reith, he had learnt the use of spade and plough before he could read. He carried the muscles formed in boyhood to his maturity. He had, too, tucked away beneath the dark encircling garments of professional reserve, a boisterous sense of fun. He had a story at the tip of his tongue which only awaited the end of the chess and the taste of Glendruigh whisky for its telling. He spoke out loudly to the doctor's back view.

'Don't overdo a good thing, Thomas. One dram gives me a sense of charity and two the wind. Steady, man, that's enough of your gug-gug-guggling.'

'The gug-gug-guggling's for masel', Jock. I've had a queer kind of a day, what wi' a dead wumman, an incompetent howdie, a daft man, and a bairn—aye, a bairn. Never heed that the noo, Jock, I'll tell ye a' aboot *thon* when Glendruigh and masel' are closer thegither. Now, prick your lugs, Jock! Gug-gug—and thon'll dae the meenister wi'oot ony guggling.'

The doctor returned from the cubby-hole of the lobby, a filled glass in each hand. The Reverend Jock McFadyean gave thanks. The doctor raised his glass.

'Here's tae us, Jock!'

'Wha's like us, Thomas?'

'Nane that shouldna be, let's hope. Noo, Jock, before we ging ony ferther, I want your advice.'

'Who's the lassie, Thomas?'

'It's no' a lassie, it's a bairn.'

'Thomas, Thomas——!'

'Na, na, Jock. You ministers are like the lawyers. You must aye think the worst o' a body. It's about a bairn that was born in the glen this day.'

'Is this a serious matter, Thomas?'

'Aye, serious enough if the faither's nae found.'

'Some evil-disposed lassie trying to compromise you, Thomas? A doctor runs that risk.'

'You're aye barking up the ae tree, Jock laddie, and it's the wrong ane. This bairn was born in holy wedlock, but the bairn's nae holy by the look o' it. It's mair like a monkey than a bairn. Thon body Darwin would gie a five-pound note for ae keek at it.'

McFadyean's face changed from pink benevolence to red anger. 'Don't mention that abomination to me again, Thomas! We might do well to borrow the red mantle of the Inquisition from the harlot of Rome with which to try and with which to condemn that man. What think you, Thomas, will overtake mankind should they ever come to believe themselves the spawn of monkeys rather than the children of God? This man Darwin will allow us no divine creation, neither one to last until the day of judgement nor a succession of creations, each more perfect than the one preceding. He will allow us no Garden of Eden, for which he would substitute a pond or ocean with nameless slugs crawling and procreating in its filthy mud. He will allow no Fall of Man by divine wrath. No! He would call it an accidental tumble from the tops of trees with natural selection of the thickest skull. I've read his book, Thomas. Dirt, slime, foul blasphemy and ignorance. Aye—and ignorance, Thomas. He listens to the puffings of pigeon fanciers and calls it evidence. He talks nonsense about cattle, how the best always leave the best. Why, I remember the best bull and the best cow in Glenbrannochie where I was myself born and bred, and the calf they left was for all the world like a crofter's mongrel stirk from the island of Lewis. Man, Thomas, this fellow Darwin brings in the Creator like an apology on the last page of the last chapter of his book. "Origin of Species" he calls his heresy. Pray God it does not prove to be the "Origin of Error." Man is all too ready to return to the beast, to grovel in the slime, without being consoled that, in therein doing, he returns to his natural home.'

Dr. Thomas Reith stood erect, his blue eyes round in surprise, his lips pursed out with the same emotion. 'Jock!' he said, 'I'll sweir that's the first time ye've preached a sermon on a Monday night. Ye'll need mair nor a gug-gug to ease your thrapple aifter thon eloquent discourse. Your gless, man, and nae refusal! I'se awa' ben tae mak' it a "gug-gug-guggler" like ma ain.'

When the peat streams of Glendruigh, after passing through a namely distillery, had begun to enter the heads of the learned professions, the Reverend Jock McFadyean insisted on telling his story. 'I've had it on my tongue all evening, Thomas, and I'll have no serious discussion before it's told. I couldn't laugh when it occurred, because it happened in Kirk yesterday evening, and I must tell it to you now, and then I can laugh as I dared not do in the House of God.—You know Peter MacBean, the Glendarroch herd? Well, he was sitting away in a back pew with his wife and bairns, and somehow the weeest wean, wee Cherlie, got loose. I saw it happen, but I was coming to the end of my sixth heading, and what could I do? Well, Cherlie began to travel underneath the pews, bobbing up here, bobbing up there. My eye, that should have been fixed on Peter MacBean, for he's always the first to be falling asleep, kept looking out for Cherlie's yellow head. When he came up beside old John Taylor, who follows every word I say with his silent lips, John looks

42

down, lifts his Bible, and "Yout!" with it on Cherlie's head. I didn't see Cherlie for a while then, although I couldn't help but seek for him. Then a commotion started in the second front pew. Mrs. MacCulloch, her that's been a widow these five years past, poor body, was sitting next to Willie John, the saddler. First I saw some kind of a commotion under Mrs. MacCulloch's skirts, like a breeze filling a black sail, and thinks I—"There's Cherlie got hanked in Mrs. Mac-Culloch's merino!" Sure enough, out popped his yellow head. Mrs. MacCulloch she looked down, saw Cherlie, and lets out a loud cry of surprise—"Good Lord deliver us!" Cherlie bolted back underneath the pews to be safe beside Peter MacBean. Meanwhile, Willie John turns to Mrs. MacCulloch and says in that dry way of his, in a half-whisper but loud enough for me to hear. He says, "Madam, this is neither the time nor the place," and I had to keep from laughing and get on to my seventh point. But I'm going to laugh now, Thomas, sin though it may be. If you'd seen the commotion of black flannel, then Cherlie's yellow head peeping out, then heard Willie John say in that dry way of his, "Madam, this is neither time nor place." You'd have laughed then, Thomas, and I'll laugh now.'

They sat back and laughed together, each in a brown leather arm-chair on either side of the peat flames, and as their big bodies shook so also did their glasses, until the pale distilled waters of Glendruigh splashed like the sea against shingle. Dr. Reith ceased laughing first. He composed himself all of a sudden lest his whisky spill. 'Have a care, Jock!' he cried. 'Fun's fun, but Glendruigh's abin price.' And the Reverend Jock McFadyean also achieved instant composure.

'Well, Thomas,' he said, 'there's my laugh out on what passed in the Kirk yestreen. Now I can look on Cherlie's yellow head come Sabbath and never blink an eye. If I hadn't had my laugh out now I might have had it then, and who would forgive a minister of the Gospel giggling like a tickled servant lass to the fine old tune of French? Now, Thomas, there's something more than your weekly bag of corpses and confinements on your mind this night. Tell me about the bairn!'

'Weel, I'll nae deny but it's been in ma heid a' day, Jock. I wis thinkin' on it when ye rummled ma queen in atween yer randy auld bishop and a couple o' pawns. Which minds me, Jock, it's past time we got haud o' a book tae tell us how the game's right played. I whiles think what we ca' chess is some kind o' a confusion atween draughts and dominoes. But niver heed that the noo. I'm tae tell ye of the bairn. An' afore I dae that I'm going to shut

44

oot thon damn draught that's whistling atween ma collar and the carbuncle that's been sitting on ma trapezius muscle for the last eight days.'

Dr. Reith, after laying down his glass very cannily on the sheepskin hearthrug, crossed over to the window to make his cosiness more secure against the night. As he had half suspected, he found that his housekeeper, old Bella Pringle, had left the upper sash unsnecked. The doctor looked out for a moment on the wild night before making all secure. A full red moon was being chased through the sky by a pack of scudding clouds, the rain and the wind raced across the road and across the garden to attack the house. The puddles shook like ill-made jellies, and the lamp at the street end swung to and fro as though an unseen gigantic hand shook it in alarm. Through the thick pane came the deadened sound of the sea lashing against the harbour pier. And Dr. Thomas Reith muttered to himself, 'Wha would pit a bairn frae his door tae stairve on sic a nicht!'

'Were you speaking to me, Thomas?'

'Aye, Jock, I was saying I'll need tae close the shutters. Nae gless window in Lochend will haud out a nicht like this'n. Man, did-ye-iver-see-or-hear-o'-sic-a-damn-awkward-contraption-o'-a-damn-ill-jinted-thing-tae-ca'-itsel'-a shutter. —Noo, Jock, aboot the bairn.' And the doctor sat down again—and between sips of distilled barley and peat water, which in moderation gladdens the hearts of all good men and in excess has broken that of many a good woman, he related to Jock McFadyean the strange events in Glendruid on that day.

When the doctor had finished his tale, McFadyean said, 'Thomas, I fear that Sandy Macdonald will never return, though we must search for him. Indeed, if you had told me sooner I'd have had on my hill-boots and been out on the Sliaghmhor to search for him ere now. But I doubt, Thomas, we'll never find him. There's too much green moss up yonder where the Sliagh draws down to the Pot to hold up a man that can't see for the tears of his sorrow that cloud his eyes.'

'I did ma best tae hold him, Jock. I thocht I had the strength in me yet to hold ony hill herd. They're supple and swack, but there's nae great weight tae the maist o' them. But it would hae ta'en twa ootsize Partick *pol*icemen tae hae kept a grip o' Sandy Macdonald this day.'

'I'm real sorry about this, Thomas. Sandy and Janet Macdonald, though no great church-goers, were grand people. Can the love between man and woman be too great, Thomas? I think it can. I think that Sandy and Janet Macdonald gave some of that adoration to each other that is only fitting when offered to God.

Oh, Thomas, Thomas, can a man imagine that in the great tribulations of life he can stand alone?'

'Maybe no, Jock, maybe no, but ye've preached me ae sermon the nicht, for which I'm muckle obleeged, but I'd gar ye mind it's Monday night. Ye were on your high "Doh" yestreen, and ye're doon tae low "Doh" the nicht, and ye've a' the ither five days tae work up the scale again through your "Re," "Me," "Fa's." Dinna think ye'll stick on high "Doh" a' week or your voice will crack, and ye'll come a maist awfu' tummle doon among the low B's like masel'! Ye'll gae doon as the Reverend Kenneth MacWhirtle aince said in ma hearin' —"Ye'll gae doon, doon, doon amang the neegers, the teegers, the Hottentots, the cannyballs, the Black Moredrates and the Caatholics." —What'll I dae wi' the bairn, Jock, noo that its mither's boxed and its faither's drooned hissel' in the peat-hags as like as not? I feel masel' kind o' responsible, Jock. I've niver lost a confinement case in the glens before, except for poor Mrs. Macgillvaray that's deid, that went five months over her time because she swore she an' Timmy, as she ca'd her man, had niver deen mair nor say "Tootie-Pootie" tae each ither until ye'd blawn yer fustle, Jock, and waved your wee bit sacramental flaggie, Jock, and said tae them baith, "Noo, there's your tuckets and aff ye go." But ae thrawn wumman lost doesna mak' a record like Dr. Macinlay's, wha should ha' been a vet—though it's nae for me tae spak' ill o' a brither practitioner. It's nae medical ethics, which means, Jock, if ye didna ken it afore, that ilka doctor's in a gless-hoose hissel', and that he's naething but a fule to start chuckin' stanes. But as I wis sayin' aboot this bairn, I feel kind o' responsible for him, Jock. Forby, it's an interestin' case. I shouldna wonder nor the bairn had a patent foramen ovale, or but the ae kidney, or its pancreas is hankit up aboot its thrapple, or maybe it's like a case I saw when I wis a student in Aiberdeen that had nae guts ava, just twa-three bit stringies a' ready for the fiddlin'. If the bairn was tae dee, which God forbid, for I feel kind o' responsible for it, if the bairn *wis* tae dee, I'd hae Professor Rust doon frae Aiberdeen wi' a wheen bottles and spirit for the p.m. But if it's like tae live, and Sandy Macdonald deid, what'll I dae wi' it, Jock?— I dinna like tae pit it tae the poor-house, and there's nae couple living going to adopt an orra thing like thon.'

'Had you not better wait a day or two, Thomas, before making a decision? Perhaps Sandy Macdonald will come back, or perhaps the poor babe will be taken. Where have you it now?'

'Upstairs in ma bedroom a' snug in a drawer o' ma kist o' drawers. Come and have a keek

48

at it, Jock, and maybe ye'll nae be sae doon on
Darwin! O' a' the orra wee creatures ye iver
saw in your born days. Come, have a keek at it,
Jock!'

Dr. Reith lit a tall candle and led the way
through the lobby and upstairs. The tread of
the two heavy men shook the old house within,
the wind drove the rain and the sea-spray against
its walls without, but the babe lay snug in its
improvised cradle.

The two men stood looking down upon it,
the candle held high above the doctor's head,
shedding down its kindly light and drops of
grease falling 'plop-plop' upon the carpet.

'God save us a',' said Thomas, 'but it's an
orra like thing right enough. Old Jessie Mundle
doon the road, she's a quey new-calved, and I've
given the bairn a sup o' the beestings tae put
life in it and a sup o' the warm milk aifter. Eh!
but it's an orra like thingie, Jock. Ye'll need
tae christen it Cherlie—aifter Darwin, no' the
Prince.'

'And are you keeping it here, Thomas?'

'What else can I dae wi' it, Jock? I canna
pit it oot on sic a like nicht!'—The doctor bent
down to straighten the shawl it lay in.—'Keep
yersel' happit, bairnie! Keep yersel' weel happit
on sic a like nicht!'

Dr. Thomas Reith and the Rev. Jock McFadyean tramped downstairs together with the air

of men bearing responsibility—a little pompous, perhaps—but filled with a sense of duty as became grown men of their day and generation. They parted in the lobby.

'A dram afore ye go, Jock. Sic a like nicht for spring!'

'No, no, Thomas, we've done well—uncommon well.'

When the doctor opened the outer door it blew back upon him, making him stagger. The rain and the sea-spray wet his face. The Rev. Jock McFadyean forced his way into the night.

The doctor shouted, 'Nae keekin' up closes tae find a job for the elders. It's ower weet the nicht.'

But the minister did not hear the jibe, for the wind drove the words with the rain and spray over the house-tops and over the hills. In his mind there rang like a silver trumpet—a favourite text:

'Whoso shall receive one such little child in my name receiveth me.'

IV

THE boy was tired and now he would go home.
All afternoon he had been down on the seashore,
squatting amid the shingle, half-way between
the pier and the ribs of a ship blown in on a
winter's night ten years before. All afternoon
he had watched the small waves follow each
other like a succession of smiles on a happy face,
to break into quiet laughter amid the shingle
and the sand.

There had been but few ships on the sea-loch
that afternoon; one white sail far, far away out
where the hills grew close and bowed to each
other across the blue ribbon at their feet; one
puffing paddle-steamer bringing two calves and
a tup, a man in a top-hat and a young woman
with a sad face to Lochend pier; a rowing boat
with the sound of the oars in its rowlocks a quiet
melody that put a boy to sleep, or would have
sent him to sleep had he not been told to be in
before six o'clock for his tea or he would get
none, but a thrashing instead.

The beach had been very quiet that afternoon,
no barking, snarling dogs on it as there some-

51

times were; no rough-voiced boys or men
shouting and throwing stones at the laggard
gulls drifting in peace on the rhythm of the
waves; none to shout after him calling him
Alicky Mag or the Daftie. Just peace and the
water lapping against the shore. Peace and the
sun sinking. Peace, and a silver pathway across
the sea. Peace, and the wings of birds caught
and made fine in the evening light. Peace, and
none to break it, but now he must go home. Old
Bella would be waiting for him, a scolding on her
withered lips, gingerbread in her crooked hand.

The boy rose from the friendly shingle and
the face of the quiet sea. He turned to meet the
streets of Lochend, the dangers of the baker's
dog that would chase him were it about that
afternoon, the butcher's boy who would shove
suet down between his hard collar and skin were
he about that afternoon, the men or the women
or the boys or the girls who would stare at him
or laugh at him, or shout Alicky Mag or Daftie
after him were any of them about that afternoon!
But if he crept home quietly, keeping in the
shelter of houses, looking round corners before
he ventured round them, he might reach home
without these dangers. He walked up over the
shingle beach, trying to make as little noise as
possible lest the baker's dog, the big black brute
with the white teeth and snarling lips, would
come barking down to the mouth of the close

leading from the beach to the High Street. If the dog should come to meet him there, Alicky did not know how he would ever win home.

There wasn't much size to the boy—there was many a child in the town of Lochend bigger at four years than he was at six. There were no looks to him either, with yellow, wrinkled skin to his face, like an old, old man's; bald as a coot under his heavy grey cap; his small blue eyes sometimes twinkling with merry mischief among friends, but so easily startled into animal fear by the new, unfriendly, or the strange; his milk teeth turning to black decay before they were shed. He was well enough dressed in the thick clumsy clothes of the time, in grey Norfolk jacket and corduroy breeches, grey stockings and heavy black boots, a starched collar and black bow tie about his wizened neck. He clutched a bunch of sea-pinks he had picked to take home to old Bella; but he dropped them half-way up the beach because he was afraid that the butcher's boy, seeing him, might laugh at him carrying flowers through the High Street of Lochend, deriding him for a lassie. He dropped the flowers and they lay scattered and forlorn among the shingle, to wither and die like poetic thoughts amid the world's hustle. He crept up over the beach, trying to control the heavy tread of his boots crunching the gravel. He never looked back at the sun and the blue sea and the quiet peace of a summer's evening, because, did he look back, even for a moment, the baker's dog might steal up behind him, and then he would have to stumble back to the water's edge again and so be late for his tea.

He reached the mouth of the close without being seen by dog or by man. Between the tall grey houses with blank, empty windows the sun died and shadows grew. Between the old grey houses on the cobbled lane were the ghostly echoes of smugglers straining their muscles against the weight of casks, of Jacobite agents whispering vain hopes to cloaked figures while the waves lapped against the sides of a sailing ship bound for France. On the cobbles between the tall walls of the houses in days long past they had found the body of a foreign, bearded sailor with his pockets filled with gold, who had struggled from his wrecked ship through a December sea to die from exhaustion in the dark close leading to the sleeping High Street of Lochend.

Of course, even when Alicky Mag was a boy stealing his way through imaginary dangers to the doctor's house—even then, the High Street of Lochend slept deeply of a summer's afternoon. The life and the pride of the place died long before, when the laws of England gave Highlanders their freedom to forget their ancestors and earn a wage. But when Alicky Mag was a boy one could still hear the Gaelic, the old tongue—the soft liquid flow of it—spoken freely between old men with the beards of patriarchs and the carriage of princes who met together to talk of the weather and the next boat's arrival.

Alicky heard the sound of men talking Gaelic in the High Street of Lochend as he made reconnaissance from the close. He peered round the corner and felt reassured. It was only old Sandy Maclean, who had been to America and returned without a fortune, conversing with Willie his brother who was said to have gathered his fare to America on twelve separate occasions and to have drunk it each time before the weeping and the wailing at the pier-head was ended, and *he* left behind while the boat sailed. Two old wizened men, nut-faced, white-bearded, dressed like gamekeepers in green knickerbocker suits, although they kept the gardens for their wives who kept summer lodgers, and that was all that the old men did, but they talked earnestly together in the language of warriors, hunters, and poets. Alicky could not understand what they said, but he knew that the old men were kindly and safe. They might not notice him pass, or if they did they would shake hands with him and ask in the English how the doctor was and were they all well at home. Kindly, quiet old men living in past memories; coming again to life when a friend was buried

55

or the ice held. Alicky slipped past them without being noticed.

The High Street seemed deserted. Away down the street he could see the green railings of the doctor's house he called his home, where he saw much of the kitchen and old Bella; a little of the study and the doctor when work was easy and Dr. Reith in good humour. The green railings seemed a long way off for a small boy to reach without dangerous adventure, but there was no one in sight and the way seemed clear. Something of the peace of the hills and sea had crept into the High Street of Lochend. Shadows from the tall houses stretched like quiet hands stroking the evening sunlight on the pavements. The breeze stealing down from the hills over meadows and corn-land that lay by the sea, brought the scent of clover and wild herbs. Black swifts flashed in and out playing hide-and-seek and follow-my-leader around the eaves. The clock on the town-hall grumbled to life and struck six strokes. A striped white and green canvas shielded buns and pastry in Inglis the baker's shop from the sun's fading heat. From a window high above Wishart the chemist's shop a woman's voice sang—

> *Hobhan, hobhan, Goiridh og O,*
> *Goiridh og O, Goiridh og O;*
> *Hobhan, hobhan, Goiridh og O,*
> *Gun d'fhalbh mo ghaol's gun d'fhag e mi.*

56

Alicky stood wide-eyed and open-mouthed in the High Street of Lochend, listening to the fine singing. The song had the rhythm and the solace of an off-shore boat lying easy to the swing of the tide in quiet waters. Alicky looked up, and the woman who had been singing, seeing him, mistook his admiration for mockery.

'Away home with you, Daftie!' she called, and Alicky ran for the shelter of the green railings up the street. Half-way there he again fell into his quiet walk, for a dog that would leave a walking boy alone would chase one running. Thus, now anxious of danger, now calmed by nature's peace, he reached home and went past the bay windows in the front of the house, along the gravel path past the meat-safe to the back door. He hesitated there a moment wondering whether he dare go in, for it was after six now. Bella would be angry at him. But she would be still more angry were she to find him hiding behind the meat-safe, frightened to go in, as she had found him before. While he was trying to make up his mind what was best for him to do, Bella came out. She said:

'Come away in, lambie, or your sowans will be cold.'

So Bella wasn't really angry after all! Her gingerbread must have risen in its centre for once that afternoon.

Old Bella had looked the same ever since

Alicky could remember, which wasn't so long, after all. She was so tall and thin that they called her 'Bella Broomstick' in the village. She had such a grey lined face, her white hair was so unkempt, she had such a huge hooked nose, that the boys in the village called her for a witch. The black shadows beneath her sunken brown eyes were marks made by the devil's thumbs, or so folks in the village said. They could say what they liked about her to her very face, for she was growing deaf as a post. But although she was deaf, she was not dumb.

'Come away in to your sowans, my lambie,' she said. 'And if you're a good wee boy and sup every drop of them I'll give you a piece of gingerbread. But if you don't sup every drop of them I'll skelp you till you're sore. D'ye hear me?—Answer, can't you! Are you dumb as well as daft?—Ach! What am I saying to you, my wee pet? It's not your blame that you're not as other folks. The doctor, God bless his kind heart, would have been better to have drowned ye than to father ye, when all's said and done, but then he aye says he feels kind of responsible for ye, you poor wee lamb, because if he'd had his mind on his job the day you were born, your mother might be living yet, aye, and your father too. Did I ever tell you, Alicky, ye poor daft wee soul, that your father and your mother were the best-looking young couple in all Argyll, and that their own bonnie, bonnie bairn was stolen away by the good people the minute it was born and you put by them in its place. They say it was the good people that did it, but more likely it was the *Donas*, the work I've had with ye! But never heed old Bella's blethers, my darling, come in to your supper before it's cold.'

Alicky had heard the story of his parentage from old Bella's lips, if once, then a hundred times. He had heard it so often that he troubled little about it. It might be true like the Bible stories or false as the fairy tales. How could a wee boy know? It might be like the skelpings old Bella was always threatening and never gave him. In any case, if he could force down his sowans—the sour, slimy stuff that they were— there was a piece of new-made gingerbread to follow. So Alicky went straight to the table and got busy with his spoon while old Bella went about her business, putting kettles on the fire and taking them off again; washing pots and pans and clattering plates and glasses together under the swishing water in the scullery sink. Alicky sat at a deal table facing the window, and his bald head and yellow, wrinkled face came just to the level of his mug of tea. Through the window he could see the high grey stone wall, a strip of gravel, a corner of the meat-safe under the assault of bluebottles, and the house-martins with their clean white rumps flying up to their mud nests beneath the eaves. To have destroyed their nests would have brought misfortune to the house, or so old Bella believed.

To the left above Alicky's head high up on the green-papered kitchen wall was the box containing the bell-indicators. That labelled Bedroom No. 3 was wagging, which meant that the doctor was tugging at the bell handle of his study. The wires in the walls of the doctor's house had grown twisted and rusty, so that the indicators had become a sort of private code. Alicky got off his chair and ran across to poke old Bella in the back, then point to the indicator settling to rest. Old Bella looked and spoke:

'Was there ever a situation like this, Alicky? On my feet all day, cooking, baking, scrubbing, answering the door, answering the bells, holding down the bairns while the doctor himself pulls flies from their eyes or peas from their ears, and work the riddle when he's seeking for the pennies or buttons the brats has swallowed. I'll not put up with it a single day longer. My notice is in this very night, and you keep your hands to yourself, Alicky, till I'm back, or I'll give you such a skelping as you've never had before.'

Alicky listened to old Bella's departure upstairs. She slammed each door behind her as though she would knock the house down before she left it. Perhaps, being deaf, she could not realise the din she made, and of course she wouldn't leave the house until she or the doctor died. She was always giving notice or saying she was about to give notice, and then staying on. It was just talk, like her skelping threats.

Alicky waited until he heard the roar of the doctor's voice shouting to make Bella hear, then crept over to the dresser where the newly made gingerbread stood solid and circular in its brown, fragrant glory. He broke off the hardened edges and ate them. When he was done the taste of the sowans was out of his mouth and the ginger-bread looked as though mice had gnawed it. Alicky was safely back on his chair watching the house-martins when Bella returned.

'Here, you poor daft wee soul, let's see if your collar's clean this once,' she said. 'The doctor's wanting to speak to you, so wash your face and hands and go upstairs like a gentleman. And if he asks you how many get their supper in my kitchen at night or who makes the *din* as he calls it, you must tell him you know nothing about it or I'll send you to bed with as sound a skelping as you ever had in your born days. Now don't stand staring at me there like a gumboil on a Popish palace. Wash your hands and face and see that your hanky's clean and away upstairs. You should be a proud boy that the doctor's sent for you to-night and him kept late on his rounds, or so he says, with taking a frog from an old man's throat.'

Alicky crept up the long dark stairs. He hadn't been up them for many a long day. Sometimes the doctor would take it into his head to father Alicky and would send for him every night to play with sea-shells on the rug before the study fire. Then Alicky would spill something or break something or would have a snuffle in his nose, and the doctor would lose his temper and send the boy packing back to the kitchen again, where he might remain in Bella's sole charge for many a long week. So when Alicky crept up the dark kitchen stairs in obedience to the doctor's summons, he felt a stranger both to the doctor himself and to the upper part of the house. He saw that the study door was ajar. He knocked timidly, hesitatingly, upon it.

'Come in!'

When Alicky heard the doctor's rough voice he wanted to fly back to the kitchen. But it was too late for that now. He must go in. Perhaps the doctor would be in a kind humour and sing a song, beating time with his pipe on an empty tobacco box. If the doctor was in that kind of humour he would be lying stretched in his arm-chair with his slippers off and his feet on the mantelshelf above the fire. But that night the doctor wasn't in his arm-chair, nor were his slippers off, nor were his feet on the mantelshelf.

62

He stood with his back to the fire, his heavy riding-boots on, and his red nose and chin thrust forwards facing a difficulty. He said:

'How old are you now, boy?'

Alicky answered in a whisper, 'Six, past.'

'God Almighty! are ye that already? I thocht ye wouldna hae been mair nor five. Weel, weel, time slips awa' as the corpse said when the undertakers' men got fou an' cam' doon the stairs wi' the grandfaither-clock. Alicky loon, when ye grow tae be a man if iver ye div, mind an' niver start a thing unless ye mean tae gang through wi' it. It wis nae manner o' use liftin' ye an' handin' ye over to a deaf witch tae dandle. I'll need tae mak' up my mind what's tae be done wi' ye. If you're six past ye'll need tae gang tae the schule this back-end.'

Alicky had heard the dread word mentioned. He had paid but little heed to what the doctor was saying until he heard the word 'school.' It was Alicky's nightmare. Night after night he would dream that he was in the school playground—the bare, bleak playground of the school, surrounded by rusty iron railings too tall to be scaled. In his nightmare he was running round and round that playground, with all the boys and girls in the village running after him. They were led by the butcher's boy, his face alight with the cruelty he called fun, and

they were coming nearer and nearer, carrying
sticks and stones, and mud and suet. They
were laughing without any gladness in their
laughter. They were all shouting 'Daftie!
Daftie! Alicky Mag!'—And Alicky running
from them in his dream tried to make his legs
work faster, but they felt like a couple of useless,
heavy pillows. His chest felt like fire and his
tongue dry and too big for his mouth. Run as
he might, the butcher's boy was almost on him,
was stretching out a red hand to grasp him by
the collar and begin the fun, when Alicky awoke.
—And now the nightmare was to come true!
The doctor had said, 'school in the back-end.'
A few weeks of summer, the birds and the sea,
and then the butcher's boy would have him by
the collar in a corner of the playground. After
he had heard the word 'school,' Alicky could
see neither the doctor nor the study, for the
vision of the bullying that was surely coming
upon him beat upon his brain. He could feel
the kicks and the blows; the hot hands crushing
and suffocating him. So, unthinking and un-
knowing, he gave such a piercing scream that
the doctor dropped his pipe, bending forwards
as though to catch the boy, for indeed he feared
a fit. But Alicky shrank away holding up
clumsy hands to shield his yellow, wrinkled face,
and Dr. Thomas Reith had never seen such
fear in a human face before. He cried:

'What are you feared for, boy?' and Alicky answered, 'The school! The school! I won't go to school.'

'Sit ye doon,' said Dr. Reith. He caught up Alicky in his arms and planted him down in the arm-chair before the fire. 'Dinna greet, bairn. Ye're maybe right.'—The doctor picked up his pipe, stuffing the spilt tobacco back in the bowl. Then he lit it, and walking backwards and forwards over the short length of his shabby study, spoke to Alicky between pauses and puffs.

'You're no' like ither bairns, Alicky. I dinna ken ye as weel as I should ken ye aifter sax years—I'd no notion ye'd been here as lang. But I ken this, Alicky, ye're no' as ither bairns are.—Some would call ye daft?—Aye!—I kent fine what they would likely call ye.—Aye, daft! —And what's that but no' being as ither folks are? Weel, is the common rut o' mankind onything sae marvellous that a body that's different maun be daft? Ye'd raither hear the birds sing than folks speak?—Is thon nae so, Alicky?—Aye!—Can a body call thon daft?— Ye'd raither watch the sea and the trees than learn hoo tae cheat your fellow-men?—Is thon daft? Ye'd raither coont birds in the sky than figures in a ledger?—Is thon daft? Ye'd raither be oot on the hills than boxed in a wee bit room learning foo mony pennies gang tae the pund. Weel, if ye wis born and bred in Buchan they'd

call ye daft for that—but here in the Heelands?
—Man, Alicky, they're a' daft onywye. Aye,
and when they were content tae be daft they
coonted for something, wi' their language that
soonds tae me like an auld wife that canna keep
her dinner doon; their bit tartan skirties, and
their bit pipies they ca' music that's naething
but wind blawn oot o' a sheepskin through a
penny fustle; their wee bit dirkies and *sgian-
dhus*, and their cerrying their ane or twa pennies
in a leathern fig-leaf; and, man, the pride and
the boost and the palaver aboot a hundred or
twa under-sized mannies comin' doon oot o'
glens where there was naething but heather, the
small-pox, and beasts they ca'd cattle nae bigger
than goats! But they coonted for something
when they were content tae be daft.

'But noo that they're seekin' tae be as ither
folks are, what are they?—Porters and clerks
ower proud for their jobs!—Not that I'd say ye
were a fair sample o' a Heeland bairn, Alicky.
God kens what ye are! But I ken this, and I
dinna need Jock McFadyean tae tell it me.
Whoever and whatever ye are, God niver sent
ye into this warld tae be pitten in fear.—Ye'll
no' go to the school, Alicky loon. When the days
draw in I'll fetch Jock McFadyean in to tutor
ye.'

And Alicky stumbled forward awkwardly,
mumbling his thanks.

V

In the years that followed, Alicky discovered that happiness was found where streets ended and the hills began. He did his best to please the Rev. Jock McFadyean, the dark solemn man who came in to tutor him each morning, beginning the lesson with the Lord's Prayer and a paraphrased psalm, concluding with a joke or story and a peppermint cream. Arithmetic, spelling, history, geography, literature, scripture, writing and Latin were all very well in their way, but happiness was to be found only where streets ended and the hills began.

On fine Saturday mornings in the splendour of summer when the Rev. Jock McFadyean was preparing his sermon and there were no lessons, Alicky would be up early, long before old Bella Pringle had risen from bed. He would get up when the sun rose over the rim of the sea to salute the hills, or before that, when the dawn wind thinned night's darkness and the birds in summer chorus sang thanksgiving to God. Alicky would steal from his stuffy little room off the kitchen to lift the sandwiches left for him on the kitchen table by old Bella Pringle. He would open the door and draw the fresh air into his lungs, like a thirsty deer drinking from an ice-cold spring bubbling through peat. He would look out on the shadows of the hills or the mirror of the sea, to rejoice in the silence, the solitude, the peace and quietness of the sleeping world. He would hurry through the echoing streets of Lochend, past the tall grey houses with closed shutters and drawn blinds, where humanity slept, and sea-gulls ruled for an hour. At every corner and at every garbage pail the big herring gulls, in their flashing white plumage and yellow shanks and beaks, quarrelled and bickered or sailed with mournful crying over the silver sea. At that early hour when the morning air was cool and birds sang in every garden, the town of Lochend was at peace. Perhaps a door of a house might open and a maid, still dishevelled by sleep, shake a mat and go in again. Perhaps a thin line of smoke might rise from the chimney of a house where a match had been put to the fire set ready in a kitchen grate. An occasional boat might be coming in from the night fishing, the rowers working the oars with the relaxed effort of work completed. And punctually at six o'clock each morning Macpherson's milk-cart came rattling in from the country over the cobbled streets.

With the town behind him Alicky took the

68

road beside the sea-loch leading to the hills. He felt happy in the solitude of dawn. His self-consciousness deserted him. He forgot that his face was withered and wrinkled and his head bald. He forgot that his body was clumsy and stunted and his teeth decayed. He forgot everything except the peace of the sea, the majesty of the hills, the glory of summer.

On his right as he walked was the long stretch of the sea-loch with the hills beyond. The water rose in a smooth swell that never broke into white waves. It was as though the sea stretched its arms in lazy awakening from sleep.

In early morning the Lochend seashore was a meeting-place of birds. They gathered there when day dawned to filch the harvest strewn on the sand by the sea during night. Gulls were there in snowy abundance; plover catching the low sunlight in their wheeling formations; the oyster-catchers, piebald black and white with long red bills; the cormorants and shags, clustered on the rocks, wings outstretched and quivering as in ecstasy of prayer. Seals, too, might slip from the seaweed-covered surface of smooth rocks into the quiet water, turn to gaze at Alicky, showing their old men's faces and dog-kind eyes above the surface, then follow the piping of a fairy piper out to sea. As the sun rose, spilling silver over water, so the wild life of sea-tangle and stones of the Lochend shore dispersed. A man, walking there later in the day, would find the imprints of its myriad feet on the wet sand.

Alicky knew most of the birds by name. He knew them all by their plumage, their flight, their cry. In the night, before dawn, lying awake in his bed at the doctor's house, he could tell the notes of the passing birds as they flew overhead. He could follow, as it were, the seasonal traffic of the air. He knew the birds as he never knew arithmetic; as he could never hope or wish to know his Latin. But while he walked along the sea-road leading to the hills the silly jangle of Latin grammar kept recurring to his mind, the list of meaningless prepositions the Rev. Jock McFadyean insisted he should learn. The silly, meaningless jangle of Latin words—

> *A, ab, absque, coram, de,*
> *Palam, clam, cum, ex, or e,*
> *Sine, tenus, pro and pre,*
> And into these if 'rest at' be intended,
> Let *in, sub, super, subter* be appended,

the only Latin he could remember; the only Latin he would never forget. But Latin would die away in his mind when a curlew came sailing over the hill's crest, spilling fine melody on the morning air. For, up to the left of the winding road by the sea lay the heather hills where moor-birds called to summer, where the black-faced sheep wandered—where the hinds

70

led their fawns to sweet pasture. And the road parted from the sea and its eternal song, stealing its white way through the red moors to the mouth of Glendruid.

When Alicky reached Glendruid, the old *cailleachs* would be at their doors, in their white mutch caps and tattered clothes, the thin blue smoke from their peat fires rising above the thatch of white-washed cottages, giving incense to hill air. The old women would greet Alicky, calling him darling and dear one in the Gaelic, recalling to him the beauty of his mother and the prideful strength of his father who had followed the sheep into Argyll from the island of Islay. They would mutter spells over him, those of the old faith among them crossing themselves as they poured blessings on him. Kind old women, those, who never called him for a daftie or mocked the quaint ugliness of his face and body, the silly swathings of his soul. Kindly old women who thought him a simple one in God's own special care. When Alicky left them to go farther up the glen they would cry their blessings on him again—*bean-nachd leat! beannachd leat!*

Past the clachan and the *cailleachs* to the narrow glen! The Druid river to the right of the road, dark and swift, with the trout in its waters black as peats—the steep hill beyond with scattered sheep clinging to its side like flies to glass, that led over the top and the wide flat moors to Glendarroch. On the left of the road, the brae face towards the North that seldom saw the sun, rising away up to the high wether grazing of the Sliaghmhor. Far ahead the road died towards the West where the glen grew narrow at its beginning as a cleft in the heel of Ben Cruachan.

Half-way up Glendruid, midway between the clachan of thatched cottages and the grass carpeted hollow where Ben Cruachan joined hands with the Sliaghmhor, there stood the shepherd's house where Alicky Mag was born. Its small garden with the potato patch and few bushes of black and red currants came right up to the road. It was always with fear in his heart that Alicky saw the tumble-down dyke of the shepherd's cottage appear round a turn in the glen road. Were the shepherd at home, his two dogs would feel the vibration of footsteps on the road and come leaping over the dyke, tearing down upon the stranger. They were small, black, smooth-coated collies with white on their throats. They were not vicious. The *cailleachs* had told Alicky a dozen times that he need have no fear of them for they would not bite. But even when Alicky knew by experience that their ferocious challenge ended in a tail-wagging recognition, even then the sight of the two dogs leaping over the dyke made his heart tumble over inside his breast and the calves of his legs quiver and go weak. He was glad when the

72

shepherd was out on the hill and his dogs from home.

The shepherd himself was an elderly man with a fine white beard and stout legs fit for any walking. He was a widower. It was said by some that he had come to Glendruid to forget his sorrow. Others said that only a bachelor or widower would come to that haunted place, for no woman would face the whispering ghosts of its winter's nights and the memory of how Janet Macdonald had died there on an April day.

It was on a fine May morning that the Glendruid herd, and Archie Campbell was his name, and he an Argyllshire man, first fell into conversation with Alicky Mag. Alicky had come up the glen in the fragrant weather of the early summer to hear the cuckoo if he could, for once the cuckoo was heard he would take off his heavy boots and woollen stockings, and never wear them again all through the summer. He hoped, too, to see the snow blossom drifting over gean and bird-cherry by the river's side. He had walked along by the seashore where the gulls cried in the soft wind of sorrows and things long past and dead; he had walked through the clachan passing the time of the day with the *cailleachs*, and still the boots were on his feet. He had passed the shepherd's cottage where the *smeorach* sang to summer in the rowan-tree. The dogs were not there that morning, for the

73

shepherd was on the hill. Alicky had walked beside the winding Druid until the road lost itself in the heather and the tender green fronds of the opening bracken. Then he came to the green cup in the hills where the Sliaghmhor met with Ben Cruachan and the grass grew sweet. The little black-faced sheep of Glendruid were pasturing there with their young lambs beside them. They were so ravenous to taste fresh grass after the long famine of the winter and cold spring that they had grown tame, merely turning to look at Alicky as he approached them, then returning to their urgent grazing. From the steep rocks that shut in the grassy hollow, the cold waters of newly melted snow dripped downwards over moss and fern, over yellow primroses, and the purple saxifrage that hid high ledges of the rock in coloured mist.

Alicky stood silent in the green cup amid the brown hills listening for the cuckoo which he must surely hear on such a fine morning of May, his boot-laces already unloosed. There was deep silence until a ring-ousel, the blackbird of the mountains, sent a hill-song to Alicky over the river. Alicky could see the brave black bird with his snow-white breast, swelling his throat as he stood on a rock beside the Druid's dark waters. The mountain blackbird finished his song and the hills were silent again. The light wind drifted over the hills, gathering warmth from the unclouded sun and freshness from the melting snow in shaded corries.

Then a brown and long-tailed bird with the shape of a hawk and dipping, undulant flight came over the river with three little brown pipits pursuing it as it flew. And on the wing and half-way over the Druid river it called out its bugle note, its réveillé to summer—'Cuckoo! Cuckoo!' And Alicky made a bundle of his stockings and boots.

He was crouched on the ground, stuffing stockings into boots and tying laces together to form an easy burden for carrying over his shoulder, when he heard a deep voice behind him saying:

'And it's yourself that's the brave boy, coming all the long way from Lochend to hear the *cutag* in Glen Druid Pot!'

As always when he heard a strange voice speaking to him, Alicky felt afraid. He turned quickly, the blood flushing the withered skin of his face. He saw the Glendruid shepherd standing over him, a smile on his brown face, that looked all the browner above his white beard, laughter in his kind blue eyes; and fear left the soul of Alicky Mag. He was not afraid even of the dogs, for the shepherd had them quietened and at heel before he had spoken. Then since Alicky said nothing, for though kind things were often at his tongue's tip, yet they stayed there through shyness, the shepherd spoke again.

'You'll be no stranger to me, boy, though I've never had the occasion of speaking to you before. But it's the *cailleachs* down at the clachan that are never done talking of you, boy, and of how there's never a fine Saturday morning but you're up the glen looking for the birds. Aye, and it's the *cailleachs* that tell me that you would be knowing the names of them all, of where they come from and where they go. Aye, and it's right you are, Alicky boy, to be watching the birds. It's the birds that are the bonnie ones. Aye, they're bonnie in every single thing that they do, in the nests they make and the fine coloured eggs they lay in them, in the colours they put on for the fine weather, and the fine notes of the music they will make. Aye, I'm thinking, Alicky boy, that if it was only the bonnie birds that were left in the world, we'd be back in the first garden that ever God made.— Aye, when we'll be done with this world, Alicky boy, and we stand on the eternal shore, then the days will aye be fine as they are this day, and the wee birds singing, and the sheep a' thriving. There'll be no lairds there, Alicky, nor factors, nor politicians, nor braxy, nor trembling in the sheep. There'll be no English there, Alicky, for the angels in heaven a' talk in the Gaelic. There'll be no promiscy dancing there, Alicky, with man and woman hugging each other like brute beasts. There'll just be the fine fiddles playing reels and strathspeys. There'll be no brass bands there, Alicky, just the MacCrimmons a' *piobaireachd* on the great pipes. There'll be no piners or eild ewes there, Alicky boy, just sappy ewes and strong, well-headed wethers, and every lamb will be a top lamb on the close, green pastures of the heavenly hills.

'But in the meantime, Alicky boy, we're in this *ifrinn* of a Glendruid grazing, where we will maybe get a taste of heaven like this day once in a twelvemonth just to torment us. If it wasn't for the Pot here, and that'll soon be all under the brackens if the factor will no' pay for the cutting of them—if it wasn't for the Pot, there'd be no meat to put milk on a gimmer in the whole of the Glendruid. If it wasn't for the Pot here, Alicky, that in winter's nothing but a death-trap with the sheep sheltering in it and the swirl of the wind from Ben Cruachan giving the poor beasts a white winding sheet no living herd is fit to dig through—if it wasn't for the Pot, Alicky boy, there'd be nothing fit for a ewe to live on in the whole of Glendruid. We'd be needing to put it under a wether stock like the Sliaghmhor. But the factor he's aye girning for "More *ewes*, Mr. Campbell, more *ewes*, that's what we want."

'And what will you be doing wi' yoursel' noo,

Alicky boy, that ye've heard the *cutag* and your brogues is off? Will ye be writing to the papers about it like a fool or will ye be keeping the music of it in your heart like a wise man?—Ach! never fear for the dogs, Alicky boy! The dumb beasts know fine when a body's in God's own care. —Will ye be for home now, Alicky boy, or would ye be for taking a turn down to the house and I'll be making a cup of tea to us both?'

Alicky always found acceptance easier than refusal. Besides, he felt safe and happy with the strong shepherd of Glendruid. He said that he would go to his house for a cup of tea.

On the way down the glen Alicky said never a word unless it were an answer to a question, but the shepherd kept him amused with the stories he told and the riddles he put. He had all the old Gaelic riddles—the *toimhseachain*—at his tongue's tip.

'I'll be asking you them in the English, Alicky, because ye'll no' have the Gaelic, though what's music in the Gaelic is just a rattle o' tin pails in the English. The Gaelic was for making love and singing together with praises to God, Alicky boy, and the English for one man making money and his brother begging at the street corners. I'll be asking you an easy one first of all, Alicky boy—"A stream running uphill."—Now what would be the answer to that? Boy, that's an old one and ye don't know it. *Mart breac a'*

78

chibeir ag ol dibhe—the shepherd's spotted cow drinking.

'Now I'll give ye another, and if you can give me the answer it's you that will be the proud one.—"I went to the hill and I did not seek it, yet I found it. I searched for it and I could not find it. I wished to throw it from me but it would not leave me. I could not see it but it came home with me.

'You won't know the answer to that one, Alicky! You might search a while and never find it. Well, I'll give you the answer myself, Alicky. It's a stab—a thorn in the foot that's in it. Now think it out for yourself, boy.—"I went to the hill and I did not seek it, yet I found it . . .!" What else could be in it but a stab?'

So they came down to the wicket-gate of the shepherd's garden and went in past the currant bushes and the potato patch to the small house itself. The shepherd bent low to go in first, and Alicky followed him. The two dogs lay down, stretching themselves on the stone slab at the door, which had caught the grateful warmth of the May sun. And all down Glendruid was sunshine, the plashing of river water, the trembling music of the whaups, and white clouds drifting across the blue sky.

There were but the two rooms in the small house, and the shepherd used one as a storehouse for his potatoes and meal. The other, where the grate was, was his kitchen, his sitting-room, and where he slept. There was the one small window facing northwards with the view of the steep hill that led over to Glendarroch, and spiders made tapestry on its fixed panes. The range was grey with unswept ashes, uncared for and unpolished. On the bare table were the cup and unwashed plate, the knuckle of loaf and kebbuck of cheese, left over from the shepherd's breakfast. Unwashed blankets tumbled over the edge of the box-bed in the wall. It was an untidy house, because no woman dwelt there.

The shepherd made a fire of wood and put the kettle on to boil, and when the kettle sang its busy song he made tea to them both. He saw that Alicky kept looking at the fiddle that lay on a shelf beside the bed, kept looking so often and so long that at last the shepherd said:

'D'ye ever get a tune at home, Alicky?' and Alicky answered that in the doctor's house at Lochend there was no music played.

'Boy, and that's the pity,' the shepherd said. 'If it wasn't for playing a wee tune to mysel' here in the quiet of the evening, I'd go daft in this dark pit o' an uncanny glen. Aye, if it wasn't for a bit tune on the fiddle or the pipes, and the sheep, Alicky. Aye, Alicky, if ever your heart is sore go out among the sheep and watch them graze. There's aye peace among the sheep.

'But if you're through with your tea, boy,

I'll give you a bit tune, if you're caring for it. I'll play you " Mary Macleod's Farewell to the Island of Skye." It's a sad, sad tune, and if it wasn't a fine day I wouldn't play it to you. Keep the sad music for when a man's heart is glad, and play nothing but reels and strathspeys when his heart is sore.'

When the shepherd played the sad old tune, Alicky forgot where he was. In the lilt of the music his mind flew out from Glendruid on the wings of a bird. It flew to where the sun sets behind high and jagged hills and the sea is drowned in a mist of blood. The shepherd, watching the dream of strange beauty steal over the quaint face of the boy, felt joy in his fiddler's heart. There was a listener to whom music was magic, a key to unlock the hidden places of a soul!

The shepherd played that fine old dance tune, 'Jenny, Catch Your Skirts Up,' and as he played the jig he saw Alicky's feet twitch into motion and then keep time. There, then, was a listener too for whom rhythm was motion and life! He saw the expression on Alicky's face change from shy self-consciousness to forgetfulness of everything but melody and rhythm. There was a boy who might make a fiddler, some day, himself.

So, on that May morning, Alicky had his first lesson on the fiddle, taught by Archie Campbell, who got the tradition and the knowledge from old Peter Campbell, long dead, who had it from John Campbell, who had it from Sandy Campbell who was with the Campbell militia on the winning side on Culloden field. It was fiddling in a fine tradition with subtleties of rhythm and time that no script could reproduce, a tradition carried on from generation to generation by unpaid teachers who chose their pupils for their gifts.

'And ye never hear a tune in the doctor's house. What do they teach you there, boy, if you're no' at the school,' the shepherd said as he put the fiddle aside.

'Latin.'

'Latin? Well, I never heard the sound of that tongue, boy. Can you say "It's a fine day" in the Latin and let me be hearing the sound of it?'

'Aye,' Alicky answered, '*A, ab, absque, coram, de.*'

'And so they have the same word for "day" as they have in the English?—*Coram de*—"a fine day." I must mind that.'

Then just as Alicky was leaving to go home, one of the shepherd's dogs crept in and laid his head on the boy's knee. Alicky, at first afraid, looked down timidly into the dog's eyes, and he saw kindness there and sympathy such as he had seldom met with in a human face. And after that, Alicky found that his fear of dogs was gone.

VI

On a mild Monday night of February in the year 1882, Dr. Thomas Reith was in finest humour. The minister's knights were unhorsed, his castles captured, his bishops unfrocked. The doctor had won decisively in three successive games, because the Rev. Jock McFadyean, having bought a chess manual second-hand in Edinburgh while attending the General Assembly, was attempting to play to a system he did not understand.

'It all comes o' too much book-learning, Jock,' the doctor said. 'I mind fine o' a student that was in ma year in Marischal College at Aberdeen. He had a' the text-books by hairt, but pit a patient afore him an' he couldna tell constipation frae a carcinoma. Ye'd hae deen better in Edinboro', Jock, if ye'd keepit your mind on Foreign Missions and Sabbath Schools, an' nae tried tae steal a march on me by ransacking a' the second-hand book shops in the High Street o' Edinboro' tae find the knowledge ye hoped tae beat me wi'.'

'It would work fine if you played to some kind of system yourself, Thomas.'

'An' sae I div, Jock. My chess is like ma medicine, plain symptomatic treatment. I aye wait on the disease tae see what it means tae dae, and when I ken that, I stop it. An' i' the same wye, I wait on ye till you're in a complete an' complex snorl, an' then I plank in a pawn amang a' your muddled manœuvres an' mak' things waur.—Well, well, the luck's been a' agin ye, Jock. We'll need tae mak' it a gug-gug-guggler tae ye the nicht.'

The two friends sat well back from the fire, because the evening was mild for the time of year. The doctor sipped his Glendruigh with added pleasure because of his medical adventures of the day. When Glendruigh had spread its warmth to his very toes, he told the Rev. Jock McFadyean something of these adventures.

'Aye, Macinlay ca'd me in for a second opinion the day, Jock. I had muckle pleesure in tellin' him that his diagnosis wis mistaken, his treatment wrang, and that I'd been ca'd in far ower late tae dae ony guid.'

'Was that a Christian act of yours, Thomas?'

'Maybe no, Jock. Maybe no. But mair sense than Macinlay's action in ca'ing diabetes a guid appetite for mair nor a twelvemonth!'

'But you doctors can't cure diabetes in any case, Thomas.'

'Maybe, Jock, maybe, but a lot o' guid meat could hae been spared that the puir body could

84

ill afford.—Which minds me, Jock, it's past time ye pit in a bill for teaching wee Alicky.'

'There's no need to mention money between us, Thomas. In any case, if I've taught the boy for six years without fee, there's no need to start talking of it now.'

'Sax year, Jock! Is it that, now? Man, time slips awa' as the corpse said. How's the loon shaping, onywye?'

The Rev. Jock McFadyean filled his pipe slowly with yellow Virginia leaf tobacco. Then he threw back his massive head in contemplation, his face not quite so young now in its frame of greying whisker.

'Alicky will never be a scholar,' he said. 'To give you an example, Thomas. He's been three years at Latin now. I started him very early in Latin, because it is the best mental discipline I know. Well, only last Friday, I asked him to decline *hasta* and he failed, Thomas, he failed lamentably.'

'Then why no' try him wi' *mensa*, Jock. It's aye *mensa*, *mensa*, *mensam* we got in the school.'

'It would make no difference, Thomas, I fear. He has made no progress whatever with his Latin, although, poor boy, he is anxious to please. The only Latin he can remember is that absurd rhyme—you will recall it, Thomas: *A, ab, absque, coram, de*——'

85

'Aye, aye, Jock. Thon's the fifth declension, is it no'?'

'Hardly, Thomas, but it means nothing to Alicky, either.—He can memorise any verse without understanding it. He can do "The Lord's my Shepherd" from end to end, but he can't remember the Lord's Prayer. His arithmetic is no better. Was it Thursday or Wednesday?—I can't remember. It doesn't matter, but anyway, I set him a very simple arithmetical problem on the papering of a room, and had his answer been correct the room would have been stuffed with paper. If I set him an exercise in composition he gnaws his pen like an animal and stares out through the window.'

'Then he'll niver mak' a doctor, Jock?'

'He'll never be a scholar, Thomas.'

'Aye, an' I tell't thon daft witch, Bella Pringle, tae feed the loon on white fish. She's nae been daeing what I tell't her tae dae. Did I iver tell ye, Jock, that if my landlady in the Spital hadna given me yellow haddies a' through my final examinations, I'd hae been in Harley Street the day like Sir Malcolm Macpherson who was in ma year and hadna half ma diagnostic abeelity, and no' in Lochend alang wi' Macinlay, wha kens nae mair aboot medicine nor ma——'

'Quite, quite, Thomas, I've no doubt that if you'd eaten more white fish and drunk less white water, as they put it in the Gaelic you

86

despise, you'd have come out better in your finals and have got the honours you deserve. But I'm afraid no diet will ever make poor Alicky a scholar.'

'Weel, weel, Jock, if that's the wye o't, ye're wasting your time, and if I was tae pay ye as I ought, me my money. We'll need tae apprentice the loon tae a trade. I wouldna hae keepit him sae lang if it hadna been for my experiment on the effect o' white fish on the brain.'

'I think we would do right in getting Alicky taught a trade, Thomas, although I shall never for a moment admit that science had any part in inducing you to give him shelter. There's no cause for pride in denying the call of the Master, Thomas.'

'Cannie, noo, Jock lad! It's a Monday nicht! Though whiles I think, Jock, I'd dae better if I heard mair o' sermons and less o' symptoms. Ony man wi' a guid Scots hairt can mak' a start on an act o' Christian charity, Jock, but it tak's the help o' God to carry a body through a job he's grown tired on. I'll no deny atween oorsel's, Jock, that I took the puir wee piner o' a loon hame oot o' charity, an' he's aye had food and shelter and claes tae his back. But whiles, Jock, when the wee gowk coups ma tobacco jar intil ma boots an' never lets on he's done it, an' I stick ma taes in amang what should be in ma pipe—! Aye, he's a trying wee loon,

Alicky Mag. Not but what I'm fond o' him or I wouldna hae keepit him sae lang, charity or no charity. Whiles, an' I'll tell ye truth, Jock, I've thought on pitting him awa', an' then he looks up at me wi' trusting eyes like a dowg, and I canna find it in me tae dae it. I'd as soon drown a dowg I'd a liking tae. I thocht maybe Alicky'd mak' a scholar. If he'd but turned oot weel, he'd maybe hae gotten a chair in King's College, Aiberdeen. He'd hae felt at hame there amang the professors that are naething but orra-looking auld wives in breeks. But, man Jock, they're scholars. There was ane o' them in ma time that could recite the whale o' Virgil backwards in the original Greek.

'If a loon's daft and a scholar he can aye find a job in a college. But if he's daft and nae scholar, like oor puir wee Alicky, it'll need tae be pit tae a trade. But what trade, Jock?—He canna be a butcher, for he canna pass the butcher's shop for thinkin' o' the meat that was aince living beasts. He canna be a tailor, for it tak's him a' his time tae pit on his ain breeks right side foremost. He canna be a jiner, for if he lifts a hemmer, there's gless broken somewhere. Can ye dae onything for him yoursel', Jock?— Yon beadle o' yours will no' last long. I niver kent a man ower saxty that married on a quean o' twenty-ane that lived mair nor a twalmonth.'

'A stupid match, Thomas. A stupid match.

But if you're serious about putting Alicky to a trade, let it be a country trade. The boy is unhappy in towns. He's something of a naturalist too. He knows all the birds on the Lochend shore. He loves flowers and the butterflies. He loves music and a sunrise.'

Dr. Reith blew out a cloud of smoke, and drawing his chair closer to the fire, kicked off his slippers and planted his stockinged feet on the mantelshelf.

'Noo, is Alicky ane o' that kind!' he said. 'I mind o' a student when I wis in Aiberdeen, Jimmy Craig he wis ca'd. Weel, I wis walking doon the Spital wi' Jimmy Craig ae nicht an' a queanie keeks oot o' a close, gies a bit giggle, an' says, "Fine evening, Mr. Craig." He didna answer like a man, but started tae sing—"Oh beauteous time! Oh evening hour." "Who's thon, Jimmy," says I—"John Sebastian Bach," he answers like a fool. Aye, his mind was a' on music and fine evenings an' he never kent that Jeannie Baxter, for that's what she was ca'd as I found out that verra nicht, had been eating her hairt oot for him till she fell in wi' masel'.— Aye, puir Jimmy Craig. He didna dae ower weel in his finals, his mind aye being a' on oratorios and nae on ossifications, an' the end o' it a' was that a' he could get when he was through was an assistantship to a club doctor doon aboot the Midlands o' England. Weel, ye niver ken how things will turn oot, Jock. When he'd been there twa year, Jimmy Craig wrote and tell't me that the toon he wis in was a gey bleak and smoky hole, but says he, "The part singing in the oratorio choir is magnificent and a November sunset through the town's smoke a marvel of changing colour. I've never been so happy in my life. Yours aye—Jimmy Craig." Sae ye niver ken wha they daft musical bodies will be content, Jock. Maybe we should send Alicky doon tae rowl peels tae Jimmy Craig—if Jimmy's aye livin'.'

'I don't think Alicky would be happy there, Thomas. I'm sure Alicky would never be happy in a town. I've been talking with the shepherd up in Glendruid, a great friend of Alicky's that teaches him the fiddle. I think the shepherd, and a decent, godly man he is although a red-hot radical—I think the shepherd would learn Alicky the sheep. There's worse jobs than a shepherd's, Thomas.'

'Aye, fairly, Jock, fairly. Stand on a bit heathery knowe, fustle through yer fingers, an' let the dowgs dae a' the work.—Aye, I ken Archie Campbell. Aye, Macinlay made him a widower afore his time. Aye, Macinlay ca'd a cancer gall-stones on thon occasion.'

'You are too hard on Dr. Macinlay, Thomas. The best surgeon in London could have done nothing for poor Mrs. Campbell.'

'Fairly, Jock, fairly. But if Macinlay had made a correct diagnosis when the signs were patent tae a first year student, Archie Campbell would hae had time and opportunity tae seek a second wife. Instead o' that it a' came sudden on Archie and he up and awa' tae Glendruid herding where he'll never see onything female but the *cailleachs*, a collie bitch, and the auld yowes.—Well, we might dae waur than apprentice wee Alicky tae a herd. If he can coont the yowes in the buchts that'll be a' the arithmetic he's needing. An' it's nae hard work. Skin the deid an' coont the livin'—thon's herding in Argyll. Guid sakes, Jock, some o' them'll nae even condescend tae skin a corpse. They'll yabble Gaelic at the fit o' a hill while the craws dae the undertaking at its tap. Aye, but I'll see Archie Campbell the morn. I'm riding up that wye, onywye. I'll have tae dae something wi' Grannie Maclean at the clachan. She's been sittin' in a claes basket this week past makin' on she's a clockin' hen. That's gey near the limit when behaviour ceases tae be merely Heeland an' becomes certifiable, Jock.

'But I'll speak tae Archie Campbell. He'll likely tell me that a boy will no mak' a herd unless he's heard a yowe "Baa" within an hour o' his birth, but a few bob a week'll pit that right or ma name's Macinlay.'

The Rev. Jock McFadyean became very

serious. He put on the stern expression he adopted in the pulpit before embarking upon his final peroration. He leant forwards, speaking softly, with an eye on the door lest old Bella Pringle should have hers at the keyhole.

'Excuse me talking of a matter which does not concern me, Thomas, but is Alicky mentioned in your will?'

Dr. Thomas Reith thrust his red face forwards—'Na!'

'Would it not be proper after all these years, Thomas? Just a small legacy?'

'Na!'

'But you have no other dependants, Thomas.'

'Have I no'? That's a' ye ken, Jock. I've the brawest loon ye iver clappit eyes on that's being reared by his mither's folk in the Buck o' the Cabrach.'

The minister drew back, rebuffed. He had thought there were no secrets between the doctor and he.

'I didn't know you were married, Thomas. You never told me of it.'

'I wouldna tell ye a lee, Jock.'

'Oh, Thomas, Thomas!'

'Ye needna "Oh Thomas" me, Jock. I'm prood o' the loon as I wis o' his mither. I wis prood o' her and would hae married on her if God had spared her, though she wis just a hilty-skilty bit servant lassie aboot ma faither's place.

I'll nae dee a rich man, Jock. I canna get ma bills oot o' the folks here. Eggs and cheese will no' keep. What siller's left will be for Jessie's boy.

'He's ca'd Gordon, and if ye'll but hand me your gless, Jock, we'll drink a gug-gug-guggler thegither tae his health, and tae the memory o' his mither, wha wis naething but a saint.'

VII

It was in the month of March and a fine day for the time of year. Alicky said farewell to Lochend, old Bella Pringle, and the house of Dr. Reith.

He was not sorry to be leaving and yet he was sad to go. There were times when he had not been happy, and yet when the hour for leaving came it was the glad times he kept in mind. When he awoke that morning and heard the chorus of bird song in the garden, and looked around the stuffy little annexe to the kitchen in which he had always slept, he felt afraid of his adventure. The room was so familiar to him that it seemed a friend. There was the green wallpaper peeling at the wall's angles which he had looked on first thing every morning for years. There was the text above his bed, painted by some forgotten hand and bought for sixpence by Bella Pringle at a sale. It said, 'Thou, God, seest me!' There was the view of the apple-tree through the window. The left-hand bottom window-pane had been cracked ever since Alicky could remember. There was the cane chair with his clothes thrown in a clumsy pile upon it. There was the dressing-table with the year's collection of shells, sea-urchins, feathers, dead flowers, and lumps of quartz shining with the mica he thought to be silver, the year's collection which Bella Pringle threw out in the dust-bin at each spring-cleaning. It was just about all the cleaning she gave to Alicky's room. Sometimes Alicky had thought his room a dark and dreary place, but on the March morning he was to leave for Glendruid, it had a peace, familiar and all its own.

He got out of bed and began to wrestle into his clothes. He always found dressing a difficulty. He couldn't keep his mind on the job. He would be thinking of the nest the missel-thrushes were busy building high up in the apple-tree, or of the fine tune he was learning on Archie Campbell's fiddle. When he was finished it was like as not that his stockings were inside out, his braces twisted, or his tie in a knot instead of a bow.

On that morning on which he was leaving for Glendruid he felt that he was doing things for the last time and it made him sad. All the time he was dressing he could hear the sound of Bella Pringle's snores coming through the wall, and the squeak of her mattress when she heaved herself about. The old woman was not a good riser, and Alicky was out and about, as was usual, before she was astir.

95

The dawn was fresh with a cool wind off the hills where the snow still lay. The sea was white-capped; the waves attacking the shore. Over Lochend, still sleeping, wild geese in formation sped northwards. A new moon and the morning star were fading shadows in a clear sky. Alicky went out to the streets and the seashore to say good-bye to Lochend. He liked the old town when the houses were places of secure sleep and only the gulls cried to him as he passed. He liked the town in the very early morning when the streets were deserted by mankind, when there were no grown-up people to laugh at him, no children to shout after him as he hastened by.

He walked down the High Street between the tall houses. The herring gulls busy at the garbage pails flapped their wide white wings at him, opening their yellow maws to scream at him. He passed Campbell the draper's shop where the window was filled with a line of red flannel selling at a discount. The blinds were down in the windows of Inglis the baker's shop. One blind was tucked up at the corner showing the massive base of a wedding-cake. Mr. Macfarlane, the bank-agent, was to marry Miss Fletcher, the cabinet-maker's daughter, for love, they said. There was a placard swinging on the door of Wishart the chemist's shop, saying that an errand-boy was wanted but a girl might apply. The housemaid of Mackay's temperance hotel opened the door to let out the cat. Macpherson's milk-cart came in from the country, rattling over the cobbled streets.

Alicky turned off to the left down the quiet close which led to the sea. It made a framed picture—the white crests of waves on the black sea, a pale blue sky with the white gulls wheeling above the black sea, and the grey stones of age-old houses forming its frame.

He walked along the shore where rocks were broken down to shingle, and shingle ground to sand. He walked for an hour by the sea, listening to plover pipe of summer's coming over cold waves, watching the waves shatter against the rocks and then recede, leaving the seaweed glistening wet. He grew elated with the surge of the sea, the wind's sting and the wild birds calling. He hummed over to himself the old tunes born long past in the minds of simple men in their sorrow or joy, and no one, not even himself, could hear his humming for the crash of the sea. He would lick his lips to feel the taste of salt, and breathe in the cold salt air off the sea until he felt he might soar with the white sea birds.

When he left the sea and came back through the close to the High Street of Lochend, he had forgotten his body in the joy that filled his soul. He forgot until a message-boy coming up silently behind tripped him with an outstretched foot and pulled his cap down over his eyes. Alicky ran from him, tugging at the peak of his cap so that he might see where the green railings lay, and the message-boy shouted 'Daftie! Daftie! You're aye daft, are ye?' after Alicky running clumsily to the safety of a home he was to leave that day.

Old Bella Pringle was in tears because he was leaving her. When Alicky ran panting into the kitchen where no message-boy would follow, she raised her voice in shrill lamentation:

'Ach! my wee pet, and are you leaving us to-day? It's no' right that they should put you away like this. It's not your blame that you're not as other folks are. Sit in to your breakfast, my wee lamb. It'll be the last Christian meat you'll have for a while, for the herds just live on the braxied sheep that the craws will no' touch.

'Well, it's not for me to tell himself upstairs what's right nor what's wrong. *That's* a job for the Reverend Mr. McFadyean if he was to do the job he's been called to instead of passing every Monday night playing like a bairn wi' a parcel of ivory idols in a game of chance.

'Aye, it's not for the likes o' me to tell himself upstairs what becomes a Christian gentleman and a medical man at that. It's not old Bella's place, my sweetheart, though if I was to speak my mind there'd be some plain speaking, let me tell you that, Alicky Mag! The idea of it! To take a

98

bairn into his house and give it all but his name, and have it eddicated and all, and then when he's tired of the game that he should never have started on unless he was meaning to go through with it, to put a poor thing like yoursel', Alicky, up to Archie Campbell in Glendruid, who'll preach you up to heaven one day and fiddle you down to hell the next!

'And what would your poor mother say to it all if she was with us this day, Alicky Mag? And did I ever tell you, my lamb, that she was the bonniest woman I ever clapped eyes on, Alicky? And did I ever tell you that your father was the finest man that ever came out of the island of Islay?—Aye—I've often heard tell of the honey that came out of the braxied lion in the book of Samuel, but it's whiles the other way round if we're to believe on what came to pass in the Druid's glen on the day that you were born, my angel.'

Alicky was staring at old Bella, wondering whether she would ever stop talking of the things he had heard a hundred times before. He stared at her and forgot where his spoon was going. Bella cried:

'Can ye no' put your porridge in your mouth for once instead of on my clean floor? *Daftie* that you are! Aye, you'll be at home in a herd's house where the dogs have more manners than the men. Look what you're doing, you daft wee owl! It'll be good riddance to bad rubbish when you're clear of my kitchen.'

Then Dr. Reith roared down the stairs asking if the boy was to keep him waiting all day, and was he to be all day over his porridge, and hadn't he given orders that the boy should be ready when he was called, and what in the name——!

Old Bella Pringle heard a distant sound which she recognised to be the doctor's voice. She screamed back, 'Aye, your boots is at the stair head if that's what you're seeking.'

Alicky sprang from his chair, leaving his breakfast unfinished. He ran close to Bella and screamed up into her withered face, 'He says I've to go at once.'

'Well, wash your hands and face, and see that your hanky's clean, and away upstairs. Your bag's packed and alongside his boots at the stair head.' Bella raised her voice to a shrill yell. 'And if somebody I'll no' put a name to before witnesses has any shame left in him this day, he'll ask forgiveness for leaving a Christian deed without an end to it, and he'll never again put his hand to the plough of Charity to drop it like it was red hot just because a poor motherless and fatherless bairn that's in need of all the help that Christian folk can give him, should have couped a puckle stale tobacco into his riding-boots!'

And the doctor roared downstairs again. 'Never heed thon daft auld skirling sea-gull, Alicky. Stick a preen in her tae let oot her wind some ither gate. We'd never hae had this upset if she'd stuffed ye wi' white fush as she wis tell't tae dae. Come awa'! loon. Come awa'!'

Alicky ran upstairs. He was too scared of the doctor to say farewell to the housekeeper. He had no time to wash his hands or face or to see to the cleanliness of his handkerchief. He stumbled upstairs, calling out, 'I'm ready! I'm coming! I'm here!' He tumbled over his packed bag lying ready at the stair head. He fell headlong, bumping his forehead on the stone floor. But he was more fearful of the doctor in a rough mood than of any pain.

'Are ye hurt, loon?' asked Dr. Reith. 'Can ye no' bide on yer twa feet till ye're clear o' the hoose? Here, gie us yon bag and come awa'. Macinlay has twa cases he's bungled that are no' like tae live, sae he's taken tae his bed an' left me wi' a' his work tae dae on tap o' ma ain. Aye, nae the first occasion he's done thon!— Awa' oot and into the gig till I get a haud o' ma howdie bag. If the mare offers tae bolt, say the ae word "Macinlay" an' the dumb beast'll turn doon tae the kirk-yard and stop there at the iron gates. Aye, the varra beasts ken what cam's o' giving whisky tae an apoplexy.'

Alicky Mag ran out of the house and clambered

up into the doctor's yellow gig. He held the heavy reins in his hands, but the brown mare stood still, her head bent downwards as though repenting of her sins. Soon Dr. Thomas Reith appeared at the house door, his head turned backwards to bellow his last instructions to old Bella Pringle. And she, in a voice she thought a quiet whisper although all the town could hear her, screamed back at him:

'Aye, if it wasn't before witnesses, I'd let Lochend know of your heathen capers, feeding a poor orphan bairn on white fish to make a whale of him and put him in a bottle and send him up to Edinburgh and have yourself made a professor at a poor motherless bairn's expense. Aye, if it wasn't before witnesses, I'd——'

Dr. Reith slammed the door to deafen the noise of Bella Pringle's farewell. He hurried down the path between the crocus beds to the green iron gate, a squat figure in his heavy black clothes, his tall black hat stuck on the back of his head, his red face under it like a hunter's moon, and carrying his heavy black obstetrical bag. He heaved himself up into the gig, mumbling:

'Gie me the reins, loon, an' lat's oot o' here, or thon auld bitch o' a body will hae the whale toon on the tap o' us for vivisection or resurrection, or just tae hear a respectable party misca'd. Aye, Adam niver had ony fancy for thon apple.

He took a bite o' it tae stap Eve's blethers. Hae ye a'thing wi' you, Alicky? Then we'll awa'.'

They drove up the long road to the glen beside the sea, and the tide was going out leaving the sands bare. The plover piped their shrill note into the wind. The gulls sailed overhead crying of sorrow. Down from the hills came the cold March wind, smelling of snow. Dr. Reith fumbled at his coat collar until it was up to shield his throat. When the mare had settled to her trot and the wheels of the gig made monotonous music, the doctor turned to talk to Alicky, and Alicky wondered why barley grew from but the one side of the doctor's nose.

'It's queer kind, Alicky, takin' ye up this road. I mind fine o' the day I brocht ye doon it, and ye squealin' aneath ma oxter like a wee pig that the soo's sat her hunkers on. Aye, did I richt or did I wrang? Is it richt I'm daein' the day or is it wrang? Wha'll ken till the trumpet soonds and the deid cam' scamperin' frae their graves tae settle ootstandin' accoonts wi' their medical advisers? Aye, what will auld Jennie the hen-wife say tae Macinlay. "Aye, Dr. Macinlay," she'll say, "ye said I had a wee touch o' the wind when I wis deein' for the want o' it." Aye! puir auld Jennie! She preferred a wrang diagnosis in the Gaelic tae a richt ane in a Christian tongue.

'Weel, Alicky loon, an' ye're tae be a herd,

103

are ye? The profession had a gey reputation in the time o' Noah. It's nae sae muckle thocht o' the day. A herd the day thinks he'd deen fine if a' his bairns are policemen and ladies' maids ower a' fower continents. Or are there five o' them, Alicky? It's a while since I wis at the school. But for masel', Alicky, if I wis startin' ma life ower again, I'd as soon be a herd as treat an auld body a' winter for rheumatics tae be peyed wi' a sittin' o' pullets' eggs that winna hatch.—Aye.—Keep yer heid doon when we come wi'in sicht o' the clachan, Alicky, or a' the *cailleachs* will be oot on the road calling blessings on ye and scaring the life oot o' the mare.'

Alicky did as he was bid, crouching down with his head level with the doctor's knees until the clachan was out of sight and they were driving along the rough track through Glendruid.

'They're telling me, Alicky,' the doctor said, 'that Glendruid's the best place in the world tae learn a herd's job. The factor will hae a running stock on it, though they say the yowes will no' live here in a late spring. Weel, and it's like as not that herding's the same as medicine. It would get kind o' monotonous like if a'thing lived, and if ye can breed sheep in Glendruid, ye'll breed them onywhere else.

'And there's Archie Campbell oot on the road tae meet us. That's anither grand thing aboot a herd's life, Alicky. Your time's yer ain. Ye're

104

no' at the call o' ony daft body wha thinks ilka buzzing o' wax in his lugs is the last call. Aye, Alicky loon, stick to the sheep an' your prayers an' leave women alane, drink steadily in moderation, niver haud wind nor water in nor guid meat oot, an' ye'll niver need the attentions o' the profession tae which Macinlay has the impertinence tae belang.—Haud yer head up, mare!—How are ye, Archie? *Cia mar tha sibh an diugh?* Man, if the Glendruid wethers were as weel fleeced as yersel' there'd be nae occasion for ye tae keep yowes.'

The doctor leant down from the gig, gripping the shepherd's hand. 'Aye, Archie lad, it's kind o' queer how many herds hae fine lang beards. Whiles I'm o' the opinion it's the braxy mutton that mak's hair grow. Maybe ye'll get some kind o' a thatch tae Alicky's pow. He didna answer tae white fush, but green mutton will maybe mak' a man o' him. Ye ken Alicky?'

'Indeed, yes, doctor. It's Alicky and myself will be the old acquaintances. If he's to be living in Glendruid, it will save him many the long day's tramp from Lochend. Come in to your tea, doctor! There'll be bread and cheese and peeweets' eggs and barley bannocks and goat's milk. Aye, doctor, I put the cow away in the back-end and got a goat to myself in her place. There'll not be the substance in Glendruid grazing or bog-hay to give a decent cow an occasion to give milk, but the goat's doing well for me, and if a gentleman will trouble himself to hold his nose while he's drinking he'll never know it's not cow's milk that's in it.'

'Ye can gie me onything in reason, Archie. Plain meat and a short blessing and I'll dae awa' fine. But nae braxy mutton! I canna bide the stuff.'

'Indeed, and there will be no braxy mutton in it, doctor, until the casks come back with the hoggs in the first days of April. There would be plenty dead sheep on the hill if a gentleman was to be seeking for them, but there's not one of them at this time of the year would stand up to a swing.'

Archie Campbell led the way up the path to the little house. An old grey nanny-goat was tethered in the vicinity of a patch of green weeds. She lowered her head, presenting her horns in defiance of strangers. The shepherd said:

'It was Dr. Macinlay that was once telling me that in the old days the goat's milk was believed to be a cure for the consumption. Indeed, Dr. Macinlay was telling me that on occasion he would be prescribing it himself.'

Dr. Reith made a sneering noise, something between a sneeze and a snort. Alicky Mag backed away from the goat's horns, and Archie Campbell said quickly: 'She will not touch you, Alicky. Fine does she know who is in God's care.'

Dr. Reith muttered, 'Weel, weel, wi'oot intendin' ony profanity, the Almichty hes his work cut oot.—D'ye smoke, Archie? Because if ye dae, keep your baccy jar weel oot o' the reach o' the loon!'

The shepherd led the way into the house, stooping to go through the low door. The doctor, shorter in stature, followed him, combative and erect, his keen nose judging the quality of the barley bannocks. Alicky shambled behind, wondering shyly whether the invitation to tea extended to himself.

The shepherd had made a good tea. It was all set out on the deal table, newly scrubbed in preparation for the visitors. There were a half-dozen peeweets' eggs, hard-boiled and cold, lying in a basin in all the beauty of the green and brown and strange scrolled devices which hide them from sight on the fresh-turned ploughland. There were oatcakes and barley bannocks and a jug of the goat's milk. There was a kebbuck of soft Ayrshire cheese wrapped in a white napkin. Twigs of the hazel, the alder, the birch, gathered by the river-side, blazed a welcome on the hearth. And the tea itself was thick and brown and strong with the tang of the peat water in which it was made.

The doctor said, 'You're fine and cosy here, Archie.'

'Aye, doctor, all that a man could be wanting would be here. Indeed, if a gentleman was to be left in peace to work away with the sheep in the way they should be worked, there might be worse places than Glendruid between the months of April and October. But sit in to your tea, doctor, and you too, Alicky, and tell me what you will be thinking of the Ayrshire cheese and the goat's milk. But maybe Alicky will be giving us a Latin grace. Will ye no', Alicky?'

'Dae as ye're bid, Alicky,' said Dr. Reith.

So Alicky bent his head obediently, muttering:

> *A, ab, absque, coram, de,*
> *Palam, clam, cum, ex, or e.*—Amen.

'Fine!' said Dr. Reith, 'that brings back ma college days.'

But Archie Campbell was staring hard at Alicky, surprise mixed with admiration on his brown face. He said:

'Indeed, and the Romans must have been uncanny people to pass the time of day with the Almighty before sitting down to their meat.'

'Aye, Archie,' said Dr. Reith. 'The Romans had a God for ilka occasion. Jupiter for a'thing, Ceres for the white crap, Mercury for medicine, Juno for merriage, and Venus, a grand upstanding woman wi' a fine roomy pelvis, for a' the tootie-pooties nae sanctified by the Kirk. And the geese cackled on the Capitol whenever it wis like tae be rain—Aye!'

'Indeed, doctor,' said Archie Campbell, 'and

it must be a grand thing to have all that education. Indeed yes.'

Then they ate together and ate well, and Dr. Reith accepted a splash of the Auld Kirk in his third cup of tea.

'Noo, I must awa',' he said. 'I've ma ain patients the day tae keep richt, and the patients o' a sick professional brither, wha shall be nameless, tae *pit* richt. And it's mony a lang mile atween Glendruid and the outbye hirsel o' Glendrochater, whaur the herd's wife is hoping for a lassie an' will fairly brak' her hairt if it proves tae be a seventh son.' Dr. Reith rose from the table and wrestled into his heavy black cloak. 'Goodday tae ye, Archie. Keep an eye on the loon. Mak' a guid herd o' him, but see that he doesna forget a' his Latin.—Alicky, if ye iver tak' it in yer heid that I micht hae deen mair for you, pit the blame on auld Bella Pringle for no' haudin' the white fush intil ye. And when it comes tae the lambing, mind on the first law o' obstetrics, human or veterinary, which a sick professional brither wha shall be nameless whiles forgets.— Niver pu' till ye ken what you're pu'in' on.'

Archie Campbell and Alicky followed the doctor to his gig. The mare was three parts asleep, the reins thrown over a fencing post, a thick rug over her back. The doctor turned her face towards Lochend and settled himself in the driving seat for a quick run down the glen.

Archie Campbell said, 'I'd have liked fine if you'd taken the occasion to hear Alicky play you a tune on the fiddle.'

'Na! Na!' the doctor answered. 'I niver could bide tae hear guid cat-gut mishandled.—Guid-day tae ye a'. Guid-day tae ye a',' he called as he drove away.

Alicky, struck suddenly with shyness, loneliness, and panic fear, started to run after him. But the shepherd laid a gentle hand on the boy's shoulder, restraining him.

'Come away in, Alicky,' he said. 'I've a new trick of time in "Robin robbed the weaver" that I've been meaning to show to you this month past. If you can but put your mind to the fiddling, there will surely come a time when you will never feel lonely like. When I would be sleeping alone in this house on a dark night and the sorrow comes over me for Mairi, my wife that's gone, I stretch out my hand and lay it on my fiddle, and—oh, Alicky!—the comfort of the feel of the wood and of the strings. Come in with me, boy, till I learn you that fancy trick of time.'

And Alicky turned and went in.

VIII

SUNSHINE streamed in over the potato sacks and the meal kist, over the piled sheepskins and the bags of loose wool, over casks of smearing grease and a litter of old sacks, broken spades, empty bottles and rusted shears. It streamed over the dusty floor to the chaff bed on which Alicky lay. It fell on his withered face, making it look comely for a moment, then growing stronger, it showed the bald head, the thick nose and lips, the lifeless, withered skin of the boy.

Alicky Mag awoke. He started up, wondering where he was—wondering where was the painted text, the cracked window-pane, the collection of shells, dead flowers, and sea-urchins of his room at home. Then he remembered where he was—in the shepherd's house at Glendruid—how he had fallen asleep the night before listening to Archie Campbell playing old, sad tunes on his fiddle in the room next door. So he lay in bed watching the dawn grow, monstrous shapes loom out of the morning mist into the shape of hills, the crimson of a space of clear sky fade to carnation pink, the peeweets and larks rise calling and singing from the green turf by the river-side, a shower pass in silver over the sun's face. He saw that the door of his room was open, the outer door of the house open too, and the morning air swept over the garden and through the open doors to greet him as he lay in bed. He could hear the goat rattle her chain, the larks' vibrant melody of spring days, the cock grouse calling on each other from knowe to knowe to 'Go-back,' 'Go-back.'

Alicky scrambled out of bed and dressed himself, never heeding whether his tie was straight or his collar turned up at the back. There was no Bella Pringle in Glendruid to send him back to his room to straighten this and to tidy that. Archie Campbell wore no collar and tie. Indeed his clothes looked as though he slept in them. So without bothering much about his clothes and with his boots half laced, Alicky stumbled out to meet morning in the glen.

When he stepped from the house, small birds, chaffinches, linnets, and starlings, rose in a cloud from the place where hens' food had been scattered. The birds flew out over the river which sang its quiet song down the glen. Alicky went down the garden, stepping wide of the path to keep clear of the goat's lowered horns. He came on the narrow dusty road where birds were scattering the fine dust among their feathers. Everywhere there was the singing of birds and the whispering of water and wind among low trees by the river-side.

Alicky heard a shrill, far-carrying whistle from the hills above the house, and looking back, saw the tiny figures of Archie Campbell and his two dogs away up on the brae face. Alicky set off to overtake them, stumbling into drains and over stones in his awkward haste, stopping every now and then to look up to the place where the tiny figures gradually grew larger. Archie Campbell was awaiting his coming. The two smooth-coated black collies came racing down to meet Alicky, but the shepherd called them back to his heel. There could be no playtime for the dogs of a hill herd.

Alicky felt the blood rush to his face. To meet an old friend for the first time in the day was to him the re-making of friendship. He had gone out into the morning sunshine with such pleasure, even with gaiety, and yet, when he saw Archie Campbell awaiting him, sitting on a lichen-covered boulder with his two dogs lying quietly at his feet, Alicky felt shy of him. He wondered whether the shepherd would be displeased with him for sleeping in after the sun had risen and the work of the day begun. He wondered whether the warmth of evening kindness had faded with morning. But Archie Campbell was kindness itself.

113

'And it was me that was slow to waken you this morning, Alicky,' he called, 'and would I have been keeping you awake now last night with the fiddling I was at? I couldn't keep my hands off it till the night was well through. And it's a grand day to be seeing the hill for the first time. Indeed, as you've risen early like a herd, you'll be coming with me round the sheep. There may be a lamb or two in it the day. Indeed and there was a yowe like kebbing out on the Sliaghmhor heft yesterday morning. The yowes are no' due for a week yet, but it's a hill that's bad for kebbing as for all things else. It's no' fit for yowes, but the factor he's aye girning about more ewes, more ewes, Mr. Campbell, when it's a wether stock like the Sliaghmhor itself that should be in it indeed. Lace your boots up like a herd, Alicky, and we'll away out to see what the sheep will have been doing since I saw them last.'

Archie Campbell took Alicky all round the hill with him that day. It was a fine day for walking. Mist rose before the sun, gracefully, lifting the gossamer lace of its veil from the hollows of the hills. The mist cleared until the sun shone out and the pools and the river were all blue. The sheltered rocks gathered and held the spare warmth of a spring morning. The wind gossiped in the bare branches of stunted rowan and birch-trees, in the ravines where streams sang. Birds everywhere, in a multitude of voices, gave thanks.

Alicky followed Archie Campbell for mile upon mile, over heather and moss, across the bare tops of the ridges where the peat was cut by water into fanciful shapings, down into the hollows where the peat-brown water of the streams foamed into white, along the steep and shaded rocks where snow still lay in the early days of April.

The shepherd knew where each heft of sheep would be found. He knew too each sheep as a man will know his acquaintances in a village. He knew their faces, and their history, their parentage, peculiarities and behaviour. He would point his stick at a lean ewe, saying to Alicky:

'Aye, and it's herself that's the lean one. She's been like that in the spring for the last three years. You would be thinking, indeed, that it was fluke that was the do with her, but never yet has she been poked below the jaw as a fluky sheep will always be. And the last three years, though you'd be thinking it's eild that she was by the look of her, she would have as bonnie a lamb at her foot as any ewe on the heft, aye, and milk it well.'

He would point his stick at another, saying:

'Aye, she's a good yowe indeed as her mither and her granny were before her. She would never be leaving a lamb that wasn't a top. But

115

it's a fair bit of grazing she would have as her gang.'

Again, he would point to a strong and heavy wether. 'It is the bold one that's in it, indeed. He would have been away two years back, but I will be keeping him on a whiley yet, for there's no drift of snow that he's not fit to break through, and the weak yowes following behind him. Aye, and he's the bold strong sheep he is indeed and after the best tup we ever had on the place.'

So, on a fine fresh morning of early April, Alicky Mag was introduced to the small-boned, hardy sheep of Glendruid grazing, by Archie Campbell, their shepherd, who knew every one of them by sight if not by name. Alicky would come to know them all himself in the days that lay before.

The shepherd circled all round the rim of the elliptical cup that was Glendruid. He pointed out the unfenced boundaries to Alicky, the twisting burn that lay between Glendruid and the wether grazing of the Sliaghmhor; the crest of barren rock between Glendruid and Glendarroch, the high precipice that rose from the Pot to the feet of Ben Cruachan. And far over the crests of Ben Cruachan lay the Western sea. He pointed to the far distant house over on the Sliaghmhor, saying:

'And yonder's where Duncan Ban Macgregor would be living with his wife Anna who had an eye pecked out by a hoodie crow when she was but a baby lying in the heather while her mother was at the cutting of the peats. Aye, and yonder there lives with him Donald Mor, his grandfather that fought with General Campbell in the Indian Mutiny, and who has heard with his own ears from the lips of those who saw it all with their own eyes when they were bairns, of what Cumberland's redcoats would have been doing to the decent, quiet, Hieland women when their men were scattered and beaten in the "45." Indeed and it's the sad, sad story that Donald Mor can tell. And Duncan Ban Macgregor has the two lassies with him, Mairi and Janet, and it's two wild lassies that are in it and all. We must be taking a walk over to the Sliaghmhor to see Duncan Ban on some fine evening when the lambing's over and by——'

From a high point on the ridge between Glendruid and Glendarroch, Archie showed Alicky the view of Lochend and the sea-loch where it lay. The town, so far away, looked like a toy; the first boat of the day seemed a model ship steaming across a small pool of water. The pier looked the size of a match. Yet so clear was the air and so still the hills that the piermaster's bell, signalling the approach of the first boat of the morning, rang like a fairy chime that could be heard even on the high ridge between the sheep grazings of Glendarroch and Glendruid.

Then Archie Campbell led the way down the steep brae opposite to the house, through rank heather and the brittle fronds of dead and frosted bracken. To reach the cottage they had to cross the Druid river by an old bridge where the stones were buried in cushions of green moss and the ferns grew out from the cracks where mortar had decayed. The bridge was humped like a bent back with a high parapet on either side. They stood on the bridge for a moment watching the dark waters swirl beneath them, and as they stood a salmon leapt like an arrow in his silver glory, leaving ringed ripples spreading to the river's banks.

'It's a whiley since I saw one so far up the Druid,' Archie Campbell said; 'it's a grand burn for trout that's in it, and fine trout they will be, with the skin on them black as coal with red spots like a toad's eyes and the flesh of them red as any sea-trout's. You'll be having more than one to your tea before you're through with Glendruid, Alicky Mag.'

Over the bridge, the fine springy hill turf was under their feet all the way to the glen road, and the larks above it were specks of living melody in a mist of blue. The grass itself, too, had the fresh green of spring-time spreading like a thin green mist over the dead mat of winter herbage.

'Indeed,' said Archie Campbell, 'and you'd be thinking, Alicky, that this was a fine bite of meat for a weakly ewe. But if you would be wanting a weak ewe to live to be cast in the back-end, *you* keep it clear of the green turf by the burn's banks. There'll be no' a worse bittock of ground for the trembling in the whole of Glendruid. I was once asking Dr. Reith what the cause of trembling in sheep might be, and he says it's nothing but the poor beasts shaking themselves to death with excitement at the sight of some decent meat. Indeed, and the doctor must always be having his joke.'

They crossed the road more used by the wings of birds in their sand-baths than by the feet of men coming and going about their business. They crossed the road, and went in through the little garden past the goat to the cottage. Archie chained his two dogs in a ramshackle lean-to shed behind the house, and then he led the way to the kitchen to make breakfast.

'You be getting the fire going again, Alicky, and a kettle on the boil and I'll make porridge to us both. I'll be making porridge to us, Alicky, the like of which you will never have tasted in your born days. You will find those who will say that porridge is made by the mixing of oatmeal and water. They would be thinking that every meal and all water is suitable to the purpose. The poor things that they will be! If you would be tasting *real* porridge, Alicky, you must know the land where the oats were grown, the weather that was in it at the harvesting, and the mill where the meal was ground. And the finest meal in all Scotland, the country that should be called Alba if a man would but be using his tongue to make the music of the Gael and no' misusing it to mouth the rude noises the Sassenach would be calling speech, the finest meal in Alba will be that grown in machair land in a late year and ground in the mill of Glengrassochy by old bald Donal with the steel hand. If that be the meal and the water be the melted snow that would have passed over rock and then through peat and then over rock again, you will have the materials to make the porridge that was fed to Fionn by the two wise women. Indeed, and it's likely it'll do more for you, Alicky, than white fish and education. Porridge will be making something better than a scholar. They will make a herd. Indeed, Alicky, and that's something better. Any old bodach can write a book, but it would be taking a man to herd Glendruid, indeed.'

When the fire was a flicker of live flames and the lid jumped on the kettle like a little old man capering to amuse his grandchildren, Archie devoted himself to the making of the porridge. He poured the water into a big black pot with the remains of a year's breakfasts in its ample depths. He sifted the meal through his fingers in fine dust, with reverence as though assisting at some mystic rite, letting it fall in a fine cloud into the boiling water, stirring with a short spirtle encrusted with dried meal.

'Never clean a spirtle, Alicky,' he said, 'for it would spoil the flavour of the porridge. Indeed, it would ruin it. Now I will let the porridge set while I milk the goat. You be getting out what's left of the bannocks and the cheese and a plate or two and a knife to us both, for it's like gentlemen indeed that we take our breakfasts in Glendruid.'

After the goat was milked, and Archie put the jug of warm milk on the table, they sat down together to meat.

'Maybe you'll oblige a gentleman with a Latin grace, Alicky?' said Archie Campbell, and Alicky, the blood rushing to his face, mumbled awkwardly, '*A—ab—absque—coram—de.*—Amen.' Archie covered his bent face in his cupped hands.

Then for the breakfast! For the porridge and warm goat's milk—the barley bannocks and the Dunlop cheese! And while they ate breakfast the sunshine and the breeze gave a blessing to their meal. The river and the hill-birds' song played music to them, the honey scent of the willows' golden catkins came in through the open door.

'And who would be thinking,' said Archie Campbell, 'on a morning like what's in it the day, that we're sure to have winds yet, and rain yet, and maybe snow yet. Whiles I'm thinking, Alicky, that it's yourself that brings the bonnie weather to the glen, for I can mind of many a fine day that I've met with you, or spoken with you, or caught a sight of you coming down the road. You'll never have been in Glendruid in storm, Alicky?'

Alicky shook his head.

'Because if you had,' Archie Campbell went on, 'you might have heard some queer things, no' cannie at all. On the wild nights here, Alicky, when I'll be sitting alone with the dumb fiddle across my knees, and the wind coming down the glen like the trumpets of the heavenly host calling sinners to repentance—whiles, Alicky, I'll be hearing some queer like noises in the voice of the gale. Whiles I'll be hearing the sough o' the wind in the branches o' trees. Whiles I'll be hearing a cry in the glen like a people in sorrow. Whiles I could swear that there's horses out on the road and whiles that there's men talking and whispering together out there on the road. And I sit here by the fireside, listening to it all, the dumb fiddle across my knees.

'But—ach, indeed, but it's only the wind that's in it, indeed. Stretch out your hand, Alicky, and help yourself to the bannocks and the cheese. Eat well, boy, for when the lambing's on us, you'll need it all. Eat well!'

All that April day it was fine weather in Glendruid, with whaups sailing with stilled wings over the valleys and hills, spilling liquid melody. All day it was fine weather in Glendruid, with the cock grouse speeding over heather and moss. All day the bees sang lullabies in the willows by the swiftly flowing river. All day it was fine, but at evening the wind changed.

It grew cold by evening, and when the dogs were chained Archie Campbell made a big blaze of wood and peats on the hearth, and brought the fiddle down from the shelf above his bed.

'And to-night, Alicky Mag, I'll teach you as fine a jig as ever was played. "Lady Mary Douglas" it's called, and this is the way of it.'

Archie played the fine tune and Alicky studied the manner of his playing of it, then took the fiddle in his own hands, making discords and some music. But Archie kept him at it until the night grew late and the fire had settled itself down to sleep in a warm glow. By the time they were finished Alicky could make something of the jig called 'Lady Mary Douglas.'

Somehow that night, when the fiddling was over, Alicky felt unwilling to leave the companionship of Archie Campbell and the friendship of firelight. He hung about trying to make his tongue move into speech to delay the necessity of his departure. He went on asking silly questions about the sheep until Archie yawned,

123

displaying a gaping cavern of red above his white beard.

'This will no' do in the morning, Alicky,' he said. 'It's time you was in bed.'

Alicky wished he could sleep within sight of the glowing fire, near to Archie Campbell. But he could not force himself to confess to fear—fear of darkness—of loneliness—of the whispering voices in the gale—of nothing. So he lit his candle and crept out to the lobby, then to his own bed in the farther room littered with implements of the shepherd's trade. He lay in bed with the lighted candle beside him until it spluttered as though in agony, and then died.

Darkness, thick darkness, and the wind outside dying to a whisper, then rising to a scream. —Darkness, and the wind.

Alicky lay quite still, every muscle in his body tense with fear. He lay still, biting his lips in fear. Until he could lie still no longer and was sufficiently afraid to face scorn. He felt that he must escape to the firelight and to Archie Campbell or he must surely die of fear. Yet when he attempted to move he could not, because of the threatening shapes in the room that might leap upon him as he passed, stifling his cries with suffocating hands before he could call for help. He dare not move! He lay in the darkness, listening to the wind.

Far away—it must have been in the hills at

the very top of the glen—from there—from out in the darkness—there came a cry—the cry of a human soul who knows that death is on him. And the cry grew louder and louder, coming down the glen—coming down on the shepherd's house—growing louder and louder.

Alicky sprang from bed. He could not lie there waiting for that awful crying to come over his head. He plunged blindly into darkness, screaming, 'Bella! Bella!' forgetting where he was in his misery of fear, tumbling over the piled sheepskins and bags of loose wool. He imagined that monstrous soft hands were gripping his legs, pulling him downwards until he should fall and be choked by them. He had lost his sense of direction. He did not know where the window lay or in what direction he might find the door. He had forgotten the crying of the wind in his mad panic. Thinking he saw a chink of light he rushed towards it, and something heavy and soft descended on his back.

Alicky lost all reason. He imagined himself buried alive with the earth falling in on him. Deep down in utter darkness and alone. Then he screamed, forming no name with his lips, just the pitiful scream of the trapped animal.

Archie Campbell came in, holding a lamp, his long blue shirt down to his knees. He pulled Alicky from under the pile of sheepskins that had fallen on him.

'Boyan! Boyan! Have no fear!' said Archie Campbell. ''Tis God Himself has us all in His care! Come through with me, boyan, and you will sleep on a blanket by the fire I shall make up for you until daylight will come. Pray you to God and you will find peace, and no fear, in your heart. Pray to God and watch you the firelight till you sleep.'

And lying on a blanket before a fire of twigs Alicky slept until morning.

IX

It was in the last days of April, and only the late ewes left to lamb, when the Glendruid factor rode up the glen road. Alicky was out at the well drawing up a bucketful of the clear water when he saw the grey horse coming round the bend of the road at an easy canter. The horse was unknown to him, but he thought the rider must be a grand horseman because the horse and the rider seemed as one. Alicky left the full pail standing by the well and ran into the house to tell Archie Campbell that a visitor was on his way.

'A grey horse, did you say, boy? Then it's the factor himself will be in it! And is it no' like him, indeed, to be coming just when folks is setting down to their dinners, and before the lambing's through and all. It's "And how many lambs will you reckon to have to sell this year, Mr. Campbell, and how many wethers and how many cast ewes, and what weight of wool?" he'll be asking of me, as though a gentleman was a magician and could poke his nose into the insides of sheep, or was a prophet fit to tell what like a September will be in it the year, and April no' through!'

But even while he poured scorn on the factor and his ways, Archie Campbell was combing out his fine white beard before a broken splinter of mirror glass. He strode down the garden, a tall handsome figure of a man, his age sitting lightly on clean living, his lips courteous to a visitor whatever scorn there might be in his heart. Alicky fled to the lumber-room where he slept. With Archie Campbell and the dogs he could often forget his stunted frame and withered face, but before a stranger he remembered them. Hidden in his sanctuary he could hear the horse being led round to the empty byre, and then the voices of the two men talking as they came towards the house. The factor, saying in a south-country accent unfamiliar to Alicky Mag, 'And what do you reckon to have to sell in the back-end, Campbell? The sales last year were no use at all, not with the price sheep and wool are at. Wethers are not worth the keeping, to-day.' And Archie Campbell answering:

'Indeed, sir, and the wethers are worth the keeping if it's only to break the snow for the weak yowes in storm. And there's more than there should be of yowes on the place just now without seeking to carry any more. If I was to have my way of it, sir, I'd have Glendruid a wether-grazing like the Sliaghmhor. Yes, indeed, sir.'

'If the place won't carry a running stock, Campbell, it's not worth having sheep on it at all. In another twenty years there'll not be a wether grazing in Argyll. I want to see your tally, Campbell.'

'Well, indeed, sir, and you'll find it all in order this day. Maybe there'll be one or two yowes that I never come on the horns of, but— ach—they'll not be more than two or three that's in it altogether.'

'And what will have come over the two or three ewes that you haven't found the horns of, Campbell?'

'Well, maybe they went down the burn, sir, when the spate was on in the last days of February, or maybe they got sunk in the moss and went down out of sight, or maybe they'll be over on the Sliaghmhor. I was thinking of taking a turn up there myself one fine evening and having a bit crack with Duncan Ban Macgregor. He's maybe seen something of them.'

'Maybe, *maybe*! You can't keep accounts on "maybes," Campbell.'

'And allow me to say, sir,' said Archie Campbell, and Alicky could hear the nasal whine in the shepherd's voice which meant the end of his patience, 'allow me to tell you, sir, not meaning any offence, indeed, sir, that sheep were created to graze grass, sir, and no' to make sums wi', and that when a yowe dies and canna be found, her account is with her Maker and no' wi' the factor. There's no living body fit to herd sheep from an office, sir, not meaning any offence, indeed, sir. The very idea o' it, sir, minds me o' the story, sir, of the London merchant, sir, that sent a letter to his shepherd in Sutherland, saying "Wool a very good trade. Have the sheep clipped immediately." And when the shepherd wrote back that he was in the middle of the lambing, as, indeed, we are here, sir, the merchant wrote again giving orders to stop the lambing immediately on receipt of his letter and to get on with clipping, as he had ordered, while Cheviot wool was a good trade. Indeed, sir, and Solomon with all his wisdom was no' fit to manage sheep without seeing them nor to find a yowe that's gone down to the sea or the bottom of a peat moss. But you'll be hungry after your ride, sir, for it's a long road from Dunblair Castle and a cold raw day that's in it, indeed. Maybe you'll do us the honour of taking a bit dinner with us, sir, and a dram to put the sea mist from your lungs.—Alicky boy! Come ben and fetch the water for the kettle. Mr. Scott, the Dunblair man o' business, is stopping for his meat!—Step in, sir, and I'll show you the figures that's in it, for it's little time I have for the clerking and the yowes needing me on the hill.'

Alicky, carrying the full and water-slopping

pail with both hands, found Archie Campbell and Mr. Scott, the estate factor, sitting at the living-room table, the plates shoved backwards in an untidy collection to make room for the shepherd's records of births, deaths, sales and purchases, diary of notable spates and storms, and detailed transactions with the petty cash.

At first they did not look up when Alicky Mag came in, having their heads bent down over the books. But Alicky, confused and awkward as always in the presence of a stranger, stumbled over the edge of the sheepskin which did for a hearthrug, and sent the water out of the pail in deluge over the factor's riding-boots.

Mr. Scott jumped up with an oath, shoving the table from him so that plates and cheese and milk and bannocks fell in the expanding pool of water on the floor.

'In Heaven's name, Campbell,' he cried, 'where did this clumsy old idiot of a man spring from?'

'Indeed, sir, and it's no' a bodach that's in it at all but a boyan that's in God's own care that's giving me a bit hand with the lambing.'

'Well, Campbell, if that's a boy, he should be in a circus side-show and not on a hirsel. Where's his hair? Where's his teeth? Surely he wasn't born like that, was he?'

'Wheest, sir, wheest, you should aye be minding that the sun's behind every cloud and a soul in every body, never heed what queer kind of a

131

body there is that's in it.—Alicky boyan, never heed what Mr. Scott would be saying to you, for with all thon cold spring water in his boots, the hot blood will have gone to his head.—And indeed, without offence to you, sir, the Gall will have no' the manners of the Gaidheil!'

'And do you call it Gaelic manners to souse a man's legs in cold water, Campbell? Is it some kind of ancient feet-washing custom you have in Argyll?'

'Indeed, sir, and the boy never meant any harm. But think you, sir, on the surprise that came over him, and it the first time he set eyes on the Laird's factor! Take off your boots and stockings, sir, and we will dry them to you!— Alicky, get a hold of all the clean clouts you can lay your hands on, and see if it's no' possible for you to make some kind of decent order out of the boorach of baps and dishes that's lying yonder on the floor!'

Alicky did what was possible to retrieve the elements of the dinner and to make the floor dry. He fetched a second pail of water from the well, and as he went backwards and forwards on his tasks the factor and the shepherd paid no further heed to him. Alicky was thankful for that.

But of course his ordeal merely was postponed, for when the meal was prepared he had to share it with the men. It seemed that Mr. Scott was in some sort ashamed of his comments of surprise on Alicky's appearance, for he paid but little attention to him when seated opposite at table. He addressed all his conversation to Archie Campbell.

Alicky hated both the conversation and the man. It seemed that for the factor everything in existence had a price, and that if a thing had no price it was without title to existence. Every opinion the factor held was laid down as though opinion were law. The man talked fast, thrusting forwards his thick neck and highly-coloured face. There was no blemish on his face; many would have called it a handsome face, for the skin was clear if red and the features regular, but the blue eyes had the hard stare of a man who found opportunity for gain rather than charity in his dealings with the weak.

'There's some good bits of sheep-grazing left in Argyll yet,' he was saying, 'if we could get the crofters cleared out, Campbell. But if you as much as turn out a man that's behind with his rent there'll be questions asked in Parliament about it. Unless we can get more land cleared I don't know what's to come over the sheep. Half the land the sheep are on is sheep-sick and the other half won't carry ewes. There's nothing in wethers now to what there was, and there was a ship docked at London the other day with a cargo of frozen mutton from Australia or New Zealand, I can't remember which.'

'*Frozen* mutton!' Archie Campbell exclaimed. 'And what use would frozen mutton be to a body, sir? It's an axe we'd need to be taking to our meat, sir.'

'They thaw it out, Campbell, and they say that when it's thawed out it's better than any braxy mutton and not far short of fresh.'

'I dinna believe it, sir! It's no' right at all, sir! The Almighty would never have been putting warm blood in a beast if it had been His Will that it be frozen.'

'Perhaps not,' said Mr. Scott, 'but whether it's right or wrong, it's going to play the devil with the Highland sheep trade. Yes, Campbell, the Liberals with their Free Trade will soon clear the Highlands of men although they won't allow the lairds do it, and they'll clear them of sheep into the bargain. We'll not compete against Australian mutton once it starts coming in. They can run thousands of sheep to one man out there and no rent or taxes to pay.'

Archie Campbell sneered. 'And will they be thinking in London, indeed, that an Australian sheep that's maybe kangaroo and no' mutton at all, and that's been a matter of months at sea, will have the flavour of a black-face wether from Argyll that's full of lean meat from climbing of the hills, and the fat put on it on the turnips of Lothian, and that's been well bled and hung for no more than a week before it's sold?'

'That would be all right, Campbell, if they kept on sending mutton. But what's to hinder them freezing lamb in the back-end and keeping it frozen until Christmas? Will an Argyll wether, fresh, be any better than a New Zealand lamb frozen?'

'Indeed, and you canna go against Providence like that, sir. If folks will be eating meat that's been dead a six months, frozen or no' frozen, their bellies will rot within them, sir. It will be a judgement on them, sir, for going clean against the good seasons the Lord made for them to enjoy.

'Aye, indeed, sir, the Devil himself will aye help ignorant man to think he's improving on what God ordained for him to do. I was reading in the papers last year of a daft body in America that tied wings to his back and jumped off the top of a house. He gave but the one flap and down he came. And when the poor daft body was dying, sir, he says, and these were his last words, sir, "Men will surely fly one day." Aye, and maybe they will, sir. But God gave wings to the birds because they are but innocent beasts that will be using their wings to fly to the top of a tree to send a bit song down the glen in summer. But if men could fly, sir, with the Devil's aid, what kind of work would they make of it, sir?'

It seemed that Mr. Scott, the Dunblair factor, was not a religious man. He gave scant heed to what Archie Campbell was saying, being more concerned with the sappy excellence of the Ayrshire cheese. When Archie Campbell had paused for lack of breath to carry on with, the factor said, 'Flying? I don't think there's much in that. Railways will be a safe investment for a long time yet. But I'd take the Devil's help any day to get ten per cent. and full security.'

And Archie Campbell quoted the old words:

'*Amadain, air an oidhche so fein iarrar d'anam nait: an sin co dha a bhuineas na nithean sin a dh'ulluich thu?*'—'Thou fool, this night thy soul shall be required of thee: then whose shall those things be, which thou hast provided?'

But Mr. Scott knew no Gaelic and Archie Campbell did not translate. Instead, he asked the factor:

'And would you be caring to take a look through the sheep now that you are here, sir?'

'No need for that, Campbell, I have the figures. You'll let me know if you come on those missing ewes.'

'Indeed yes, sir. I'll be sending the boy here running all the way to Dunblair Castle if we should come on a horn.'

Mr. Scott's face grew a deeper red at this remark. He realised the impudence behind the courtesy. But, as he was fond of saying, the hand that signs the cheque rules. He said:

'You understand that if you can't account for

missing sheep, their value comes off your wages, Campbell.'

'Indeed yes, sir, that was always the way of it wherever I was herd. Except in the one place, sir, where the gentleman himself managed his own affairs.'

Mr. Scott took no heed of the insult, or perhaps he did not notice it. Instead, he nodded in the direction of Alicky Mag.

'You seem to manage your own affairs in your own way, Campbell. Who is this boy you've got and what is he doing here?'

Archie Campbell gasped in simulation of surprise. 'And did Dr. Reith not tell you of him, sir? Indeed, and I thought he had taken the occasion to have a word with you before he sent the boy to me here. He's a boy that Dr. Reith has an interest in and that was to have come out for a doctor if he'd had the makings of a scholar, but Alicky's mind is all on the hills, and the birds, and the beasts, and he's taken it in his head to work among the sheep. And it's shaping well at them he is. He's been real handy about the place this lambing.'

'So Dr. Reith put him here, did he? The boy is one of *that* kind. You'll be getting something for keeping him, I suppose?'

Archie Campbell motioned to Alicky to withdraw, saying:

'Indeed, and we'll not discuss that before the

boy himself, sir. I'll tell you of the arrangement privately.'

So Alicky wandered out into the garden while the two men talked of him inside. He felt very miserable. He always did feel miserable before strangers. He wondered whether life were worth the living. It would be fine if he could live all alone with the dumb, friendly beasts—the birds, the dogs, the sheep. He went round the little house to the tumble-down byre, once inhabited by the cow that would not give milk on Glendruid pasture, and there he found the grey horse whinnying. Its saddle and bridle were off, and there being no halter in the byre, the horse was looking out on the unfamiliar glen over the lower half of the swing door. Alicky thought the grey horse looked lonely too, and went over to speak to it, and the horse stretched out its head to be stroked, whinnying so loudly that its whole frame shook. Alicky stayed to comfort the horse until he heard the men coming round from the house, then he fled out of sight behind the byre. He stayed there until he heard the sound of hoofs go down the road—first the walk changing to a trot, then breaking to a canter—and the sound dying away in the distance. He crept out and found Archie Campbell gazing after the horse and its rider. When Alicky came up, Archie laid a gentle hand on his shoulder.

'Alicky,' he said, 'if this were Ireland and me

myself an Irishman, I'd put a bullet down that road that would go quicker than any horse. Aye, indeed, and that's what I'd do if this were Ireland and me an Irishman. But that's never been the way of the Highland Gael. It's the great sorrow that's on us for the grand days of our race that are gone. We'll weep for those days in the *ceilidh*, and make the sad songs of them to play on the fiddle or the *clarsach*. But we'll no' do nothing now to bring the grand days back again. It's nothing but the shooting from behind dykes would bring them back, and it was never the way of the Highland Gael to do that. If only the Campbells and the Macdonalds could have agreed together, we'd have given the Sassenach a wee bit of ground round about London to build their general merchant shoppies on, and put the fine grazing of England under black cattle and sheep. But we'll no' descend to shooting a body when he's expecting a bit rise in his pay for the grand way he's factoring the Dunblair estates. But—eh—Alicky boyan, I whiles wish I was Irish! Run in for my gun, Alicky, and a cartridge for it! I'll make on my name's Patrick and thon birk tree called Scott. Run in, boyan, for my gun!'

And Alicky, because he thought the joke good and one after his own mind, wrinkled his ugly face into a weird smile, and ran to do the shepherd's bidding.

X

WHEN the lambing was all by and past, and in the milder days of May the cuckoo called to summer in Glendruid, Alicky went with Archie Campbell to visit Duncan Ban Macgregor on the wether grazing of the Sliaghmhor. They took the rough track through the heather which had been a foot-path over the hills in that direction since the first Irish emigrants stood on the highest vantage-point they could find to gaze out over the Western sea, searching for a glimpse of the green hills of Ireland—the land of saints. Archie Campbell led the way because a man must know the tricks of that track among the heather before he can find it. The path gets lost every now and again. At times it disappears in the spate course of a hill burn. At times it dies away on bare places where weather has scarred and furrowed the peat's face. But if a man should but know the vagaries of the track he will find it again, where it winds in and out among the heather and the moss between Glendruid and the Sliaghmhor.

Alicky found the going heavy, because Archie

Campbell had the same steady pace on the brae
as on the plain. The shepherd was hard of
limb and superlative of wind, for he could talk
fast and climb fast, all together without losing
his breath.

'You should understand, Alicky,' he said,
'that the wethers on a wether-grazing are all
bought in and not bred on the place. They
come in as hoggs, and they'll be on the place a
matter of two, three, aye, even four winters before they come to be sold. They're grand sheep
for living, boy. There'll not be one wether lost
for four or maybe five yowes that will die on the
same ground. Aye, and you'll graze three
wethers well where two yowes will be needing
all their time. Aye, if I had my way of it, Alicky,
I'd have a wether stock in Glendruid, and not
they poor wee yowies that think they're doing
grand if they will rear but the one lamb in two
summers.'

Alicky clambered up behind Archie, too
breathless to do more than nod assent to the
shepherd's assertions. Behind him came the two
black collies, panting like railway engines getting up steam.

They came to the twisting burn—the boundary
between Glendruid and the Sliaghmhor—a brown
peat stream running swift and strong amid the
privacy of birch trees. They crossed by the age-
old ford, scene of ambushes and the flash of

targe and sword in days long dead. The track went down over the lip of a ravine, using the exposed roots of birch trees as steps in its steep descent. There, at the bottom of the ravine, was the deep brown stream breaking into cream over the crests of rocks. Stepping-stones suited to the stride of an active man made an easy and dry crossing for Archie Campbell and his dogs, but Alicky Mag hesitated in the middle of a stride between the last stone and the farther shore, tried to step back, spread arms and legs in an effort to regain his balance, and went splashing in to the waist in the ice-cold water. He pulled himself out again, protesting to Archie Campbell that he was only a little wet and not at all uncomfortable, and the shepherd said that on a mild evening of May there was no harm done in clumsiness having its own reward. Alicky didn't mind the coldness of the water so much as the exhibition of his ineptitude. It seemed that he was doomed throughout life to make a fool of himself. Whenever he began to fancy himself as a shepherd and no mere daftie, something would happen to prove to himself and to others that he was not quite as other boys were. Still, if he walked hard, most of the water would have dripped off his clothes before he reached the shieling of the Sliaghmhor. Archie Campbell had told him how in the old days before men and cattle went and sheep came, there was no winter stock on the Sliaghmhor, but that the best bit of grazing where Duncan Ban Macgregor had his house now, was once on a time a hill shieling, summer pasturage, for the stock of the people of Glendruid. But now there was the family of Macgregor living there all the year round— Duncan and Anna his wife; old Donald Mor the grandfather, and Mairi and Janet the two daughters of Duncan Ban—wild lassies and full of daft ploys, it was said. Alicky wished he had kept dry and of a respectable appearance, instead of looking like a drowned rat when meeting with new friends. But Archie Campbell went up the hillside at such a pace that soon Alicky lost interest in everything except his pounding heart and aching legs.

'We'll no' be far from half-roads there,' cried Archie Campbell to encourage him, and Alicky wondered how he could possibly survive the second half of the road. But instead of death overtaking him on the open moor as he had feared, he got fresh wind, and settled down with greater comfort to complete the journey up the hillside.

Over the crest of a ridge they saw their destination and resting-place for the night, for Archie Campbell said that they would spend the night with the Macgregor family and return down the hill again early in the morning in time to milk the goat and feed the hens, seeing to the sheep on the way down.

The ancient shieling of the Sliaghmhor is built on the side of a loch of clear water entrapped in a cup of the hills. People living in the shepherd's hut of the Sliaghmhor can open the door, take a few strides downwards over fresh, green grass, and fill a pailful of water where the shore of the loch is quartz rock and where no water weeds grow. In the dusk of a winter's evening at the shepherd's hut of the Sliaghmhor, people sitting before the warm fire can hear the rustle of the water in the loch when the duck come down from the cold sky to rest on the calm placidity of moon-lit water. So close is the dwelling to the lochside. There are tales told of the loch—of the water-kelpie—'*an t-each uisge*, who in the old days when the quiet-spoken maidens of Glendruid would follow the cows and the milk-goats to the sweet summer grazing of the Sliaghmhor, met them in the guise of a splendid youth, and in the calm of evening led them through love to a wet grave in the loch of the Sliaghmhor. And there the wild fowl sung them a coronach and the white water-lilies formed their shroud.

'And yonder,' said Archie Campbell pointing towards the house beside the loch, 'will be Duncan Ban Macgregor coming down the hill to meet us himself. You'll no' need to wait long now, Alicky boy, before you'll be sitting in to your tea.—Aye, Duncan!' he shouted in Gaelic, 'and are you all well at home?'

Duncan Ban Macgregor strode forwards to meet his guests, and on his lips was courtesy and in his blue eyes shone the kindness of his heart. 'Archie Campbell,' he said, 'and it's me that's glad to be seeing you again. And will this no' be the boyan that they're telling me knows every living bird by its whistle and every living beast by its track in the peat. You will both be a thousand times welcome to the Sliaghmhor!'

Alicky Mag looked up to the tall man in green knickerbocker suit and green cap, his brown beard and ruddy face with hundreds of wrinkles running outwards from the corners of his blue eyes. And in those blue eyes was kindness. Duncan Ban and Archie fell into the Gaelic talk and walked on ahead, with Alicky, and Archie's two dogs at their heels. They came to the low house of grey stone set by the shore of the still loch.

They went into the house and there, seated around the table, were the others of the Macgregor family—old Donald, the patriarchal grey-bearded grandfather, sitting by the fire, the great family Bible open on his knees, and Anna, the wife of Duncan Ban—her once comely face worn with the fear that loneliness brings to women who always must wait, and with the anxious work and cares of long years. Her body had grown gross and her legs swollen with much standing over pots and pans. One eye was dead glass, the other dark and twice alive. There were the two girls—fair Janet and dark Mairi—Janet solid, heavy, with the placidity of a calm evening on her happy face, Mairi lithe and dark, with the restlessness of a troubled sea. And after one fleeting glance Alicky knew that he could die for Mairi.

But old Donald was reading a chapter from the big family Bible spread on his shaking knees. Old Donald was reading the Word, and everyone was still. Archie Campbell and Duncan Ban Macgregor stood on the threshold of the room, their bonnets clasped in their hands before them —their heads bowed. And Alicky Mag stood silently behind them.

Old Donald read on, and it was in Gaelic that he spoke the Word of God. He was reading from the twelfth chapter of the Gospel of St. Luke the fine old words — *Thugaibh fainear na lili-ghean, cionnus a tha iad a'fàs*—'Consider the lilies, how they grow.' He read on without raising his head until the chapter was ended—*Tha mi ag ràdh riut, nach téid thu mach as a sin, gus an ioc thu eadhon a pheghinn dheireannach*—then he laid the Bible down with reverence on the table beside him, covered his face with his aged hands and prayed. Alicky Mag peeped out between the webs of his own spread fingers to let his glance linger on dark Mairi. He saw that she too was peeping, that she was looking at him and that her

146

mobile lips were twitching in efforts to control her laughter. Alicky thought that she must surely be laughing at his absurd appearance—he closed his fingers together before his eyes to hide his burning face.

After his prayer was ended old Donald rose and his family rose with him. He drew himself wonderfully erect to welcome his guests. His head shook a little from age, but his blue eyes were keen yet kindly, his hand-clasp genial and firm. To Alicky Mag he gave special courtesy and consideration, as though to prove that here was no deformed object, but rather a handicapped soul—as though to show that those who were in God's care were sure of protection and special privilege in the shepherd's house of the Sliagh-mhor. Old Donald could speak only in the Gaelic, so that Alicky could understand but little of what was said, but he could see gentle kindliness shine in the old man's eyes.

Anna Macgregor had a meal ready for them all. Soon the low-ceilinged kitchen was filled with the reek of braxied mutton. But Alicky, since the return of the young sheep—the hoggs dead and alive—from winter grazing to their home in Glendruid, was accustomed to that reek.

He sat between Anna Macgregor and her daughter Janet. Opposite him was Mairi, her lips still twisting in amusement at his appearance.

The three men at the table's head talked of sheep and of sheep again. Alicky knew of what they were talking because the words *caorach*, *uan*, and *treud* kept recurring, and he knew these words to mean, 'sheep,' 'lamb' and 'flock.' He heard too the Saxon words 'heft' and 'hirsel' spoken, words that had come to the Highlands with the sheep when the sheep came north. All the talk was of sheep.

The women folk, out of courtesy to Alicky, spoke in English. In their quaint accent and with many idiomatic twists of speech taken straight from the Gaelic, they asked Alicky of his life in Glendruid, of his long walk over the hills that day. Archie Campbell interrupted to say that he had clean forgotten that the boyan had fallen in the burn and that, even yet, his breeks must be wet to the very skin. Anna Macgregor gave a little cry of distress, 'Eh! but he will be catching his death of cold. He shall be standing with his backside to the fire until he will be dry.' She insisted that Alicky's wet clothes were steamed out in this so ignominious a manner. Alicky wished he were invisible or dead. Dark Mairi laughed outright. Alicky knew that she was laughing at him, at his absurd appearance, at his undignified posture, standing as he was like a boy waiting to be whipped—his trousers steaming. But although he knew Mairi's laughter was at him, yet he loved her laughter. It was like

148

the music of birds in a festival of song in the sun-lit gardens of heaven. But old Donald thumped his fist on the table, calling '*Mairi!*', and Mairi's laughter was stilled.

When Alicky's clothes were dried out and the meal ended, Duncan Ban took Archie Campbell out to see a young dog working. They asked Alicky to go with them but Alicky looked at Mairi and said that he was tired. Then he blushed helplessly, again and again, so that Mairi turned away her head to hide her laughter.

Mairi said that she was going out to bed the cow and would Alicky care to come with her. He was made silent by her invitation. He grew redder than ever in his uncomely face. But he could not refuse her. He followed her, in dumb reverence, as though she were something too precious to be addressed in earthly language. He followed her, and in his boy's imagination he was a humble serving-man ready to die in defence of his lovely queen. And, indeed, had there been danger to be faced that evening, Alicky Mag would have died gladly for the sake of Mairi Macgregor.

To Alicky there was something unbelievably precious in every movement of that calm evening in May. The hills were still, brooding in their age-old majesty. Peace lay dreaming on the loch's still waters. The very crying of the hill-birds seemed distant and unreal, transmuted to

149

the voices of angels singing the beatitudes. The Sliaghmhor was the carpet of heaven on which he and Mairi walked together.

In her laughing, teasing way she was so kind to him. She called him 'Baldie' and the 'Wee Bodach' and 'Junket Face.' But she laid her slim hand on his sleeve and said that she liked him.

She was so tall, and slim, and agile, with the grace of the willows in their spring glory. Her hair was so dark, with the light and the laughter of peat streams in its two long plaits. The dark oval of her face held all the beauty and mystery born into the world since its beginning. Her brown eyes held the joys and sorrows of all things living, gathered and held together as in the facets of rare jewels. Her voice could caress with the softness of its melody or thrill with the vitality of its happy laughter. She was Mairi, dark Mairi, and creation was her setting.

She and Alicky went down to the lochside where the bank was white quartz with threads of silver mica in its chaste embrace. Together they looked out over the still waters, where the ripples left by the rising trout, the spreading wake of disturbed water-fowl, were mere apology to motion.

Mairi said she would be sixteen in June and asked Alicky his age. Fifteen he told her, and she said he was terribly wee for his age, but maybe he would grow yet. 'And you'll be right hardy though you're wee, Alicky,' she said. Laughing at him again she told him he would be right bonnie if he could but persuade Archie Campbell to buy him a fine, curly wig. She laughed at the idea, finding it irresistibly funny, and Alicky could not resent her teasing. He loved her so. Had she said, 'Alicky, you'd look right bonnie if you was drowned,' he would have plunged to the loch's deepest depths to please her.

They became children together for a while, searching the loch's banks for flat stones which they sent skipping over the water in games of ducks and drakes. They raced each other from the quartz pool to the sheep-pens they called *fanks*, and Alicky won the race. When Mairi caught up on him, she flung herself down in the heather and the sweet-smelling bog myrtle, and laughed up at Alicky again. She said, 'You run real fast, Alicky, but I couldn't race you for laughing. For all the world you looked like a bandy-legged old bodach chasing bairns from his garden!'

She sprang up again, smoothing her white blouse and blue skirt. 'I forgot I'd my Sunday clothes on on a Thursday,' she said. 'Mother always will have us dress up for strangers. Do you like my blouse, Alicky?'

Something snapped the shyness of his soul. He blurted out his thoughts—that the whiteness of her blouse was the sea-mew's breast and the clouds in a summer sky, the white crest on the sea-waves, the cool snow-drifts in shaded corries amid the hills.

She laid her long fingers on his arm, saying, 'I'm sorry, Alicky. I shouldn't be flirting with you. It's time we went in.' So the magic of evening must always end.

But as they walked towards the house, Mairi spoke strangely.

'Oh! Alicky,' she said, 'maybe after all you're *'an t-each uisge*! But maybe, again, you're not. When I saw you first, Alicky, I thought surely you must be he. I thought when we were out here alone by the lochside, that I would turn round and find that you were *he*—the bonniest lad that ever yet was seen. That you would laugh, saying, "Will you come with me to the golden cave beneath the loch where you will be my lovely queen?" But, Alicky, I doubt you're not *'an t-each uisge* at all. I'm thinking you're just a boy that's not grown very well.' She sighed, then laid her long fingers for the last time ever so gently on his sleeve.

'But I do like you, Alicky Mag. I *do* like you,' she said.

XI

WHEN Alicky and Mairi came into the house, dusk had fallen already and the faces of the Macgregors and of Archie Campbell were palettes on which the caressing fingers of the firelight painted dreams. Old Donald himself was talking, spinning tales of the dead past, and in the urgent passion of his speech there lived again the proud boasting of the unconquered Gael. Round about him sat the others on a miscellany of chairs. Archie Campbell whispered to Alicky that old Donald was telling his favourite tales of the morrow of Culloden, of how brave men and true women had been treated like beasts, how children had fled from their quiet homes amid the crackle of flames, how the poetry of a pastoral people had been destroyed—how machinery had gained another victory over men.

Alicky could not follow old Donald's talk— the impassioned rise and fall of the Gaelic tongue —the syllables and words flowing together like liquid silver to form the music of a phrase. Indeed, had he been able to understand, he would not have listened to the words nor have cared for their meaning. He sat quietly beside Mairi, watching the shade and mood of her face's beauty change as the peat flames rose or fell. But Mairi, all through the evening of talk, never touched his sleeve again.

Anna brought out a bottle and the drams went round. The whisky was white and raw, fresh from the still which Duncan Ban kept hidden from the exciseman's eyes in a lonely glen of the Sliaghmhor. Alicky was not offered a glass, but he marvelled how the talk grew louder and the laughter more free once drink was taken. He wondered whether, had he himself been old enough to drink, his tongue would have loosened too, and the poetry in his heart have risen to his tongue in praise of Mairi. For he had it in his heart to praise her.

When Alicky went to his box-bed in the kitchen-wall's recess that night he knew he could not sleep. Solitude was no reason for his sleeplessness. In box-beds round the wall slept old Donald, Duncan Ban, and Archie Campbell. Two collie dogs and a cat lay before the dying fire. The women were in the other room. It was not solitude that kept Alicky from sleep, nor was it lust. He had no lust for Mairi. But he worshipped her. He lay watching light die away on the kitchen ceiling. He day-dreamt of Mairi. When he thought that she was near him— sleeping—indefinable peace spread over him so that he quivered in an ecstasy of worship. He whispered her name 'Mairi,' and in the name lay music's soul. He pictured her lying in the heather and sweet-smelling bog myrtle, lying there in her white blouse that was the sea-mew's breast and in the blue skirt that was the summer sea. In his mind he painted imaginary adventures where Mairi was in danger, and he, Alicky Mag, sacrificed ten lives to save her from a moment's peril. Thus day-dreaming did he lie awake until the first bird rose calling over the loch outside. Only then did he sleep, and it was only when he slept that he dreamt of how he was indeed *'an t-each uisge*—the water-kelpie. He dreamt that he and Mairi were by the lochside and that he suddenly changed to the most handsome of all youths and bent to sweep the strands of Mairi's dark hair with magic lips. But when Alicky awoke and passed his fingers across his face he knew that dreams were only dreams.

He rose early, yawning dully from insufficient sleep. He put on the few clothes that he had troubled to take off the night before, and pulled on his heavy boots, while one of the dogs kept thumping its tail in friendly welcome. Then Alicky crept out past the sleeping men to greet the flood of morning glory sweeping on silver wings across the loch. He wandered down to the gently lapping water, and duck rose in hurried flight, speeding like living arrows to the farther shore.

Alicky stood for a time watching the rebirth of the world which happens each morning. He hoped that Mairi would come out to join him, but only Anna was up and about, carrying pails of water from the loch, milking the cow, feeding the hens, before she had the heart to waken her daughters. To her they were still little children who needed their sleep. So Alicky helped Anna with her morning tasks and was happy with her. She was a quiet contented woman in the summer months. Only when snow lay for long weeks in mid-winter did her heart fail her and she feel trapped and surrounded by white bars. She told all her troubles to Alicky as they wandered together among the out-houses and barns. She treated him as though he were a dumb animal in whom she could safely confide. When all the morning tasks were done she wiped her soiled hands on her apron, saying, 'I must be going in to waken the bairns.' She meant Janet who was eighteen, and Mairi who would be sixteen next month.

Alicky wandered down to the loch again hoping that Mairi would come out. Down there the water lapped against the white quartz rock, birds sang, and the whisper of a breeze stroked the face of the waters, but Mairi did not come. So Alicky went back to the house, disconsolate, knowing that breakfast would be a mere satisfaction of hunger, eaten quickly before he and Archie Campbell returned down the long track to Glendruid.

It was as he had feared. The three men were eating around the table when he entered the house, and Archie Campbell told him to join them quickly for they had no time to waste. So Alicky sat down to the porridge and milk which Anna placed before him, and still Janet and Mairi were not up. It was only when the men had finished eating and Archie Campbell getting ready for the road that the two girls appeared, first Janet, fair and sleepy, then dark Mairi with an other-world look on her dear face. She smiled at Alicky and explained that she had slept late because of dreaming of *'an t-each uisge.*

Alicky knew that he must leave her. Archie Campbell had his bonnet in his hand and was thanking Anna for her hospitality. The two black collies were at the door, switching their tails, impatient to be gone. All around was the bustle and chatter of impending departure. Alicky, in unwilling obedience, followed Archie Campbell as he said farewell, shaking hands with Anna, old Donald, Duncan Ban, Janet—and Mairi. She said to him, 'See and grow a bit, Alicky, before you come up for the shearing next month. If you are really *'an t-each uisge* and never let on, it's me that will never be forgiving you.'

Then they were off, past the loch and down the track which only a man who knows its vagaries could find. They looked back before they slipped over the shoulder of the hill, to wave to the Macgregors. Alicky could see the white blouse where Mairi stood alone, a little way apart from the rest. She waved and he waved back to her, while a strange lump in his throat seemed to choke him. Then the shoulder of the hill hid Mairi from view.

XII

Summer fled past on the wings of sunlight. The festivals of sheep were talked of, prepared, and performed—the clipping of wethers, the eild ewes, and the hoggs in the month of June, the clipping of milk ewes in July, the lamb sales after Lammas, the smearing of the winter stock as the dark days approached. Alicky worked hard in the *fanks* and tramped the high hills among heather and fern. He became strong and hardy although he did not grow, and always the song of the birds brought his heart to the portals of heaven. He thought and dreamt of dark Mairi and the sleeping waters of the loch of the Sliaghmhor. He thought and dreamt of her but he never saw her. For Archie Campbell, although oftentimes he took the hill-track over the hill to the Macgregors' home, went there alone. He went there for the clippings and smearings, and the drawing of the wethers, but he went there alone. He went there sometimes in the long summer evenings when the sun merely dipped itself in the sea behind the hills to rise again, and when there was no special task to be performed at his journey's end. He went to the Sliaghmhor. He went there often and he went alone. And it seemed to Alicky during that summer that Archie Campbell changed. The old shepherd grew young again. He talked less of heaven and more of the world. He would sit for long hours with the dumb fiddle across his knees, but no longer was there sorrow in his eyes but rather a strange joy. When he played the fiddle there was a new vitality of rhythm in the jigs, fresh yearning in the melancholy airs. He unearthed the bagpipes he had not played for years. He spent a week in the cleaning and tuning of them, fitting new reeds to the chaunter, adjusting the skirling of the drones. When the job was completed in an evening of September, he marched backwards and forwards on the road, and Glendruid echoed once more to the music of the Gael. He played a pibroch up and down the glen road, swagger and challenge in the set of his shoulders and the proud swinging of his hips. His fingers danced like magic over grace notes and round the turns, the *tur luath*, the *tur luath mach*, the strange music of his playing drifting down the glen to the clachan, over the river to Glendarroch, up the high hills to the Sliaghmhor, and the pibroch he played was 'I Got a Kiss of the King's Hand.' He would come into the house after his playing, his great chest heaving, his blue eyes ablaze, saying, 'And do you think they will be hearing that on the Sliaghmhor, Alicky Mag?' He went daft on pipe music, setting Alicky to learn the chanter instead of the fiddle, and Alicky soon learnt the scale notes, then the grace notes, then the turns. He learnt that sweet tune 'The Green Hills,' and the fine march 'The Red and Blue Hackle,' but for Archie Campbell the only true pipe music was the pibrochs on the great pipes in the unwritten tradition of MacCrimmon. He forbade Alicky to attempt a pibroch until he had played the chanter for three long years.

In early October, when the first stags were belling in the corries, Archie Campbell came down from the Sliaghmhor with a smile in his eyes and laughter running like summer lightning over his red lips.

Alicky had been sitting alone with the chanter in his hands and the fiddle beside him, the two dogs lying for company at his feet. The lamp was lit because darkness had thickened. The rumble of the stags' bellowing never ceased. Then outside on the road there sounded the rush of horses' feet at swift gallop. Alicky thought it must be the factor, Mr. Scott from Dunblair Castle or Dr. Reith from Lochend, riding on a late errand through the glen. The dogs growled, creeping on their bellies towards the door with bared teeth, then whining. Alicky opened the door and looked out but there was nothing there, no movement, no light, no sounds but the rumble of the stags' roaring and the song of the Druid river flowing to the sea. Then far away up on the hill-track leading down from the Sliaghmhor he heard a man singing. At first the singing was distant—a mere echo among the hills. It grew louder, the words and music of a Gaelic marching song. The voice of the singer was the voice of Archie Campbell, the Glendruid herd. The music came nearer and nearer and Alicky crept into the lamp-lit kitchen. He sat down on his chair, and on one side of him was the silent chaunter, on the other side of him the silent fiddle. There was great sadness in his heart, for in some strange way he knew what was to come.

When Archie Campbell entered, he was all swagger and brag, crying out, 'And will a gentle-man no' be excused an extra dram or two on an occasion like what's in it this night? Alicky Mag boyan, bring out the bottle like a man for it's great news indeed that I will be telling to you.' Alicky did as he was told, knowing full well that Archie already had had enough. Archie lay back in his chair, throwing his bonnet down beside him, his head back, his shirt open at the neck, his white beard seeming strange against the smooth skin of his massive chest. He laughed quietly to himself, then said, 'Great news, Alicky! Great news for you, Alicky! And if it's not dark Mairi Macgregor of the Sliaghmhor herself that has promised me this very night that she will be married on me before a year is past. And is it not me myself that is the proud, proud man this night, Alicky Mag. Me myself, indeed, that was thinking that it was me that was growing the old man, and never more to speak the one hundred words of music that mean "loved one" in the language of the Gael; never more to play a pibroch with the love of my soul on the chaunter's lips and the beating of my heart in the singing of the drones; never more to be holding the warmth of a woman in my arms'—he spread out his arms, boastfully—'these great arms of my own. Never more to see the mist of love spread over the eyes of a woman that Archie Campbell loves. Never more—' He stopped, ashamed, shuffling his feet awkwardly on the floor, saying, 'and indeed that's no way for me to be speaking to a boy like yourself, Alicky Mag, that's too young indeed to be understanding the like of what I've been saying to you at all, but—Oh! Alicky—it's the *Ghruagach dhonn gun ghò, gun fhoill*—the brown-haired maid with witching smile, that's made a new man of Archie Campbell himself this very night!'

Alicky hated Archie Campbell for his blasphemy. It was not jealousy that troubled his boy's heart. He did not love Mairi in that way. But to Alicky, Mairi was something so holy and so precious—the very memory of her dark self beside the waters of the loch of the Sliaghmhor something so nearly divine, that for any man to boast of holding Mairi in his arms, to swagger of the mist of love falling down over her dark eyes —that was blasphemy—nothing less. For Archie Campbell to come half-drunken and singing down the hill-track after Mairi had given the promise to marry him that year—what was that but blasphemy? He should have come down the hill-track quietly with reverence in his heart, a quiet prayer upon his lips!

Alicky sat crouched upon his chair with the hatred that filled his heart staring out from his eyes—the little, twinkling blue eyes that were sometimes merry and often afraid. Archie Campbell saw the hatred and misunderstood. He jerked forwards into a more respectable posture than his relaxed ease. He blurted out— 'Indeed, Alicky, and it was no more than a dram or two to the lassie's good health that was in it up at the Sliaghmhor. There would not be more than the half bottle that we had taken altogether. But it's the cold night indeed that's in it this night, Alicky Mag. And when a gentleman will be coming out from a close room into the night air, it will maybe happen that even a dram or two will bring a bit song to his tongue and a bit swagger to his feet. But there's worse things in this world, Alicky, indeed, than for a gentleman to be taking maybe more drams than he would be accustomed to take on an ordinary occasion. Yes, indeed!'

And Alicky, in his thoughts, echoed those words, 'Yes, indeed! There were far worse things in the world.'

Archie Campbell seemed to resent Alicky's silence. 'Can ye no' speak, boy?' he asked, 'have ye no' a tongue in your head? From the way you're carrying on a man would think you had a fancy for Mairi Macgregor yourself!'

Alicky crept from his chair to go ben to the lumber-room where he slept. He did not speak. He did not raise his head. He escaped to his room silently, to be alone.

Archie Campbell watched him go. He did not bid him stay, but Alicky heard him whisper as in prayer, 'God! Oh merciful God! What way did You come to make a mistake like thon! To put the soul of a linnet in the body of an owl!'

'The body of an owl!'—Alicky kept those words in his memory as he lay in bed. Yes, he often forgot what he looked like when he was alone in his dreams or on the hills, forgot his stunted frame and thick unliving skin, his silly bald head and black, decaying teeth. He forgot these things in dreams or on the hills. He had forgotten them when Mairi touched his sleeve with her slim fingers. But now he remembered them. 'The soul of a linnet in the body of an owl!'

So it would always be like that with him. People would miss the poetry of his soul in derision of his face. Men and women would never see anything in him but a foul figure of fun. Who would take the trouble to probe his mind when there was easy laughter to be had for the looking at his body? Likely enough dark Mairi herself had found him ridiculous, a mere object for mirth. Maybe she had laughed with Janet over his ugly clumsiness and absurd talk. No!—that was impossible, for Mairi was a saint.

But in his dreams that night Mairi was something of a woman as well as a saint, and Alicky Mag himself the handsome young man, splendid in tall strength, comely of body and face. He dreamt of the Sliaghmhor, of the rustle of ducks' wings stroking the sleeping waters of the loch, of dark Mairi waving to him from its quiet shore.

Thus for the brief space of a dream the linnet left the owl's body. It sang boldly and free in its own gay feathering from a fine sprig of hawthorn on a morning in May.

XIII

ALICKY and Archie Campbell were silent and strange with one another for many a long day. Something had come between them on an October night that could not be forgotten all at once. Alicky never held Archie Campbell in quite the same reverence again. To Archie, Alicky Mag was no longer quite a boy. They did not quarrel, and through the autumn months they worked side by side, but the quiet unspoken confidence between them had gone. Glendruid, to them both, was a more lonely place than before. To Archie Campbell the loneliness of his life was a transient thing, because in the spring of the year Mairi Macgregor would be his wife. But for Alicky the coming of spring held no promise of release. Only his fiddling brought joy.

Now Archie Campbell was known as a fiddler of repute over wide districts of Argyll. He held the secret of the rhythm of a jig and the swing of a strathspey. He could play fatigue out of tired feet and reserve from the over-shy. He could make princess dance with ploughboy and a Scots bailie forget the dignity of his office. His playing was called for at weddings and dances throughout the countryside. In the winter before his marriage to Mairi Macgregor he took Alicky with him when he played. Of course there was a reason for his doing so. At some of the dances nearer at hand Mairi herself might be there, and Archie on occasion would wish to desert the platform and take the floor with her, leaving his fiddle for Alicky to play.

The first dance at which Alicky played (and he was to play at many in his time) was in the Assembly Rooms in the High Street of Lochend. The Assembly Rooms were on the same side of the street as the house of Dr. Reith and opposite the sea. On rough nights the boom of the sea was bass accompaniment to the fiddles' treble.

Alicky and Archie Campbell reached their destination after a long walk down the glen against cold rain blown in their faces by an easterly wind. When they came out of the cold darkness of the winter night into the warmth and brightness of the Assembly Rooms, Alicky felt they had reached fairyland indeed. The ballroom was so vast and white, lit by so many huge and sparkling candelabra, with tall palm-trees in green pots beside the band platform, and with the flags of all nations draping the gallery's walls. It was early, a full half-hour before the dance began, and the hall was empty, echoing in an exciting way as he tramped with Archie Campbell in heavy boots across the glassy floor. They went across the whole length of the hall to the raised platform from which they were to play. There they were joined, first by two other fiddlers in rustic clothes, young men with bronzed faces and plastered hair, and finally by Mistress MacQueen her very self.

Mistress MacQueen was a legend in Lochend. She was the local goddess of provincial music. Should a lassie play her piece exceptionally well, the neighbours would say, 'Indeed, and Mistress MacQueen herself could do no better.' There could be no higher praise! When any other lady ventured to play at a local dance held to repair the church steeple or to send a new life-boat to sea, somebody was sure to remark that the lady in question 'wasn't a patch on Mistress Mac-Queen.' If anyone wished to suggest that the end of the world was at hand he had only to hint that Mistress MacQueen was beginning to fail.

She was an aged lady composed of sinew and bone, with but little flesh and no fat whatever. She liked her own way and she got it. She loved bright colours in her dress. Her hair was white and stiff as wire, her face painted so thickly that the paint cracked into lines when she smiled. She wore a multitude of rings which she removed before playing. In the Assembly Rooms in the High Street of Lochend the rattle of her rings beside the keyboard of the piano was the inevitable signal that the Grand March was about to begin.

Mistress MacQueen ruled her orchestra by force of will and the strength of a dominating right hand on the keys of the piano. The only fiddler who could get his way with her was Archie Campbell. When she sailed like a gaily painted ship to take her place on the piano stool Archie Campbell accosted her. 'You will be excusing me, Mistress MacQueen, but I have the one favour to ask of you this night. I will be playing on the one condition that I get a bit dance to myself. You will maybe have heard, Mistress MacQueen, that I am to be married on Mairi Macgregor of the Sliaghmhor in the spring of the year, and I shouldn't wonder though she might look in at the dance the night.'

'No fool like an old fool, Archie,' she said.

'Mistress MacQueen, I will not stand here to be insulted.'

'Well *sit*, man, until the poor girl comes in. Who's your substitute?'

'Wee Alicky here, that's as good a fiddler as I am myself, indeed.'

'No better?'

'*Mistress MacQueen!*'

'You're a big, conceited idiot, Archie Campbell. If I hadn't known you for twenty years I'd tell you to go to the devil and to take your substitute along with you. I'll not allow you more than six dances with poor Mairi. The girl deserves her freedom while she's got it.'

'And would you be suggesting, Mistress Mac-Queen, that it's myself that's the old man?'

'Not old, Archie Campbell, *ancient, pickled,* well preserved in sanctity and sheep sharn.'

Archie rose from his chair with studied dignity and deliberation, his eyes ablaze with injured pride and resentful anger, his fiddle beneath his arm. He said, 'I will not stay here one minute longer to be insulted, Madam, I bid you a very good evening indeed.'

But Mistress MacQueen was fit for him. She was fit for any Highland fiddler who marched off the platform as protest against insult, real or supposed, and every Highland fiddler was liable to take offence and to show his protest by sudden abdication of a position in her band. She cried after Archie, 'Come back at once, Archie Campbell, you big bairn. You're behaving like a fool. If you're going to show Mairi Macgregor that you can't dance, you can at least show her that you *can* fiddle.'

Archie swung back on to the platform. 'Then you will at least acknowledge that I can fiddle, Mistress MacQueen.'

She smiled her hard and glittering smile. She looked at her band—she said, 'You're one of the three best fiddlers in Scotland, and that's in the world.' Archie Campbell sat quietly down and got busy with his resin. Alicky sat on a chair behind him, ready to take his place when

Mistress MacQueen should give Archie permission to dance. Sitting there, Alicky watched the dancers assemble.

There were the three classes of dance in Lochend —first, second, and third class. In autumn, at the conclusion of the shooting and after the Annual Highland Games, the lairds and the ladies, the shooting tenants and their ladies, officers of the Services and their ladies, met together in the Assembly Rooms for the Highland Ball. The gentlemen wore kilts and the ladies tartan sashes, and they all talked very good English. The dance, as distinct from the dancing, was first class.

A little later in the year the second-class dance was held, where the bailies and merchants, doctors, lawyers, and the customs and excise assembled together with their wives and daughters. Most of the company spoke Lochend English, and the company were so determined to make the second-class dance a first-class function that some of them could scarcely dance at all.

But the dance at which Alicky fiddled for the first time was quite distinctly a third-class affair. The men and the women, the boys and the lassies were there to dance with the companions of their choice. Many of them spoke Gaelic. The men and boys wore blue serge suits; the women and girls white or coloured print dresses, and the males were arrayed on chairs along one side of

172

the long Assembly Hall, the females down the
other. When the band, led by Mistress Mac-
Queen, struck up the first bars of the Grand
March, there was an almighty pushing back of
chairs and slithering of feet when the line of blue
serge advanced across the floor with a rush to
claim the white dresses or coloured print frocks.
The Grand March was followed by the Flowers
of Edinburgh, and Alicky itched to get his hands
on Archie Campbell's fiddle. But Archie was
still at his post, for Mairi and Janet Macgregor
were late on their journey from the Sliaghmhor.
So Alicky sat beside Archie, keeping time to the
music of the dance.

Some people wondered who he could be, the
funny dwarfed figure who followed every beat
of the rhythm with his hands, his feet, and with
a comical swaying of his hunched shoulders.
Some recognised him as the quaint protégé of
the eccentric Dr. Thomas Reith. But most of
the dancers were too intent in keeping their
places to pay him much attention, and indeed,
when they did observe the platform party they
were dominated and dazzled by the legendary
figure of Mistress MacQueen.

The fourth dance, a Highland Schottische,
was nearing its energetic conclusion when Mairi
came in. Alicky noticed her at once, and the
twitching of his body in time to the music ceased.

She was so beautiful. Her slim figure all in

white. The surprising grace of her carriage. The dark oval of her face. The dark hair of her head raised high on the nape of her neck for this special occasion. The quiet dignity of her bearing. The mystery of her presence.

Suddenly all the other figures in the room grew faint and obscure in Alicky's eyes. He saw everything in a dim haze with the figure of Mairi shining through the mist like a bright star. He saw her like an angel coming towards him through a summer evening's haze. He worshipped her so. She was smiling in his direction. Coming towards him, swaying like a tall willow in a mild wind. She raised her slim hand, waving as in invitation to him, but it was to Archie Campbell she was waving, and Archie thrust the fiddle into Alicky's hand before swinging himself down to the floor.

'Take partners for Petronella!' The M.C., a lad who had won the prize for the best-looking ploughman at the Lochend ploughing match, called out the announcement as though hurling a challenge. Who would dare sit motionless while Mistress MacQueen led her band through the tune of Petronella? Mistress MacQueen, herself, gave the opening bar—'Ta-ta-*tum*, ta-ta-*tum*, ta-ta-*tum*, *tum*, *tum*,' and Alicky saw Archie Campbell leading Mairi to the top place in the top set just below the band. Mairi would dance with all the grace of tall flowers in the gardens of heaven no more than three yards from where

Alicky sat. But it was with Archie Campbell she would dance. And her eyes were all for Archie, standing opposite her, tall and strong as a forest tree, the muscles of his limbs beneath the cloth making the blue suit he wore look over-tight. His face was alive with life and fun, the blood pulsing in the veins of his neck and under the brown, lined skin of his face. Only the white hair of his head and beard showed his age.

Alicky Mag must play music for Mairi to dance with another. He could not play. Fiddle and bow were slack in his hands. He lost time with the others. He introduced discords. Mistress MacQueen thumped ever harder to drown the squeals of tortured catgut. From time to time she turned her face sideways to snarl at Alicky, the dry paint cracking on her face, her thin lips stretched tightly across her teeth driving the blood from them so that they looked ghost pale. That made Alicky's playing worse, because he was deeply afraid of Mistress MacQueen.

At the end of Petronella, Mistress MacQueen called Archie Campbell to come to speak to her, and Alicky overheard the substance of their conversation.

'The boy's useless, Archie, he'll never make a fiddler. He's got no confidence, no authority in his playing. We can't let him play a second time, Mairi Macgregor or no Mairi Macgregor! You'll need to play yourself.'

'Oh! but Mistress MacQueen, and it's Alicky Mag that's the rare fiddler when he's in form. I'm speaking the God's truth when I'm telling you, Mistress MacQueen, that up yonder in the bothy of Glendruid I've seen the white hares stop in their tracks and listen to the playing of Alicky Mag. I've seen the dog-otter on the river-bank standing up keeping time with his wee paws to the playing of Alicky Mag. I've seen——'

'Never heed what you've *seen*, Archie Campbell. I've *heard!* I'm neither hare nor otter, but an L.R.A.M., and to my suffering this night, my ear is endowed with absolute pitch. The boy shan't play again.'

'Oh! But Mistress *MacQueen!* Will you not be giving the boyan the one more chance?'

'Giving you the one more dance with that poor, innocent, deluded girl, you mean, Archie! Well—there's just a possibility it's nerves that's wrong with him. We'll see what some Dutch courage will do.' Mistress MacQueen opened the immense hand-painted handbag she always kept beside her. She turned to Alicky. 'Come here, boy!' she said, 'you need some medicine before you attempt to play any more.'

Alicky approached her like an ugly toad hypnotised by a brilliantly coloured and evil snake. She handed him a silver flask, saying, 'Take a drink from that, boy! A *good* drink!

Go on! That won't do you any good. More than that! Good heavens, boy, you'll never make a fiddler if you can't take a drink without spluttering and choking like that. Now, go back to your seat and don't dare put your bow to your fiddle until you feel you'd die unless you played. Don't play at all unless you *have* to play! Off you go!'

'*Take partners for the Duke of Perth!*' That was a dance and tune that Alicky loved. But at first he did not want to play. Once again Archie Campbell and Mairi were at the top of the hall, in the top place of the top set, and Mairi was looking at Archie proudly, with the mist of love in her dark eyes. Alicky could not play—at first. But then a curious feeling of sorrowful boastfulness overcame him. He felt a spirit of selfish sacrifice—of self-pity—grow within himself. He would play, he thought, as he had never played before. Out of his sorrow he would make music for Mairi to dance to. He would play so that she would be forced to turn and smile at him, to thank him for his music if not for himself. And as he played as he had never played before, with a verve and a swing and a rhythm he had never equalled before, Mairi smiled at him indeed, and Archie Campbell clapped approval with some of the old warmth of affection in his eyes. Alicky could see people unknown to him nodding towards him, then asking

others who he might be. Even Mistress Mac-
Queen herself half turned her dragon's head to
nod approval of Alicky's playing of that grand
and rhythmical tune 'The Duke of Perth.'

So Alicky played three dances in succession.
The vitality of his fiddling affected his band
companions. They played with new life. Folks
said, 'Trust Mistress MacQueen to pick on a
good fiddler! The boy's great!' Alicky felt an
almost physical warmth of comradeship and
affection grow between himself and the men
and women for whom he played. Their approval
and applause, the response of their feet and
bodies to his playing, which was the essence of
his mind, brought peace and repose to his uneasy
soul. While he played he had so many friends.
He was no longer alone.

When the 'Duke of Perth' ended, the other
fiddlers leant forwards to congratulate Alicky
Mag. Mistress MacQueen left her stool to pat
his shoulder. Archie Campbell called out, 'Was
there ever fiddling the like o' yon heard in
Lochend before?' Many strangers called up,
'And it's yourself that's the fine fiddler, boy!'
Mairi laughed up at him, saying, 'Junket face,
you're the best fiddler that I ever heard play,'
but she turned to have the next dance with
Archie Campbell, who was straining arteries and
heart to regain the unforced agility of his youth.

Alicky played until the Interval. The band

went through to a side-room where refreshments were laid ready for them to eat, and Alicky was easily persuaded to drink more of the magical liquid which had snapped the strangling bonds of inhibition in his brain and hands. He came back to the dance hall half-forgetful of his stunted frame, ugly face and bald head. His self-consciousness had vanished in a burst of confidence and exhilaration. He was king of creation —the world, even Mairi, was at his feet. He had proved to her he could fiddle, he would show her how he could dance. The first dance after the interval was a reel, and Alicky was determined that he would dance it and that Mairi should be his partner. Before Archie Campbell could make a move Alicky had rushed across the hall to take Mairi by her slim hand. 'Dance with me, Mairi,' he implored, 'give me just the one dance, Mairi Macgregor of the Sliaghmhor.' She looked at him reproachfully out of her dark eyes. 'Oh! Junket face,' she said, 'it's awfully drunk that you are. But I'll give you this one dance if you will but promise me not to ask for any more!' His face lit with happiness, for he could not know that Mairi would have refused him as a partner, even for the one dance, had he not been acclaimed by the dancers present as the finest fiddler that had ever played at a Lochend ball.

Alicky knew nothing of the correct steps of a

179

Highland reel. He invented them for himself. His movements were strange and grotesque, but so perfect was his rhythm, so surprising his agility, that everyone thought his instinct was an art, and the weird capers he cut an expression of originality rather than of ignorance. Mairi shouted with laughter as he leapt like a frog in the dance before her. She could not know that he had forgotten his clumsy deformities, and that in his released imagination he was a splendid young man dancing to the glory of the woman he loved.

Everybody laughed at and applauded Alicky's weird dancing. Archie Campbell on the platform fiddled until the sweat cut rivers in his beard. Mistress MacQueen kept the rhythm going with the swing of her angular body, something that had never been seen in Lochend before. Other sets stopped their hooching and dancing to stare at the capering antics of Alicky Mag. At the end of the dance they crowded around him, telling him that they didn't know which he could do best—fiddle or dance. In one evening Alicky had become a public personage—a character in Lochend. He felt proud of himself—happily boastful—unrepressed. He told his flatterers that he was no mere dancing fiddler but an educated person as well. He struck an absurd attitude which he imagined expressed dignity. 'Perhaps you wouldn't think to look at me that I could speak Latin. You will maybe believe me when I say the Lord's Prayer in that tongue. And it's this way that it goes:

> *A, ab, absque, coram, de,*
> *Palam, clam, cum, ex, or e,*
> *Sine, tenus, pro and pre.*

'Yes, I can speak Latin if I'm wanting to, but I'd sooner fiddle and take a wee keek at the lassies' legs when they come birling by.'

Everybody roared with laughter and approval when he said that. They felt happy and familiar with the owl once the soul of the linnet had flown away. The boy was a great fiddler, there could be no two opinions about that, but in other ways he was just a plain person like themselves. 'A wee keek at the lassies' legs when they come birling by!' Had they ever heard the like? Who would have thought the queer little body had it in him to say that?

But the waters of the loch still lapped against its shores on the high Sliaghmhor.

XIV

ARCHIE CAMPBELL was to leave Glendruid at the May term to take a married herd's place on a wether-grazing of high Lochaber. He would take Mairi with him there. What should be done with Alicky Mag? Dr. Thomas Reith rode up the glen on an April day to discuss the situation.

Alicky hadn't seen the doctor for many long days, and when the familiar black-coated, red-faced figure swung itself off the brown mare, Alicky felt himself a small and frightened boy again. Dr. Reith shouted to him to take the mare round to the byre, and Alicky had to check himself from running to do the doctor's bidding.

'Ye've grown, Alicky,' said Dr. Reith, 'I'll nae perjure ma immortal soul by saying ye've grown bonnier. I'll nae venture tae sae ye've grown langer, for I havena ma tape wi' me the nicht. But some wye or ither ye've growed. Weel, weel, awa' roond wi' the mare, loon, and I'll awa' in to see Archie Campbell. It's nae likely we'll see him muckle longer, for I never heard tell of an auld man marrying on a young queanie that ever saw the twal' months oot.'

Alicky stabled the mare and then hung about in the garden, aimlessly, not wishing to go too far away unless he were wanted, not willing to go into the cottage for fear his presence were considered an intrusion. But he had not long to wait before Archie Campbell called him in, 'Alicky boyan, the doctor's wishing to speak to you.'

Alicky hastened into the house. There he found Dr. Reith sitting in a chair by the fireside, his riding-boots discarded, resting his stockinged feet on the wall, puffing at his pipe, just as he was wont to do in moments of ease in his own study in Lochend.

'Come in aboot, Alicky,' he said; 'aye, ye've growed, loon. Aye, fairly that! Archie and me's been talkin' ower what's to be done wi' you, loon, and afore we come to any final decision affecting a future that's maist likely o' more importance to yersel' than to onybody else, I'd like to ken if you're aye set on the herdin', or whether ye've had enough o' ploughin' through dubs tae yer oxters ahint a few score rabbits o' beasties that folks ca' sheep in this county o' Argyll?—Aye, Archie,' he said, turning to the shepherd, 'I'm fairly with you in this, for the maist pairt o' it is grand country for wethers, but nae fit for ewe stock ava. But that's nae to the point the noo. What I was at was askin' Alicky whether he's still on for being a herd, a job that leaves a body free tae fiddle and pipe and poach and get into a' kinds o' trouble wi' drink, women, the *po*lice, the excise, and faithers expectin' a plain answer tae a plain question, or whether he's tired o' seeing a' the work deen wi' dowgs and wouldna sooner learn an honest trade wi' a reputable master in Lochend.'

Archie Campbell interrupted, whining through his nose in the way that was a sure sign of his displeasure. 'And would you be suggesting, indeed, sir, that all shepherds will be lazy rogues, indeed, sir, and I myself no respectable master to have a boy under my authority and charge?'

Dr. Thomas Reith spat in the fire. Then he puffed at his pipe for a full half-minute before speaking.

'A' ma life I've spoken plain, Archie. I ca' a pneumonia a pneumonia and nae congestion o' the lungs. I ca' consumption consumption and nae a decline. I ca' a fit a fit, and over-eating over-eating. Aye, plain speakin' has lost me patients, I'll nae deny that. Folk dinna like truth. They prefer it coated wi' sugar like a peel. I mind fine tellin' an elder o' the kirk that there wis nae ither cause for his chronic bronchitis but his habit o' keeking up closes seeking for scandal in the congregation in a' kinds o' weather. I says tae him, "There's Ane wha sees a', judges a', pities a', wha made lads and lassies as they are and kent fine what He was at when He made

them.   Tak' my advice," I says to him, for I kent
fine he held a bond on some o' the worst property
in Lochend, "tak' ma advice and ask for guidance
whether or no the unsanctified tootie-pooties that
occur in the back streets o' Lochend, as nane will
deny, are nae due to a shortage o' decent houses
and nae to a surfeit o' original sin"—Aye, he
didna come back!   He took his bronchitis and
his fees tae a professional brither wha shall be
nameless.   Aye, plain speakin' or no plain
speakin', Archie, truth has a gey wye o' comin'
oot in the end, like the bailie wha tell't his wife
that business took him to America ilka spring,
and in the hindmost end got weel and fairly
caught in the siege o' Paris.   Aye—and I've this
ae bit o' truth for you, Archie Campbell, though
it's no concern o' mine tae tell it tae ye.   I niver
heard tell o' an auld man like yersel' marrying
on a young queanie that ever lived mair nor a
twal'month.   That's nae to say that I dinna
believe in second marriages.   I div.   But ye
should hae socht oot a decent cannie widow body
wi' a puckle siller laid by wha would hae kent
that there's a time o' life that comes tae ilka man
when what he needs maist from a wumman is
guid meat, warm claes, and a mustard plaister
on his chest when his cough winna loosen.   Aye,
tootie-pooties when you're young, and guid
cooking when you're auld—thon's common
sense worth mair nor medicine.'

185

Archie Campbell's rage was immeasurable. He drew himself to his full and imposing height, his blue eyes turned by fire to grey steel, the blood beating visibly in his neck veins, his fists clenched, his knuckles ivory white.

'Dr. Reith, sir,' he hissed out, 'it is not right that a gentleman should be so insulted in his own house. If it was not, sir, that you are a guest under my own roof I would have the greatest pleasure, indeed, sir, in throwing you out of here into the midden where you would be finding yourself much more at home, sir.'

Dr. Reith roared with laughter. 'Now, is that no' a typical Heeland dilemna you're in, Archie! Ye canna throw me oot o' your hoose because I'm in your hoose. We're nae sae particular in Buchan. Weel, weel, Archie, if I've offended ye, ye have ma apologies and a'thing o' the kind. I spoke plainer than I meant, Archie. But I brocht Mairi Macgregor intil this warld o' sorrows, and I dinna think she's seen enough o' men awa' up there on the Sliaghmhor to mak' her choice and she nae mair nor seventeen if she's that. But be guid tae her, Archie, be guid tae her. I had a maist awfu' job pu'in' her through the measles, and she's nae what ye'd ca' a robust lassie yet.

'But I canna bide here bletherin' a' day. I've a call to mak' on auld Grannie Maclean at the clachan. She's taken to mewin' like a cat and

winna gang tae her bed but sits up a' nicht seekin'
tae catch mice. I doot I'll hae tae dae something,
but I'm sweir tae pit the auld buddy awa'. Aye!

'Weel, weel, if ye'll cool doon for a minute or
twa, Archie, we'll need tae settle what's tae be
done wi' Alicky. What div ye say yersel', Alicky
loon? Are ye for bidin' at the herdin' or no'?'

Alicky liked his job—there was no doubt of
that. He liked the walking over rough country
in all kinds of weather. He liked going out in
the very early morning when the world was
fresh, before all the living creatures that went
about their business during night and hid during
day had had time to conceal themselves. He
liked the hills where the startled deer stood out-
lined on the skyline, gazing downwards towards
danger, until they turned to seek the high places
where springs are crystal clear and air is wine.
He liked the quiet restful peace he found among
the sheep. But he loved Mairi Macgregor—
loved the very music of her name. They—Dr.
Reith and Archie Campbell had been speaking
of Mairi. She was going away to Lochaber with
Archie Campbell, but Archie would live no more
than a year, and then Mairi would return, to
stand again in all the mystery of her grace on the
shores of the loch of the Sliaghmhor. And when
she returned, he, Alicky Mag, must be there to
stand beside her—to watch the duck fall down
out of the sky to ripple the quiet waters of the

loch, to throw the flat stones slantwise so that they skipped across its surface, to feel the touch of Mairi's slim fingers on his sleeve. He must stay in Glendruid to welcome Mairi back to the Sliaghmhor when Archie had died. So when Dr. Reith said, 'Speak up, loon, I havena a' day to bide here,' Alicky answered that he wanted to be a herd and that the only herding he had a fancy for was Glendruid.

On hearing Alicky's decision, the doctor reached for his riding-boots, muttering, 'Weel, weel, it tak's a' kinds tae mak' a warld.'

Archie Campbell protested, 'I wouldn't like to be leaving Alicky here by himself, doctor. The glen's no' canny at all.' Archie lowered his voice—'There's whiles in the winter's nights here, doctor, that there's strange noises, indeed, that are in it.'

Dr. Reith looked up, his face very red from the effort of pulling on his riding-boots. 'What noises?' he asked.

'Och! Doctor! Ye'll surely have heard. There's whiles that we hear the gallop of horses on the road outside, and when we open the door and look out there's nothing that we can be seeing or hearing at all but the shadow of the clouds on the hillside and the river roaring. There's whiles again that we hear folks speaking the Gaelic outside on the road and the sound of many's the pair of brogued feet on the heather

188

outside, and when we will be opening the door and looking out there'll be nothing but the black darkness of a winter's night. There's whiles, doctor, that you will be hearing a crackling of flames and you will see the light of the flames of destruction passing across the very sky. There's whiles that you will be hearing the "Cry," but it wouldn't be canny at all to be talking about that, doctor, no' canny at all.'

Dr. Reith's face became ever more red and scornful during Archie Campbell's recital. He blew through his nose so that the bristles in his left nostril stood out like a shaving brush.

'Weel, weel, and that's a gey Heeland wye o' saying that a man's nerves are awa' wi' it! What like nonsense to hear from a grown man in the reign of Queen Victoria! A body'd need tae gang to the Heelands tae hear the like o' that right enough. Horses, Gaelic, flames, cries! Aye, in the Heelands it's enough for a white craw tae be seen for a'body to talk o' sudden death. Aye! I've heard a' thon talk and palaver aboot this glen doon in the clachan, Archie. Aye, I've heard it many a time in the clachan from the old *cailleachs* that live there. Aye, it was after saying she'd heard the "Cry" that auld Grannie Maclean started to sit in a claes basket tae hatch oot eggs. Aye, that was afore she started tae mew.

'Weel, I'll tell ye the meaning o' these noises, Archie. For aince it's no wax in the lugs which in ma medical experience is the maist common cause o' noises in the heid. Na, it's nae wax. What ye think is horses galloping is deer that's got a fleg farther doon the glen. What ye think is Gaelic is dooks gobbling thegither doon on the saft groond by the river, and I'se warrant ye there's nae muckle difference atween the soond of dooks gobbling and the soond o' the Gaelic. They're a' the same tae ma lugs that can diagnose a pneumonia afore consolidation has begun, which is mair nor a Gaelic-speaking brither practitioner wha shall be nameless can dae. Aye!

'The crackle and the flames is the Aurora Borealis, which is naething more than sparks struck aff the North Pole by the rapid revolution of the earth on its ain axis.

'The "Cry" as ye ca' it is naething but wind at a high velocity skirlin' through a crack atween rocks. Aye, Archie, there's a natural explanation for a'thing whether or no ye ken what it is. Aye.

'Na, I'm nae saying it would be a guid thing for Alicky to bide by his lane in Glendruid, although there's something to be said for biding alane, as ye'll find in the Book o' Genesis afore the introduction o' Eve. There's twa quick ways o' going daft. Ane is to live amang daft folks and the ither's tae live alane. But if ye tak' oot the three coonties o' Aberdeen, Banff, and Kincardine, the whale o' Scotland's daft onywye. Soond minds and hill air dinna agree, that's ma experience aifter a lifetime o' general practice in the Heelands. Aye.

'Weel, Archie, and what's your opinion of Alicky steppin' intil your hill-boots? In the first place is he fit for the job, and in the second place is he like to get it?'

'Indeed, doctor, and I wouldn't just like to say that Alicky's fit for the job yet awhile, willing and all though he is. But fit or no, he's like to get it if he's seeking it, for the want of any other gentlemen considering the position.'

'What's the do with the job, Archie?' the doctor asked.

'Well, indeed, sir, and there's not much right with it. There's the sounds a gentleman will be hearing on a winter's night that, be what they may be, are no' canny at all. There's no married herd that would be willing to bring his wife here after what came on Janet Macdonald here on a day you might be minding on, doctor. There's no' many single herds likely to bide here with no living soul in the glen to be speaking to except the *cailleachs* down at the clachan that will soon all be gone. The situation has no' a big wage to it, and Mr. Scott, the man of business, is no' good to please. The stock's no' what a gentleman could be calling a good one, and there's no end to the work at lambing time with the ewes aye being short of milk.'

'Then there's nae muckle richt wi' the job by

your wye of it, Archie!' said Dr. Reith. 'Weel, maybe Alicky will get what he's wanting wi'oot muckle difficulty. Maybe it's right that he should herd Glendruid. In one way or anither, Alicky, you're kind of responsible for the bad reputation the place has. Aye.

'I'll pit in a word for you, Alicky. I've attended the Dowager Coontess for a' her complaints peculiar tae weemen and common to a' mankind. I've a gey lang reckoning wi' the executors when the auld buddy dees. Aye—the ae fee she iver gid me was a wee bit silver juggie wi' a crackit spoot that wis thrown oot at the spring-cleaning at the Castle. Mr. Scott o' Dunblair, her man o' business, kens that fine. Maybe I'll be able to get him to dae something for Alicky Mag on account. Aye.

'Weel, Archie, if ye've a dram in the hoose I'd be muckle obleeged to you, for I'll need a' my persuasive eloquence to get auld Grannie Maclean (puir, decent auld buddy she aye was) tae her bed when I ca' in at the clachan on my way hame. I'm gey sweir to pit her awa', for whether she's making on she's a clockin' hen or a cat wi' kitlings, she's weel enough contented where she is and can aye enjoy her cup o' tea—the puir auld soul. Aye.

'Weel, we'll take that as settled aboot Alicky, Archie. I'll see Mr. Scott aboot it, and I'll tak' a turn up here noo and again to satisfy masel' that Alicky's mental condition is nae waur than his neighbours'. I'll not be ill to please. After a lifetime o' general practice in the Heelands I'm what a body might ca' tolerant, and gey sweir tae certify. Weel, I'm awa'! Eh! Afore I forget, Alicky, auld Bella Pringle asked to be remembered to you.'

Alicky brought the brown mare round from the byre. Dr. Reith, after a succession of hops, for advancing age made mounting difficult, clambered into the saddle. He gathered the reins up in his stiff fingers and with visible effort drew himself erect. He looked around him on the hills where a thick grey mist streamed out like the fingers of a suffocating hand blotting out the sun. He muttered—'Guidsakes, what a like country tae bide in frae necessity, let alane frae choice!'

He rode away down the glen, and the grey hoodie crows swept down crying above his head.

XV

ALICKY MAG was alone in Glendruid. Archie
Campbell had gone to Lochaber, taking Mairi
Macgregor with him as his wife, and it was said
that after the long ceremony and festivities of a
Highland wedding were completed, Mairi looked
sad.

Alicky stood leaning on the parapet of the
humped bridge over the Druid river. The
weather was fine. A cuckoo was calling its May
song in the clump of alders and willows above
the bridge. Alicky remembered the day when
he had come up the glen to hear the cuckoo,
and had spoken to Archie Campbell for the first
time; when Archie had told him Gaelic riddles
and said that all lambs were top lambs on the
close green pastures of the heavenly hills. Now
Archie was away and Alicky would miss him.
And the lambs on the pastures of Glendruid were
not all tops. Not far above the bridge, on the
deadly fresh grass beside the river-bank, a lamb
lay dead, so still and white in death, and beside
it stood the ewe, her horned head hung down in
mourning, sadness in her quiet eyes. Lambs and
ewes were ever dying on the Glendruid pastures.

The evening was still. No wind, no whisper of a breeze, the cup of the hills warm in the memory of sunlight. Above Alicky's head a cock snipe flew round and round in wide circles, and when it swept steeply downwards, it drummed out its bleating love note with the flutter of its tail. The bird would be flying there hour after hour, day after day, beating the drums in the orchestra of hill-birds' song. Far away, where sunset spread a crimson shawl over the sleeping shoulders of Ben Cruachan, two eagles, distant specks, wheeled together in the perfect freedom of their flight.

The surface of the river was so calm, so still, water drifting undisturbed as a sleeping child to the bosom of the sea. It made no sound to break the hushed reverence of the summer evening, stealing through the glen to the sea, leaving the hills asleep. A small bird hidden in the depths of greenery would break into song, spontaneously, suddenly, overcome with joy, and cease its singing abruptly as though afraid that, in being overheard, it had given its soul away. But it could not keep silence for long—the ecstasy of summer was too great. Over the ridge towards Glendarroch the black-headed gulls were crying. They had their nests there on the banks of a hidden tarn. Peace that surpassed understanding —the peace of God—lay on the hills.

As yet, in the fine May weather, Alicky was

not lonely or afraid. He felt some pride that the herding, the house, the garden—the whole glen was his own to do with as he liked. There was none to interfere with his actions or laugh at his behaviour, no one to look at him. He was free.

Standing on the parapet of the bridge over the Druid he reviewed the days of his life—how the rosary of the years had been told. The house of Dr. Reith—old Bella Pringle and her gingerbread—the bullying butcher's boy—the seashore at Lochend—the teaching of the Rev. John McFadyean—the sums that would never come right—the confusion of composition—the meaningless jangle of Latin words. He recalled the early days of herding in Glendruid when his body ached all over from climbing the steep braes—when the calves of his legs in the morning felt bound and compressed with strong cords. He remembered how afraid he once had been of dogs, and stooped to touch the head of the smooth-coated black collie that Archie Campbell had left him as companion. He thought of his learning the fiddle and the bagpipes, and how with his fiddling he could open his heart and gain comfort from his fellow-men. And he remembered the Sliaghmhor with Mairi laughing at him when he ran a race.

Dear Mairi, who had gone away to be a housewife and perhaps a mother. Folk said that she had looked sad when she went away, sorrowful and trapped, as when the drink dies down in a man's eyes and he finds himself in danger. She had gone away and the Sliaghmhor might never see her again.

But Alicky knew that if he stood gazing on the gently sweeping water thinking of Mairi and the Sliaghmhor he would become so sad that not even the gayest of all tunes he played on his fiddle, the old dance tune of 'Jenny, Catch Your Skirts Up,' would serve to make his sadness flee. So he left the bridge and went up the river to where the dead lamb lay. He took it in his hand, hoping the ewe would follow him, but she was shy and unwilling to leave the place where her lamb had died. He had to keep throwing the dead lamb ahead of him, when the ewe, seeing the white lamb lying still, would run to where it lay. Thus he induced the ewe to follow him to the byre, where he had an orphan lamb penned that he had been feeding on the goat's milk. His task was to skin the dead lamb and put its pathetic shrunken skin upon the living lamb. Then the ewe would think it her own and give it suck.

Alicky loathed this dreary butcher's task. He always had loathed it ever since the first time Archie Campbell stood over him instructing him how it should be done. He abhorred the cold wetness of the raw and exposed flesh, the way the skinned body slithered in his hands. At times he

197

had a horror that there still might be life in the lamb he skinned. But Archie Campbell always told him, 'You'll never make a herd, boyan, till you learn to skin a sheep.' And that was true of Glendruid and other ewe stock grazings of Argyll.

Yet Alicky found pleasure when the task was done. The orphan lamb was smaller than the lamb that had died. The skin was much too big for it, trailing on to the ground. The lamb looked absurd, staggering around like a small child dressed in its mother's dressing-gown. In spite of its absurd appearance the ewe accepted it as her own.

His task completed, Alicky went down to the river to wash, for he could not stand the sight of blood upon his hands. He pushed his way through the alders, hazels, and willow-trees to the river-bank, to a pool where there was a narrow beach of pure white sand. The evening held such mildness and the brown, gently flowing water so cool an invitation that Alicky decided he must bathe. He stripped off his few clothes and plunged into the pool. The water was surprising in its pleasant warmth. Even so early in summer the icy coldness of melted snow coming down from the higher hills had gone. The white sand, sheltered from wind by the rustling curtain of tree leaves, and warmed by the afternoon sun beating upon it, was grateful to his skin.

First he lay in the water, feeling it glide smoothly over his limbs, raising his hands alternately and then letting them fall with a splash on the river's surface. Then he lay perfectly still, with only his head above water. After he had lain silent for a time, the tree branches above him became alive with the chirping, the graceful flutter and impassioned song of small birds nesting there. The trees that seemed deserted of life when he moved, became a city of birds' activities when he lay still. And always above his head the cock snipe wheeled drumming in its love flight.

So quiet was the world save for the music of the birds—such a mild evening in May—all the summer ahead—the hard labour and anxieties of lambing nearing their appointed end—the water so gentle in its coolness—the white sand smooth in its glittering beauty—the melted gold of sunlight reflected in a pool—the distant, mournful wailing of the gulls—the tapestry of leaves in varied greenery—the world at peace; Alicky felt he could have lain there for ever amid the peace of natural things. He knew himself one with the cool water and the sleeping earth, the insensible growth of the trees, the animated poetry of the birds. He lay there dreaming—a dream of contentment—and then he heard the voices of people drawing near.

It was so seldom that strangers came to Glendruid. Alicky had imagined his privacy to be inviolate. But a party of school-children bird-nesting from Lochend after school came suddenly upon him as he bathed.

They saw his bald head, and the sallow skin of his face above the water. When he realised he was observed, Alicky, in a panic of shame, dashed towards the shelter of the trees, seeking to hide himself.

The children saw the blood-red scar like the claw-mark of a beast upon his back. They fled screaming, believing him the devil.

PART II

BREAKING

I

ALICKY MAG herded the Glendruid grazing for many long years. People forgot that there ever had been any other shepherd in Glendruid. They forgot that there ever had been another fiddler in Lochend. Old men said, 'Aye, but you should have heard Alicky Mag and Mistress MacQueen playing thegither!', for Mistress MacQueen had failed quickly in the end, failed unto death. But with Mistress MacQueen gone, Alicky Mag was supreme.

At sheep gatherings for miles around, the shepherds awaited the coming of Alicky Mag. Of course they would say, 'The wee bodach's aye in his cups,' but the babble of his witticisms made the day's work short, the skirl of his piping or the scraping of his fiddle passed the evenings away. Then there was a mystery to the little man. His brain sheltered the wreckage of an education. Some said he had been coming out for a doctor but couldn't stand the sight of blood. Others said that he had been coming out for a minister but couldn't keep irresponsible fun from his sermons. It was so long since Dr. Thomas Reith, the Rev. John McFadyean, old Bella Pringle, had been followed with measured tread between the opened iron gates through which so many went and through which none returned; all so long ago, that the story of the orphan boy carried down Glendruid glen under the arm of a doctor penitent over a fatal delay—all that was forgotten except by the old, and nowadays the old are but little listened to and die soon.

Alicky had learnt how to overcome his diffidence in meeting other men. He knew the trick of it now—such a simple trick if a man but had the few shillings needed to afford it. Without it the rhythm of his fiddling before strangers might not come to life, the swing of a march or the shape of a pibroch might be absent from his piping, the fun in his heart die in his throat before it reached his lips. Without the simple trick that could be bought for a few shillings he was once again the clumsy boy running to shelter from the bullies who pursued him. Without the trick he was a nobody in the company of others. People said, 'Without a dram in the old bodach's no' fun at all, but give the old body a drink and he was the life and soul of any company.'

Alicky Mag—as shepherd of Glendruid he had to mix and work with all the neighbouring herds —Hugh Maclean of Glendarroch, who had succeeded the McBeans there; Mackenzie of Strathord, a grazing which had changed from Cheviot to Blackfaces within Alicky Mag's own time; the Macintyre brothers from the lower end of Glendarroch, and Jock MacCulloch, the Dunblair gamekeeper, who gave a hand to the shepherds on big sheep days. They were all strong, rough-spoken men, by nature contemptuous of the weak or timid, full of earthy humour, ready to fight and defeat any man who stood in their way. Mackenzie of Strathord was less rough since his stomach had given way because the bride he had brought to the glens from the town was too soft and lazy to cook a proper meal, but the older Hugh Maclean of Glendarroch grew, the wilder became the outbursts of his ungovernable anger. Alicky could not have faced these men unless he had known the magic of the trick Mistress MacQueen had taught him in days long past.

Sometimes when shillings were scarce or his resolution strong Alicky would set out for a sheep gathering leaving his flask behind. But as he drew nearer his destination, his heart would shrink within himself at the prospect of meeting his shepherd comrades with his sensitiveness un-dulled. He would stand in indecision, perhaps mid-way between Glendruid and Glendarroch, beside the tarn where water-lilies grew and the gulls nested, wondering whether he dare face Hugh Maclean and Jock MacCulloch, Mackenzie of Strathord, and the Macintyre men, without the flask in his pocket to give him courage, to bring the ready repartee to his lips which earned laughter, the foot-twitching magic of his playing which won friends. He always felt that if he could once win through such a day without his flask he could face many another. But such efforts ever had the same result. Before the morning was half through some shepherd, disappointed at Alicky's dullness and missing an unexpected entertainment, would call out, 'Fetch the bottle for the love o' God. The Glendruid puddock's too dry to speak.' Then the bottle would be fetched and in ever so short a time Alicky would be babbling away, amusing them all, making the work seem light, the day short. So that, in the early mornings when he stood in indecision wondering whether he should face company unaided, it was nine chances to one that he would turn homewards for his flask, and then, refreshed, set out again. From this habit, Alicky, who was up watching wild things play before dawn was fully come, earned the title of a laggard. Shepherds waiting to get on with the day's labour would say to one another, 'Will we make a start or wait on the Glendruid puddock? The bodach's aye an hour late. Aye—here he comes—he's his fiddle with him the day. Aye— he'll go down a bog-hole one day, he's fou already. Aye—he'll be at his Latin the day before he's done. He canna last long, the pace he's going on at.'

He couldn't last long, but in the meantime make the most of his drollery, his absurdity, his music—make the most of him, for when again would there be a shepherd in Glendruid who could make the lame leap, subdued kirk elders rush for the nearest buxom servant lassie to bid her dance, a Dowager Countess lift the hem of her skirt and cry 'Hooch!' with the best of them —a shepherd who could say the Lord's Prayer backwards in the Latin tongue? Keep him going—give him a dram when he asked for it, or without asking for it, seemed to need it—keep the bodach daffing and playing—keep the fun going while he lasted, for with the way that he was carrying on he could not last long.—Alicky gave his health and strength away freely, with both hands, for he knew that, tipsy, he was welcome everywhere. Sober, he was alone.

There were weeks on end when he was alone, when snow stuffed a white handkerchief in the mouth of Glendruid, when the lambing was on and he could not leave his charge—not even for a day. The passage of the years had made the glen more lonely still. The clachan was deserted, the last of the *cailleachs* gone to her rest, the thatch of the cottages in decay, the windows broken—a home of nesting birds. It was many years since the wether sheep stock had been cleared from the Sliaghmhor. No longer was there a shepherd's family beside the loch. The

Sliaghmhor was under deer that in winter came down in vast herds to Glendruid, devouring the scanty grazing on which the sheep depended. The house at the Sliaghmhor was a rubble of stones beside the loch.

A countryman was becoming an intruder in Lochend. Tourists were the only business in the small town. It slept throughout winter, each idle man dozing the cold months through, sitting opposite his wife in the smallest living-room of a large house. In summer the people of industrial towns flooded into Lochend. The streets were filled with bands of men and girls, playing accordions and mouth organs, wearing each other's caps and hats, people who found relief from monotony in rowdiness. Yes, a countryman felt himself a stranger in Lochend. Nor was fiddling what it once was in Lochend. Some of the youngest men and women there had never seen Alicky Mag. Nor had they heard of the legendary Mistress MacQueen. They could not dance to the old tunes a country fiddler played. His melodies were strange to them, his rhythm meaningless. They preferred to dance close-clinging dances to the musical idiom of negroid races. They danced very gracefully, yet missing the primitive vitality of the negro. In their dances they demonstrated the biological truths of Charles Darwin.

Each year loneliness grew upon Alicky Mag.

The hills and the creatures of the hills were the same, everlasting, stable things, but the world of men was a flux. The world of men was drifting no one knew whither on a sea of soulless uniformity, leaving originality, eccentricity, stranded on the rocks of misunderstanding and disapproval. Alicky became more and more alone.

At first he could make nothing of his growing loneliness. He would sit for hours in the shepherd's cottage at Glendruid, listening to stillness, his two collie dogs lying at his feet, the dumb fiddle across his knees. His mind would be all on the old days, the dead days, the days of distant memory. There was a night that he realised he had been talking, talking only to himself, although he could have sworn Archie Campbell was opposite him fitting a new reed to his chaunter. Sometimes of a summer's evening he would make the long journey to the ruined cottage of the Sliaghmhor, following the winding track that a man must have imprinted on his mind before he can follow it, a track that grows ever more difficult to follow from the want of human feet to tread it down. Away up there on the Sliaghmhor, where evenings are chill even in high summer, he would stand beside the still waters of the loch—the still and sleeping loch where wild-fowl rested. He would go to the corner of the loch so close to the ruined house, the corner where the shore was white quartz and the water clear from water-weeds. There he would stand while the setting sun spread cloth of gold around the black peaks of the Western hills, while soaring birds became dark ornaments on a sky tapestry of cramoisy and cloth of gold.

There he would stand while sorrow brought tears to the little pig eyes some men called evil. He would think of Mairi, dark Mairi of the Sliaghmhor, of the grace and the mystery of her, the other-world loveliness of her. He would think of Mairi and of how she had gone away as bride to Archie Campbell into High Lochaber. It was many, many years since Mairi had died, bearing a third child to old Archie Campbell in the fifth year of her marriage. Yes, Dr. Reith had been all wrong about who should die first— the old man or the young girl. Alicky had never seen Mairi since the day she went away, when folks had said that in the end she looked so sad, that a woman had cried out 'Stop it!' during the marriage ceremony, interrupting a prayer.

Mairi had been dead so many years. Yet after Alicky had stood for long beside the loch, while night swept all colour from the palette of evening, he would feel sometimes that he was not alone, that he could feel, as in a dream, the faint touch of slender fingers on his sleeve. He would whisper 'Mairi' and wonder whether the answering whisper was his imagination, the loch's water lapping, wind sighing among the reeds, or the voice of Mairi calling to him through the mist of memories and of years, the voice of dead Mairi of the Sliaghmhor. He persuaded himself that it must be indeed the voice of Mairi that he heard, and whenever he was most lonely he would take the track up the hills to the Sliaghmhor that he might speak with Mairi and gain comfort from her presence there. One evening in June, a gamekeeper, watching the movements of the deer, trained his telescope on the loch's shore at the Sliaghmhor. He saw a dwarfed, ungainly figure of an old man standing there, recognising him as Alicky Mag, the Glendruid puddock. The little man was standing facing the loch, his arms outstretched, his head bowed as though in prayer, his body shaking as with an ague. At first the keeper laughed quietly to himself, thinking that if Alicky Mag went on as he was doing for many more months the old bodach certainly couldn't last long. But there was such sorrow, such dedication, in the old man's attitude, that the keeper let his telescope sink slowly to the ground. Here was surely some strange thing, a sight too sacred to be spied upon. And the keeper, who was a young man reared in the gentility of hill places, never spoke to a soul of what he had seen that evening on the lonely Sliaghmhor.

II

Iτ was to be a fine day indeed. Mist had clung late to the face of the sleeping hills, but now it was dispersing, scattering into nothingness before the chariot wheels of the uprising sun. And as the sun rose so did the larks, suspended specks of singing glory on the blue roof of the sky. It was to be a fine morning indeed, and they were to be clipping the milk ewes at Glendarroch that day.

Alicky Mag set out over the Druid river, his pipe case and shears under his arm, his dogs at heel. That morning he had risen from bed in a mood of rare happiness, feeling that summer was a gracious thing and every man a friend. He had hurried over his morning tasks among the sheep and hens so that he could set out all the sooner over the river which was running low in summer droughts, leaving stepping-stones exposed; up the steep ridge out of Glendruid and then across the wide, flat moor to Glendarroch, where a cool breeze full of the scent of hill herbs would greet him. There would be a shimmering mist of summer heat over the wide moor leading over to Glendarroch. The moor was a great summer haunt of the golden plover. They would be piping musically to each other through the haze of summer heat.

Alicky's mood of happy anticipation lasted until he was half-way up the steep hill leading to the Glendarroch moor. There, doubts assailed him. For a time he had forgotten his customary fears in the welcome of a sunlit morning. But now the fears returned, and just because he had forgotten them for an hour they seemed stronger, more irresistible than ever. In his mind's ear he could hear the jibes as he approached the Glendarroch *fanks*. 'Aye, here comes the Glendruid puddock! Get the milk covered before it goes sour! The old bodach's piping is no' what it was! Alicky Mag! Daftie, daftie, you're aye daft, are ye?' The jibes heard in childhood mingled with those thrown at him in later years. Deep in the recesses of his brain slumbered the memory of words he had heard when still a boy: 'Daftie, daftie, you're aye daft, are ye?'

He stopped, hesitating. His dogs ran on ahead, then looked back inquiringly, trying to fathom their master's intentions. He stayed motionless, torn by the conflict in his mind, unable to decide. The effort at decision brought him agony. He felt ill. That gave him another excuse, a fine justification for turning home. Yes, in spite of the fine morning, he wasn't just feeling himself that day. It was a steep climb out of Glendruid and a long tramp over the Glendarroch moors. He would be the better of the flask in his pocket in case he felt ill and tired on the way. Of course, the flask would remain unopened unless or until he felt the urgent necessity for the comfort of its contents. So back he went, forgetting fears and fatigue in his urgent mission, hurrying over the hump-backed bridge and the smooth meadow to his cottage. In his room where everything was a jumble of unswept ashes and unwashed dishes, he sought the little cupboard above his disordered bed. He had a moment of panic, fearing that the cupboard might refuse to open or its contents have been rifled. But everything was in order, the filled flask beside the row of bottles. After a long drink he felt better, ready to face the stiff climb, the long walk, the other shepherds, hours of piping. He was ready to face anything now with his flask safely in his pocket.

Of course, as usual, he was late. When he reached the Glendarroch moors and the scent of sun-warmed herbs in the breeze greeted him over the brow of the hill, he found little Johnnie Gillies, under-shepherd at Glendarroch, had the heft gathered and was seated on a stone awaiting him.

Little Johnnie Gillies, as everybody called him, was the biggest-hearted man for miles around, defiant to the tyrant, merciful to the weak. Of

214

all the shepherds he was kindest to Alicky Mag. He was the only shepherd who treated Alicky as a human being rather than a perennial joke. Alicky was glad that it was little Johnnie Gillies and not Hugh Maclean—the Glendarroch head shepherd—that had come to meet him to drive the sheep together to the *fanks*. Johnnie got up when he saw Alicky approaching, giving a devil-may-care tilt to the old cap perched on his dark and curling hair, hitching up his trousers before he put the swagger into his walk.

'Man, Alicky!' he called, 'I thought you wasna coming, boy, and the Glendarroch clipping would be a poor-like affair. Aye, I see you've the pipes with you the day. Fine, boy, it's a grand day that's in it, there'll be a dampness on the wool to begin wi', but never heed that, we'll have a bit tune from you, Alicky boy, when the work's done. And now tell me, Alicky boy, what's the do with you that you're the hour late again to-day?'

Alicky lied as he must always lie in self-defence to his fellow-men, speaking in the over-confident, high-pitched voice that made men laugh at him, excusing him. 'Indeed, Johnnie Gillies, and I couldna get the pipes in tune at all, the day. They've been lain up this week past and it took me an hour to put them in fettle. They're going grand now.' Little Johnnie Gillies saw that already, even so early in the morning, Alicky

215

had a dram in, and wondered what he would be like at the day's ending.

Alicky found the morning fine again in the company of little Johnnie Gillies. Johnnie had such a gay swagger in his way of walking, there was always a smile twitching the corners of his broad mouth, he was always breaking into the whistling of a rare tune. Somehow when Alicky was in the company of Johnnie Gillies, he found a long journey shorter, a fine day finer still, the prospect of hard work pleasurable. If all the men he met with were like little Johnnie Gillies, he would have no necessity to return homewards for his flask.

But all men were not as little Johnnie Gillies, and Alicky Mag was glad of his flask. Before ever they came in sight of the Glendarroch *fanks*, Alicky heard the bawling voice of Hugh Maclean, 'And where in hell's the Glendruid puddock the day? Can the bodach no' be in time for once and the work that's before us this day? Has a body nothing better to do than wait on a daft fiddler till he sobers hissel' up?'

But Alicky with the help of his flask was fit for Hugh Maclean. He stopped to clean his chaunter in the burn. Then coming over the brow of the hill behind Johnnie Gillies and the mob of bleating sheep, he shouted out in his high-pitched voice so that everyone could hear:

'The bodach's here, Hugh Maclean, and early enough, for the sheep will no' clip yet with the mist that's been in it this morning. And it's no' the fiddle I've brought wi' me the day, but the pipes, man. And what's the do wi' you that you're sour on as fine a morning as ever there was in a grand summer? Was it sour milk ye got to your porridge this morning?' He cried to the two Macintyre men, standing massive, solid, and dull together like plain-clothes policemen, 'And has your mother let you away wi'oot your nappies the day?' It was well known to all that the young Macintyre men, still more their spinster sister Jenny, dare not so much as wink at a lassie or smile on a lad without their widowed mother's consent, and that such consent was so repeatedly withheld that all the younger generation of Macintyres were likely to die without mates.

Then Alicky saw the tall, emaciated figure of Mackenzie of Strathord coming down behind the Pot Glendarroch heft of sheep. With him was Duncan Gillies, who was supposed to be the first-born child of little Johnnie Gillies, but by some was said to be no child of his. Indeed, Duncan had something about him that was strange to the glens. He was a slim boy, tall for his years, with authority in the way he held his loosely knit frame erect. It was seldom such a fair, smooth skin was seen among the children of the people of the Western hills. Alicky had seen Duncan Gillies at Glendarroch before, noticing the fine, slender, long-fingered hands that might make the boy a fiddler yet should he prove to have an ear for a tune and sense of rhythm in his blood. Alicky liked young Duncan Gillies, because he loved all beautiful things of the earth, the sea, or sky, and because Duncan too, although in such a different way from himself, stood apart from the complacent uniformity of ordinary men. He liked young Duncan Gillies of the fair hair, the white skin and joyful eyes. He would help him that day in the rolling of the wool.

Alicky was glad that Jock MacCulloch, the pompous, consequential, bullying man was even later than himself. Alicky, like all hill shepherds, considered gamekeepers as nuisances who kept neither deer nor heather in proper control, thus damaging the sheep; but there was no head gamekeeper who shot fewer hinds or burnt less overgrown moorland than Jock MacCulloch, who guarded the Dunblair estates, and who by his manner of talking seemed fully convinced that he owned them as well. Every man has his special conceit. Jock MacCulloch's was his moustache, a monstrous bushy growth of sepia-coloured hair, which Alicky called the Burning Bush, because a tup could hide in it. He swore that, given the chance to catch Jock MacCulloch asleep, he would clip off one-half of his moustache so that Jock would be forced to go about for months with his head turned sideways towards his neighbours and his wife. Then Jock would forget to conceal his mutilation during night, and Mistress MacCulloch, stroking his face while he slept, would leap out of bed crying out, 'Indeed, and which of the under-keepers is it that's in it? Indeed, and I didn't think there was one of them that had it in him to do this.' In relating this plan of his, Alicky mimicked so perfectly the Englified tone of Mistress Mac-Culloch, the keeper's wife, that the shepherds interrupted their clipping to laugh. Hugh Maclean roared, 'Aye, and the bodach's in grand form the day.'

Shortly afterwards when the massive figure of Jock MacCulloch was seen ascending the hill to the buchts, walking proudly as though his feet were too precious to tread heather, Alicky Mag improved on his imagined story. 'Mistress MacCulloch she jumps out of bed, crying out, "Indeed, and which of the under-keepers is it that's in it? Indeed, and I didn't think there was one of them that had it in him to do this." Then Jock turns round his head and she says, says she, "Damn, and it's only himself that's in it!"'

All the shepherds laughed again, except little Johnnie Gillies, whose face never moved. Suddenly Alicky felt ashamed of the bawdiness which flowed so freely from his flask, remembering that young Duncan Gillies was with them, and that Duncan was only a boy.

Jock MacCulloch seemed to realise perfectly well that the shepherds had been laughing at him as he arrived. He was panting and blowing with anger and his face throbbing red as he came into the *fanks* where the shepherds were clipping. He said not even a good-morning, striding in silence to the table where Alicky and Duncan were rolling the shorn fleeces.

Alicky looked up at the keeper, saying, 'Spread out your tail and gobble, Jock, and ye'd make a grand bubbly-jock!'

MacCulloch aimed a cuff at Alicky's head, growling out, 'Awa' wi' you, ye daft wee puddock. If you go on drinking the way you're doing you'll end in the asylum.'

'Aye, Mr. Hairy Face,' said Alicky, losing his temper now, 'drink will never harm you, Mr. Hairy Face. The half of it would be seeped up by yon barley crop you grow on your face before ever it got into your belly that's too big from sticking it out wi' pride and sticking stuff into it from greed. And I'd have you remember that I'm an eddicated man and no' accustomed to be talked to in the way you've seen fit to talk to me, Mr. MacCulloch.'

'Education—my shoulder,' sneered Jock Mac-Culloch.

Hugh Maclean had had enough of the bickering. He was in supreme charge of the day's proceedings. He tugged at his brindled beard as though milking a cow, then shouted, 'Stop yabbling thegither there like a parcel o' bairns. This is a Hieland sheep-bucht, no' the London Parliament.'

After that there were no sounds in the buchts but the metallic snipping of shears and the monotonous bleating of sheep. All the men got down to the work of the day, shearing one sheep after another, while the mob of naked sheep grew larger and that of sheep in wool grew less. Only when there came a ewe particularly lean or one which through unthriftiness had shed its wool, did badinage recommence. Alicky Mag lifted a pining ewe up in his arms, crying 'Here's a yowe with less wool on her than on Jock Mac-Culloch himself.'

At mid-day, when the sun had risen to give its fullest heat, the workers went into the shepherd's house of Glendarroch for their meal. Mary, the wife of little Johnnie Gillies, had it all prepared. She was such a quiet, sad-looking little woman, fair in the hair and skin, cornflower blue in the eyes, with her body broadened and growing shapeless from child-bearing, her hands worn and chapped from work. She trudged backwards and forwards between the range and the kitchen table, carrying food and drink for eight men.

At times she stole over to a corner of the room to rock a broken-down pram where her baby whimpered. She said little, doing her work without enthusiasm and from habit, looking as though life had beaten her. Only when she glanced on young Duncan Gillies, with his fair hair straggling over his eyes, did life come to her face.

Alicky Mag always felt that Mary Gillies disliked him. He knew that she saw nothing in him but an ugly drunken little man wasting his time on bawdy stories, fiddling, and the pipes. He could see that she disapproved of the early friendship between himself and young Duncan. He could see that she feared Hugh Maclean, her father, and that she treated little Johnnie Gillies, her husband, as an old and valued friend. There was none of the magic in her that had been Mairi Macgregor. There was no poetry in her broad mouth and frank eyes, just a brave, unimaginative woman accepting fate. Mary must have noticed Alicky's scrutiny, for she turned her face away, shivering, as though she found his stare uncanny and feared to show him the secret places of her soul. To cover her confusion, Alicky made poor jokes which nobody laughed at. The men were all too busy eating, and Mary Gillies looked as though laughter was mockery of hidden sorrow.

Hugh Maclean set the pace at table as he did

in the buchts. He made it plain that the meal
Mary Gillies had prepared for them was to give
them strength for further work and not an
occasion on which to offer hospitality. He ate
as fast as he could, glancing at the cheap Ameri-
can alarum-clock on the mantelshelf above the
range from time to time. Before he had finished
his last mouthful of food his chair was pushed
back and his bonnet on his head. He muttered
through his filled mouth, 'It's time we werena
here. We've got work before us, boys!'

Without a word of thanks to Mary Gillies for
her cooking and her labour, the men filed out
again to the sheep-buchts. Before they were
clear of the room, Mary had her baby lifted
from its pram—comforting it.

The July afternoon was very hot. The men
sweated in their labour. There was now no
need for Hugh Maclean to check quarrelling so
that all could concentrate on the work before
them. They worked on until the heat of afternoon changed to the coolness of evening with
the coming of a breeze, a cool breeze like a
blessing to tired men, sighing down from the hills.

Once the sun set and the dampness of a summer
dew descended, moisture would gather on the
wool of the unshorn sheep. With moisture in
the wool the shears make slow and clumsy work.
So Hugh Maclean cried a halt, declaring that
all had striven well and a good day's work had

been done. Mackenzie left with the Pot heft, to drive the sheep to their grazing on his way over the watershed to Strathord. But the other workers called on Alicky for a tune on the pipes before they went home. Alicky swore that he couldn't play a note without having a drink first, and indeed that was true, for he was tired and sore after a day of hard labour in the hot sun.

Little Johnnie Gillies insisted that they all had tea before anyone drank or Alicky played, so Mary Gillies had to carry food and drink for eight men. They went out immediately they had finished, leaving Mary to wash up a pile of dirty dishes.

Then Alicky Mag drank long and deep from the bottle which Hugh Maclean provided. As the fire spread outwards to his fingers and toes Alicky felt that he could play. He felt he could play as none had ever played pipe music before. He felt that he could draw the souls out of the bodies of men with the magic of his music, washing their souls free of their greed and self-seeking, drawing men together in sympathy and common understanding, piping his own soul free.

He played a lament, the lament for Maclean of Ardgour, and the sob of the notes drifted out over the still peace of Glendarroch. He strode before the shed where the other men lay resting amid hay, and as he played, as his fingers got the feel of the notes and the bag answered to the pressure of his arm, as the liquid melody of the notes soared out through the accompaniment of drones, his soul won free.

He followed the lament with one of his own composition, the lament for dark Mairi of the Sliaghmhor, and in turns of the melody there was a memory of quiet water lapping against a loch's shore. He forgot himself altogether while he played, forgot where he was and who he was. He was dedicated to his playing, a proud servant to his pipes, and the chaunter and drones drained the sorrow from his soul.

The tune was altogether too sad for Hugh Maclean. Tugging at his brindled beard he shouted, 'This is a clipping, no' a burial, Alicky Mag. For God's sake play us something with a lilt in it unless you would have us all weeping together like a parcel of bairns!'

So Alicky changed his step and carriage to fit a march. He played his old favourite, 'The Red and Blue Hackle,' going out of his beat to parade before the house in salute of Mary Gillies. He thought some such honour was due to her after all the work she had done that day. He could not know that she hoped he might soon be gone that her bairns might sleep in peace. He could not know how she hated the piping and fiddling and the drinking that went with them.

Hugh Maclean called back Alicky to wet his

throat again and play them a reel. At first Alicky was inclined to accept the pay without granting Hugh's request. He protested that the fiddle, not the pipes, was the proper instrument for playing a reel, but Hugh Maclean, half-mad from the drink he had taken, swore that Alicky Mag would do as he was bid or have his puddock's neck broken. So Alicky played for Hugh Maclean, the two Macintyres, and Jock Mac-Culloch to dance to. The task angered him, because the men paid no respect to rhythm or steps, capering round about before the hay shed like the uneducated yokels that they were. Little Johnnie Gillies and young Duncan Gillies sat among the hay, laughing to see grown men make such fools of themselves. Alicky Mag lost sympathy with his listeners—the magic bond of understanding was snapped by their noisy fun. As the drink rose surging to his head he felt superior to them. Only young Duncan Gillies seemed to have something in him that the others lacked—something more than crude indulgence in bodily exertion. Perhaps the boy with his fine hands had the makings of a fiddler. Perhaps with his fine head he had the makings of a scholar. He, Alicky Mag, would ensure that the boy's talents were not wasted. 'Stand up, Duncan Gillies,' he said, 'and I will instruct you in the Roman tongue. I will teach you the Lord's Prayer in Latin. Say after me—*Unus*, *duo, tres, quattuor, quinque, sex*—' but Duncan Gillies would do nothing but giggle.

Alicky took quick offence. 'Johnnie Gillies, fetch me my pipes, and like the very good fellow you are, point me the way to Glendruid.' Without bidding a single farewell he lurched off into the gathering dusk. In a moment of sobriety he had a clear vision of himself as an ugly, unimportant old man, puffed up with drunken conceit, talking ridiculously in a mincing high-pitched voice which was not his own. But it was only for a moment. Fresh waves of the drink he had taken reached his brain, comforting him. What could he *not* do that the others could not do? Could he not pipe and fiddle and win laughter where the rest were dumb? Had he not been educated privately, while the like of Hugh Maclean had barely attended school? Which of them knew as much as one word of Latin? Not one of them! He would show them how much Latin *he* knew! In a sort of chant he recited the meaningless jangle of Latin words so that the dull companions he had newly left might hear, intentionally loud enough for them to hear.

A, ab, absque, coram, de,
Palam, clam, cum, ex or e,
Sine, tenus, pro and pre!

He would show them that he was an educated man, superior to them all!

III

When Alicky awoke his head was very sore. He could remember little of his journey across the Glendarroch moors. He wondered how he had got home. He had no accurate idea what time of day it might be, for he had forgotten to wind his watch and it had stopped at twenty-five minutes past three. But the sun was shining into the cottage through the door Alicky had forgotten to close. Indeed, he had forgotten everything, even to take off his boots and clothes. His feet were stiff and swollen, and his right arm numbed from being lain on. In his sickness and discomfort he swore that he would never touch the bottle again.

It was late before he got out on his round of the sheep. By the time he returned, exercise and the freshness of morning had chased the worst of his sickness away. He began to remember the fun of the Glendarroch clipping and the fine thing he had made of his playing of Dark Mairi of the Sliaghmhor. He comforted himself with a serial recollection of the previous day's events, of the sharp retorts he had given, the jokes he had made, the fine fettle his pipes had been in. What had seemed a tragedy in the early morning became a joke by afternoon. There were worse things a man might do than to take an occasional dram in the company of others or even by himself if it were a cold day, a hot day, or a day when a man was extra busy and needed the help of it, or on a slack day when he was the better of something to pass the time away.

Alicky was coming down off the Sliaghmhor heft. Far in the distance, in the mouth of Glendruid, he saw two dark figures bobbing along the glen's white road. He wondered who it could be coming to Glendruid so early on a week-day. Sometimes in the summer evenings or on a Saturday, children might come bird-nesting from Lochend, but on a Thursday morning visitors were unknown. Who could the two figures be? Alicky sat down on a rock with his two dogs beside him, the brindled beardie dog and the old black bitch, to wait until the figures were close enough for recognition. Ten full minutes passed before he could make out who they were. Then he saw that it was Duncan Gillies and wee Johnnie, his young brother, coming up the glen. When they reached the cottage they stopped to have a consultation together on the road, then they opened the wicket-gate, went up through the garden and into the house.

Alicky wondered what could have brought

229

them to Glendruid. Likely it was some message from Glendarroch about strayed ewes or sheep-stealers that had brought them there. In any case he must hurry down, otherwise, finding the house deserted, they might leave without his speaking to them, and when a man lives alone with no inhabited house within miles of his own, he will miss no chance of conversation with his friends.

It did not take Alicky very long to reach his cottage, but when he got there he was ashamed that Duncan Gillies should see how he lived. The wicket-gate swung drunkenly on one hinge, the garden, well cultivated when Archie Campbell was herd, had capitulated to nettles, dockens and the yellow herb called 'Stinking Willie.' Alicky knew that inside the house the boys would have found even graver disorder, floor unswept, dishes unwashed, bed unmade, all more slovenly and dirty than in Archie Campbell's time, although Archie himself had been no proud house-wife.

The dogs rushed snarling and growling into the house with Alicky at their heels. He had no fear of what the dogs would do to the boys, for they would know Duncan Gillies.

Alicky found the two brothers, sturdy and erect, their backs to the fireplace, facing the dogs without fear. Were they not a fine pair of boys and yet so different from each other? Duncan, tall and slimly built, with his fine bearing and bonnie fair face; wee Johnnie, his brother, dark and stocky, swarthy as a gipsy with his wide laughing mouth and curly hair—real child of little Johnnie Gillies of Glendarroch.

'And what has brought you all the way to Glendruid the day, boys?' Alicky asked. 'Is the school burnt?'

It was Duncan who answered for himself and his brother. 'No, Alicky, I'm wishing it was. The teacher put us out for impertinence the day.'

Alicky clapped his hands together, smiling at the boys in good humour, forgetting his smile was a grimace. 'And is that no' fine, boys?' he said. 'And you've come all the way up Glendruid to see old Alicky Mag, daft old bodach that he is. Now isn't that fine, boys? I'll tell you what I'll do, Duncan boy. I'll give you your first lesson on the fiddle!'

'I'd rather be learning the pipes.'

'Wi' those bonnie fiddler's hands of yours, Duncan, and twist thon bonnie face o' yours out of shape wi' bursting yourself puffing down a chaunter? No, no, Duncan boy, it's the fiddle for you. It's wee Johnnie over yonder I'll learn the pipes to some other day. He's only a damned wee tinker anyway. The pipes will suit him grand, will they no', Johnnie?'

Wee Johnnie giggled away helplessly, finding the old man's gestures and grimaces absurdly

231

funny, but Duncan was solemn in his determination.

'I'd sooner you learnt me the pipes.'

Duncan's persistence pleased Alicky Mag. It showed the success of his own piping the night before. Dark Mairi of the Sliaghmhor had won another heart! Maybe, after all, he would teach young Duncan Gillies the pipes, but he must learn the fiddle first! 'Now, boys,' Alicky said, 'I'll need to make some dinner to us all!'

Duncan Gillies said that he and Johnnie had their pieces with them. They had them packed away in their school satchels.

But Alicky had some fine fresh trout out of the Glendruid river—where the trout have pink flesh and black skins spangled with yellow and red jewels. He would cook a dinner of the bonnie clean trout to give to the two boys.

'It's no' your school pieces you'll eat when you come on a visit to old Alicky Mag,' he said. 'Johnnie, you wee tinker, away out and bring in some sticks to make a bit fire! Duncan boy, see if you can't get those dishes into some kind of decent order!'

Duncan Gillies protested that the plates should be washed because the dogs had been licking them. Alicky Mag would have none of such nonsense, saying that it was a poor herd that was ashamed to eat with his dogs, and that with the dry weather that had been in it there was no water in the well to spare for such Englified capers.

So Duncan set places at table, wee Johnnie brought in a lapful of sticks, and Alicky Mag fried six good-sized trout, black as the river from whence they came. When the meal was prepared, Alicky looked about for places where the boys might sit. There was only the one chair and that was spreading its legs in preparation for an early collapse, so he told Duncan to sit on the edge of the bed, and, 'Johnnie, you wee black tinker,' he said, 'ye can clap yourself down on the floor. Now, boys, do you ever hear a grace said at home?' Duncan and Johnnie shook their heads. 'Ye *don't*, ye wee heathens? Well, Alicky Mag will say a grace to you to-day, and he'll say it in the Latin it's past time ye learnt.—*Panem et circenses*, Amen.—And noo ye can make a start.'

The boys were hungry after the long tramp which had followed their eviction from Lochend school. When the trout were finished, they opened their satchels and ate the sandwiches Mary Gillies had made for them as well. Alicky asked what had happened in school, and Duncan told a long and rambling story of how a butcher had struck wee Johnnie and of how, he, Duncan, had hit the butcher back, of how the butcher had followed them into school to tell on them, and of how Miss Gray, the teacher, had scratched her face with rage until it bled and gone out to wash

233

it, and of how when she was out Johnnie had written her name in chalk on the blackboard.

'Then she turned us both out of the school and told us no' to come back till we'd apologised,' Duncan said. 'And when we were out we was feared to go home because of grandfather, and I says to Johnnie, says I—"We'll away up Glendruid and stay with Alicky Mag till it's time to go home and then we'll walk up over the moor."'

'Grand!' cried Alicky, 'and is that no' grand, boys? I'll not tell on you, boys. You can trust old Alicky Mag. And now, boys, you'll away out and take a drink from the burn. Water's easier carried in your bellies than in a pail, and when you're in again I'll let Duncan try his hand on my own fiddle that many's the ladies of title have danced to in its day. Away out, boys, or it'll be time you was away before we're right started.'

Alicky wanted the boys to be out of sight for a few minutes. He wanted to be in his best form when he gave young Duncan Gillies his first lesson on the fiddle. Duncan had the long, fine fingers for the fiddle, but had he the ear for a melody, the sympathy for rhythm? Alicky meant to play to Duncan first of all, a slow sad tune to bring dreams to his eyes, then a gay tune to put movement in his feet. He wanted to play his best so that if Duncan's eyes kept clear and his feet remained still, it would prove that the

234

Good Lord had given fiddler's hands as servants to an unmusical mind. That was unlikely, because the Lord seldom made such mistakes. Mostly He gave the body of a song-bird to a bird that wished to sing. But not always! Had He not put a linnet's soul in the body of an owl, as Archie Campbell, in days long past, had said?

Alicky wished to play his very best, to forget himself in the music his fiddle made. While the boys were out he went to the cupboard above his bed. Always, now, he had a moment of panic before opening it, that the door would jam or the row of bottles have disappeared. But all was well. When Duncan and Johnnie Gillies returned with the fringes of their hair dripping water from bending over the burn whilst drinking, Alicky Mag was in form. He was ready now to play his fiddle before any audience, secure in his pitch, flawless in his rhythm, ready to introduce the twists of melody and tricks of time which were his very own, unknown to other fiddlers, and which no written score could reproduce. He felt ready and prepared to play as he had never played before. He would test young Duncan Gillies, to prove him a fiddler or to find him wanting in music that is the Grace of God.

First he played a slow sad tune with the wail of the sea-birds in it, with the swing of the rowlocks and the croon of the waves in it, a slow sad tune born in the heart of a man of the Western Isles as he watched the small waves on a summer ocean steal rhythmically landwards to kiss the shore. While Alicky played he watched Duncan Gillies, and as he watched he saw the mist of dreaming cloud the boy's eyes, and Alicky was glad. He changed his attitude and broke into that, the gayest of all dance tunes, 'Jenny, Catch Your Skirts Up,' and watching Duncan's feet, he saw the boy's feet twitch into motion in time to the rhythm, and again Alicky Mag was glad. He had been playing for Duncan Gillies alone. His interest had been all in him. But when he had finished the jig, he noticed wee Johnnie sitting sad-faced on the floor, doubtless feeling himself neglected and eclipsed by his elder brother. Alicky thought that wee Johnnie must often feel like that, because men took so quickly to Duncan who was evidently also his mother's favourite and a companion on the hills to little Johnnie Gillies and Hugh Maclean. Alicky Mag never could bear to see a child unhappy. He had been so unhappy himself, as a child. When he was cold sober his sympathy might be killed by his shyness without finding expression, but with a dram or two taken he would do his best to help. So he said, 'I've played you two fine tunes, Duncan boy, but I haven't forgotten wee Johnnie that's clapped down on the floor there. Now, ye wee black tinker, I'll play a reel for yourself alone. Will you dance to it, boy, if I play for you?'

Wee Johnnie rolled over on the floor, helpless from laughing at the capers of the daft old man. Alicky was quickly offended, not by the insult to himself, but to his beloved fiddling. 'Away out with ye and fish for puddocks,' he cried, 'I'll not have you stopping here laughing at Duncan when he's learning to play. Out with you! Out with you, you wee tinker.' Johnnie ran out to the sunshine, glad to be free.

Then Alicky Mag gave Duncan his first lesson on the fiddle. Alicky taught as he had learnt from Archie Campbell, who had got the tradition and the knowledge from old Peter Campbell, who had it from John Campbell, who had it from Sandy Campbell who was with the Campbell militia on the winning side on Culloden field.

Duncan Gillies would make a fiddler! He would not learn with the quick instinct that Alicky himself had shown. But with time he would learn. Boys had to learn so many things in school that they took a long time to learn any one thing. It would be grand if Duncan could come across the hill to Glendruid for his lessons, but if Duncan couldn't come to Glendruid to learn, then Alicky was determined to cross over to Glendarroch to teach!

Alicky Mag could have gone on late into the evening teaching, demonstrating, encouraging, explaining the mysteries of his traditional art. When he fiddled, time ceased. But Duncan was looking out through the cobwebbed window, watching the evening grow late. Even so early in a July afternoon the sun had dipped into the Western sea behind Ben Cruachan. It was time he went home. He told Alicky he must go.

'You'll not go yet, boy?' Alicky said.

'Aye, I'm going, Alicky.'

Loneliness swept over the soul of Alicky Mag. He said eagerly, 'You'll be back, boy?'

'Aye, I'll come back, Alicky.'

'And I'll teach you the fiddle and the pipes?'

'Thanks, Alicky.'

'I'd teach you Latin, Duncan, but I'm forgetting it, boy.'

Duncan said cheekily, 'You mind it fine when you've a dram in, Alicky.'

That pleased Alicky. Yes, what the boy said was true enough indeed. If only he had enough drams, he could do anything, remember anything. If his wage were bigger and he could have bought more drams, what could he not have done? What the boy said was true enough indeed. Yes, with a dram in he could remember anything. If he'd taken one dram more, wee Johnnie would never have laughed at his playing. Just one dram more.

Alicky followed Duncan outside and there wee Johnnie awaited his brother. Alicky said good-bye to them, telling them to be sure and be back soon. He told Duncan not to forget what he had been told, of how to make common catgut the servant of God's gift. He watched the boys, walking side by side, cross the Druid bridge and ascend the steep hill-track which led over the ridge to the Glendarroch moors. He hoped they wouldn't get into trouble when they got home— two such fine boys. He saw Duncan bend down and put his arm round Johnnie's shoulder as though to reassure and encourage him. He watched the figures of the boys grow smaller and smaller as they followed the winding track up the hill. Once they stopped to look back and Alicky waved, but they did not seem to see him. He watched them until they were almost out of sight, crawling flies upon the hill. For a moment they stood out gigantic against the skyline and then they were gone.

Dusk deepened over the pit amid the hills that was Glendruid glen. A bird wailed sadly as it winged its way over the hills to the sea. Alicky turned back into his cottage. He was alone.

IV

I⊤ was October before Alicky Mag taught Duncan Gillies the fiddle again. He had seen the boy about Lammas-tide at the big Cranok sheep sales where all the lambs off the Western hills were gathered together for autumn sale. But there had been little opportunity to talk of fiddling there, where every shepherd had his mind on his own and his neighbour's sheep, comparing the prices of the produce of one grazing with that of another, the prices of one year with those that had gone before. Cranok was a market-place where sheep were innumerable and drams plentiful, but when money is changing hands, music and dancing must hide their heads in a quiet wood. One day when the sales were past and the first hoar frosts turning the bracken brown, Alicky met Johnnie Gillies in the early morning on the high ridge between Glendarroch and Glendruid. Alicky would have slunk down the hill hoping he had remained unseen, for when soberly working, to meet an old acquaintance was for him the remaking of friendship from its first beginning. But little Johnnie Gillies hailed him across the moor, and Alicky Mag was compelled to stop. Johnnie Gillies called, 'I've been seeking for three yowes that I canna find on the place. Maybe they've come over into Glendruid. Have you seen anything of them, Alicky?'

Alicky shouted back. 'There's never a strayed ewe stops in Glendruid, Johnnie. What's there in Glendruid to hold a sheep that's been used to Glendarroch meat? If a sheep strays into Glendruid it goes right on and up to the Sliaghmhor where there's a grand bit of grazing round about the lochside. If you're seeking yowes straying this way, Johnnie Gillies, it's there you should go.'

Once they had met and spoken, Alicky, even though sober and working, felt at home with Johnnie Gillies. The little dark man always looked happy, as though every day was the best day that had ever been in the world. He always wore his cap with an air and at an angle, the only bit of innocent swagger about the man. He was always breaking into the musical whistling of some fine tune, for no reason at all except the sunshine on the hills or in his own heart. Little Johnnie Gillies was indeed a fine man to meet with at the beginning of a day.

Alicky suggested that if Johnnie had the time they might take the track together up to the Sliaghmhor where they would surely find the strayed ewes had they gone that way. Johnnie answered that it would take him a good bit out of his road and make him late for the rest of his work all day, but that if a job was once begun it was as well to finish it. If there was a chance of finding the ewes on the Sliaghmhor he would go there. He would be glad if Alicky would show him the way, because it was commonly said that unless a man had a map of the track in his memory, he would never find it on the hill.

As they walked past the cottage of Glendruid, Alicky hesitated, then asked Johnnie Gillies if he would come in for a dram, because the track up the Sliaghmhor was a steep one and the day would be warm enough once the sun had risen to its height. When Johnnie refused, saying that a dram was a grand end to a hard day but no help at all at its beginning, Alicky asked to be excused for a moment that he might make sure the ashes of his fire were burnt out. Johnnie Gillies nodded his consent, not believing for one moment that Alicky would so much as look at the fire. Alicky was much more talkative and gayer when he returned.

He asked after Duncan Gillies, why the boy had not been back to learn the fiddle as he had promised. Johnnie Gillies whistled two verses of the tune, *Mairi mhin, mheall—shuileach*, before replying. Then he said:

'I'll tell ye straight, Alicky. Duncan's a grand boy the now. I'm not for him being spoilt in any shape or form. Now, you're a grand fiddler, Alicky Mag. There's no one needing to tell you that. And you're a grand hand at taking a dram, Alicky Mag. There's no one needing to tell you that either. It's no' likely Duncan will turn out a fiddler like ye are yersel', Alicky. If there's never been a fiddler the like of you in Argyll before, it's no' likely there'll be a second come oot o' the same county in such a like hurry. Now, if Duncan gets a liking for the fiddle and canna make anything like the job of it you do yourself, Alicky, the first thing he'll think on is that a body canna fiddle right unless he's a dram taken. There's plenty will tell him that the first time he canna mind on a tune they've asked for. I'd sooner Duncan never put his hand on a fiddle than kill himsel' wi' drink like Mary's father.'

Alicky had heard something of that story when, only six weeks before, he had followed the body of Hugh Maclean through the iron gates at Lochend. He had heard rumours there of Hugh Maclean having died of drink before he had time to sober up after coming home a day late from Cranok sheep sales. But Duncan Gillies would never go like his grandfather. He had different breeding in him. Nor would he ever need the help of the bottle to make friends. He had his friends made before he had spoken.

Alicky stopped on the steep track to regain his wind before defending himself. When he spoke

243

his voice was broken by sobs, and his face was twisting to hold back tears.

'Johnnie Gillies! Johnnie Gillies!' he cried, 'why would you misjudge me so? Would you think that I would seek to lead Duncan after myself and me only seeking to lay the little that's of good in me at the boy's feet? Duncan will never see the bottle in my house. And would you be thinking, Johnnie Gillies, that Duncan would need the help I myself must have before I can be forgetting myself and letting the fiddle play? Duncan needs no help but what God has given him with both His hands. You can let Duncan come over to Glendruid each day of the week and there will be no harm come to him.'

But little Johnnie Gillies would not give way. It was easy to see that he did not wish to hurt Alicky Mag, but that he was equally determined that there be no chance of harm coming in Duncan's way.

'I tell you what I'll do, Alicky,' he said, 'if it's no' putting you out of your way too much. I'll allow Duncan learn the fiddle, if you're set on teaching him, and if it's no' too much trouble to you to step over to Glendarroch of an evening. The boy's never through till then with all thon nonsense they stuff into their heads in the school nowadays. But I'll not stand in the way of Duncan learning the fiddle if you'll come over to Glendarroch and teach him there.'

'I'll come over this very evening,' said Alicky.

'You'll be welcome there, Alicky, and you'll stay to your tea.'

With matters so amicably settled it only remained to find the strayed ewes and drive them across Glendruid to the Glendarroch moor. As Alicky had predicted, they were found on the old summer shieling pasture of the Sliaghmhor. Alicky and Johnnie kept well out of sight coming down the hill lest a gamekeeper should see them and there be a noise and complaints about disturbing the deer forest in the stalking season.

Johnnie said farewell at the hump-backed bridge over the Druid. He told Alicky to be sure and not forget that he was expected to tea that evening.

Alicky was unlikely to forget because the invitations he had had to neighbours' houses within the preceding ten years could be counted on the fingers of his two hands and then leave his thumbs free. He was ready to leave for Glendarroch long before evening. He had a dram or two to put him in form for an evening of social entertainment, tucked his fiddle-case under his arm, called his two dogs to follow him for company, and set out in the gathering dusk for Glendarroch. It was almost dark when he reached there, but a rising moon and a frosty sky showed that he would have light to find his way home.

The boys were not back from school when he

reached Glendarroch. The old man who drove them to the glen head was scared of night driving and was always late in the autumn and winter months. Mary was in the house with the baby girl Jean, and little Johnnie Gillies came in from the byre when he heard dogs barking. Alicky went with Johnnie to tie up the dogs, and as they came back to the house they met Duncan and wee Johnnie hurrying up from the road to get their tea. Duncan had grown taller since Alicky had seen him last.

Alicky shouted, 'You're getting too big for the school, Duncan, and thon wee black tinker of a brother of yours, can he dance yet?'

Wee Johnnie could never keep solemn before Alicky Mag. The old man's grimaces and capers and high-pitched voice amused him so. When he'd done laughing he said, 'Can you drink water yet, Alicky? Are the puddocks deid yet?'

Then Alicky remembered that after the two boys' visit to Glendruid, every second bucketful of water he had drawn from the well behind his house had contained a living frog. It had beaten him to know how they had got there.

'Aye, Alicky,' wee Johnnie squeaked, 'ye tell't me to go out and fish for puddocks. I did as I wis tell't and when I'd got a dizzen I plunked them doon your well, Alicky.'

Wee Johnnie raced away through the yard and round the byres, laughing all the time.

'It was *you* did it, was it, ye wee black deil! Wait till I get a hold of you! I'll sort you, boy.' Alicky gave chase, but he might have saved his wind because he could not catch wee Johnnie. He came back to the door gasping. Duncan said, 'Ye'll never catch him, Alicky. Johnnie's the best runner in the school.'

Alicky panted out, 'It's my idea it's nothing but impertinence they teach you in the school, boy. But it wasn't to learn manners to wee Johnnie that I came over to Glendarroch this night. It's to learn you the fiddle that I came, Duncan boy. I met your father looking for ewes out over the Glendruid march and he gave me permission to come over this evening. Indeed, he was good enough to ask me over to my tea.'

'And how'll you get home the night, Alicky?' Duncan asked. 'Ye'd be best to spend the night here, would ye no'?'

Alicky did not like to confess to Duncan that his invitation from Johnnie Gillies did not extend thus far. So he answered:

'Dinna fear for me, Duncan boy. I'll find my way home fine. Give Alicky Mag an October moon to see by, his fiddle to make the daft white hares dance on the top of the high hills, and the deer come creeping round about him to hear him play. Never heed about how I'll get home, Duncan. There's many's the time folks have sworn that I'd *never* win home, but I've aye *won*

247

home, and maybe disappointed them.—But it's the fiddling we're to be at the night, Duncan. Mistress Gillies, your mother, has asked me in to my tea, and after that we're to go out to the byre to play so as not to waken your sister, wee Jean.'

Alicky enjoyed his tea. Mary Gillies had the art of making both a crisp oatcake and a light scone. The way she cooked a rabbit made it as good as any chicken. Her tea had a grand flavour; her home-made jams held the taste of the fresh fruit. The Gillieses, too, were a merry family, familiar and happy in each other's company. There was more talk and laughter round the table now that Hugh Maclean was dead.

The only silence that was painful followed a remark of Alicky's, when he said, laughing, 'It's the queerest thing in the world, Mistress Gillies, the difference that's in it between Duncan that's the real gentleman and wee Johnnie that's the gamest wee tinker that ever I saw.'—There was silence, Mary turning her head away and Johnnie drumming on the table with the fingers of his right hand. Alicky recalled, too late, the rumours in the neighbourhood concerning Duncan's birth. However, the boys broke the agony of silence with their chatter about school and of the imbecile doings of their teacher, Miss Gray.

After tea Johnnie Gillies put a well-trimmed lamp in the byre for Alicky and Duncan to see by, and the lesson on the fiddle commenced.

The two cows rattled their chains and turned their mild eyes to stare at the intruders on their evening privacy. Alicky sat on the meal-chest, his short legs dangling above the ground. Duncan sat on an upturned feeding-box. He had forgotten almost everything he had learnt from Alicky on his day of truancy in Glendruid. He had to go back to the very beginning again of how to hold his fiddle and bow. He made a great many screeching and discordant noises, but Alicky was pleased with the progress made.

'You'll be a fiddler in no time, Duncan,' he said. 'Now I'll play you a wee tune myself just to show you how it should be done, and then it's over the hills to Glendruid for me. I'll play a wee tune to the memory of Hugh Maclean that's gone, may peace be with his soul. I'll play a tune that was learnt me by a young herd that came over for the smearing of the sheep from the Island of Skye. He swore to me that when he was in a boat and fell to the playing of that tune, the seals would gather in the wake of his boat and would follow him with the salt tears from their dogs' eyes falling into the salt sea. Wheest you, Duncan boy, while I play it to the memory of Hugh Maclean that's gone.'

Alicky played the sad, sad tune in a minor key that was timed to the gentle rocking of a boat in a calm sea while a man sat resting on his oars. He played it to its end and then he listened.

It seemed to Alicky that there was a dim sound on the cobbles of the yard beyond the barn door as of a man walking. It seemed to Alicky that the latch of the door rattled and then moved as though someone were trying to come in.

'Wheest! Duncan,' he said, 'did ye hear anything the now, Duncan?'

'Hear what, Alicky?'

'Did ye no' hear the noise of a man clumping across the yard? Did ye no' hear the latch rattle? Did ye no' see it move the now, Duncan?'

'Away, Alicky, you're hearing noises in your own head,' but Duncan's voice was shaking as he tried to reassure himself.

'You're maybe right, Duncan. Who would it be coming creeping to a door through the night and when you open the door there's no one there? This is Glendarroch, no' Glendruid we're in the night. Ach! dinna listen to an old bodach's havers, Duncan. I'll play a reel, Duncan boy, that'll cheer the two of us up, and then we'll be going, for the moon will be full up by now to light a bodach home.' But Alicky stopped his playing, suddenly, in the middle of a bar. He was sure he heard something. He leant forwards, listening, his mouth half-open showing his toothless gums. 'Wheest! Duncan! Wheest!' he whispered. 'Did ye no' hear something that time? Did ye no' hear the sound of a big man birling about outside?'

'Ach! there's nothing, Alicky!' Duncan said in desperation to suppress his rising fear. But the dogs howled together from the stable where they were tied, and the cows rose uneasily, rattling their chains.

Alicky was sure of it now. The graves were opening, and the white hares on the high hills dancing like mad by the light of the moon. He leant forwards, whispering, 'What did I tell you, Duncan boy?'

But Duncan cried, 'For God's sake stop your daft capers, Alicky Mag!' and dashed outside.

Alicky sat still, watching the open door. He felt that he must not flee. What would come over a man who dared offend the dead? Would it be right to deny acquaintance to the cold dead? He would wait there in the barn, his feet dangling above the ground, the silent fiddle in his shaking hands. The door swung back, and there on its threshold stood Hugh Maclean.

He was just as Alicky was used to see him in life, the heavily built man with the slightly hooked nose and blazing blue eyes, tugging at his brindled beard as was his habit during life, as though milking a cow, his muscled arms bare and the brown skin of them streaked with sheep's sharn. Alicky leapt from the corn-chest to go over to speak to Hugh, for what living man would dare offend the dead? But Alicky had taken his eyes from the doorway, only momentarily, to judge the

251

distance of his spring to the ground, and when he looked up again the figure of Hugh Maclean had gone.

Alicky would have liked a word with him before he went. Hugh might have brought a message from Mairi of the Sliaghmhor, dark Mairi, who was dead so long. Alicky ran out to the yard, crying 'Hugh! Hugh Maclean!' but Hugh had gone. The dogs barked in echo to Alicky's voice, and the cavalry of the clouds sped in their squadrons across the moon. There was a mutter of stags roaring in the forest of the Sliaghmhor, but Hugh Maclean, or the shadow of the man, had gone. So Alicky went back to the byre for the lamp and then took it over to the house. His reception there was cold. Both Johnnie and Mary Gillies were angry at the fright Duncan had got, as though it were Alicky's fault that Hugh Maclean had risen from his grave to hear the tunes he loved so well.

Johnnie Gillies said, 'It was to learn Duncan the fiddle that I asked you here, and no' to scare the life out of the boy with your daft-like capers,' and Mary Gillies too, 'If there's any more of this kind of nonsense you needna show your face in Glendarroch again.'

Alicky thought all this very unfair—to rage at him for what was not his fault. How could he prevent Hugh Maclean coming back to hear fiddling, if he wished to return? Quite suddenly

Alicky realised that although people like Johnnie and Mary Gillies might give lip service to faith in an after-life, actually they believed in no such thing. Hugh Maclean was dead and buried. For Johnnie and Mary, that was the end of him. They might comfort their consciences by saying he was at peace and in a better world where Hugh might sit in his night-shirt and twang a psalm tune on a harp. They might say that, but they did not believe it. Hugh Maclean was dead and buried and that was the end of him. For Hugh Maclean to reappear was to unsettle the certainty of Mary and Johnnie's unbelief. That was what made them so angry, speaking hard words. Alicky felt a sudden contempt for the plain-minded people who heard no voices in the sigh of the wind, who saw nothing in a sunset but a coloured sky. He felt such contempt that he spoke back, although the influence of his evening dram was almost gone.

He said, 'You have gravely insulted me, Mistress Gillies. Let me tell you, madam, that if it were not for your son Duncan, who has beauty in his mind as in his face, I would not put myself to the trouble of crossing the Glendarroch moors to come to your door. I would not, indeed, madam. And it has hurt me beyond your knowledge that you, little Johnnie Gillies, that I have always thought of as my friend, should speak sharp words to me. Let me inform you, sir, that were it not for your son Duncan, who has it in him to be a great fiddler, I would not have accepted the invitation you gave me this very morning to have the honour to teach your boy and to eat in your house.'

No sooner had Alicky made this speech than he wished the words unspoken. He overheard himself speaking in a silly, Englified voice, picking a quarrel with the only friends he had left in the world. He overheard himself talking of fiddling and fiddlers as men had spoken of them in the glens two score of years before. Why quarrel with friends when he had so few? Why teach Duncan the fiddle at all? By the time Duncan had grown to be a man no one in the world would wish to dance to the old tunes played in the old traditional way. The few young people who might be left in the glens would be swaying their bodies to a Negro band. Why quarrel with friends over things without substance, the wraiths of the dead—the music that was dying? Why quarrel? Was it too late to remake friends?

He said quickly, 'Never you heed the havers of a daft old bodach that's no' quite hissel' the night. Dinna you heed my blethers, Duncan boy. I'll leave you my fiddle to try a tune or two on, and it'll no' be long before you'll be fit to give Alicky Mag a lesson himself. I'll be asking you to show me how a strathspey should be played, Duncan boy.—Mistress Gillies, it's Alicky Mag himself that's grateful to you for the grand tea you've given him this night.—Johnnie, if those yowes stray back to the Sliaghmhor I'll turn them back for you. I'll keep a look-out for them for you, Johnnie Gillies.' He heard himself blethering away, offering kindness, exposing friendship for sale after the market had closed. He was bending before them all, asking mercy on his loneliness, and Johnnie's mouth was set and hard, and Mary turned her face away.

Alicky knew what the trouble must be. It was a dram he needed to lend force to his persuasion and pleading to his words. He found that his glance kept straying towards the cupboard where he knew the bottle of reconciliation was stored. Little Johnnie Gillies saw the unspoken request in Alicky's eyes. And Alicky could see the unspoken words on Johnnie's lips, 'The auld bodach was in need of a dram. So *that* was what was the do with him !'

'You'll be taking a dram afore ye go, Alicky?' said little Johnnie Gillies, smiling at the old man's weakness.

Alicky did not care whether or no his weakness were exposed, if it should bring a smile to the face of a friend. He said, 'Well, just a wee one to drink Duncan's health, fine boy that he is.' But with Mary Gillies watching in silent disapproval, the dram Johnnie Gillies poured out was too wee to be of use to Alicky Mag.

Alicky asked if he couldn't have a wee drop more put in his flask to see him safely home. 'The cold whiles grips me when I'm out at night. I've my flask with me here.'

With his flask filled, Alicky was prepared to face the tramp over the hills in the eerie chill of an October night. He said farewell to them all. He said farewell to Mary Gillies. It was the recollection of the coldness in her eyes which told him he would never be asked back to Glendarroch again.

He set out homewards over the lonely, moonlit moors. His heart cried out for friendship to the pity of heaven, 'Mairi, dark Mairi of the Sliaghmhor!'—For Mairi, at least, had stooped to touch his clothing with the slender fingers of her spring-cool hand.

V

WHEN autumn changes to winter in the hill places, the fury of the bellowing stags is stilled by darkness and the cold, the hares show streaks of winter whiteness in their coats, the ptarmigan on the mountain tops mimic the fallen snow. As autumn changes to winter, the sun pays ever shorter visits to Glendruid, until in mid-winter it never shows itself at all over the rim of the enfolding hills. And in the depths of sunless Glendruid, melancholy and loneliness settled on the soul of Alicky Mag like a black cloak.

He went over the hill to Glendarroch on occasion to teach the fine boy Duncan Gillies how the fiddle should be played. But the lessons were held in the barn, and Alicky was never asked to stay on in the house once a cup of tea had been drunk in formal compliance with hospitality's rules. Alicky knew that Mary would have forbidden him entrance to her house altogether had it not been for the insistence of little Johnnie Gillies, her man, who would go ten miles out of his way to restore a kittling to its mother —little Johnnie Gillies who fought the sadness in others with the surplus of gaiety in his own soul!

Alicky had been forbidden the Macintyres' house altogether. He had been across there with a tup that had strayed over to Glendruid, thinking he had earned a word of friendship in so doing. But it so happened that squint-eyed Jenny Macintyre had gone in for modern poultry methods, with vast colonies of White Leghorn pullets in slatted-floor colony houses. Alicky's brindled beardie collie had never seen anything like it. When it saw the mob of snow-white birds in the fields it took them for a flock of thieving seagulls, and only found its mistake after snapping the heads off a dozen. Mistress Macintyre, Jenny's mother, would take no apologies from Alicky Mag. She told him plainly, and to his face, that he was no better than a savage Red Indian living in a wigwam, and his dogs worse than savage wolves. She said that it would be a God's blessing if they were all shot. She might have meant the dogs, but she was looking straight at Alicky himself, and as for Jenny, who had come out to see the destruction of the certain profit from laying pullets promised by the county poultry instructress in the evening classes at Lochend—who was fit to tell where or at whom Jenny Macintyre was looking?

Alicky had tried to explain that the beardie couldn't see very well for the hair that flopped over his eyes, and that the beast had never seen white hens in such numbers before—mistaking them for seagulls flocking down to steal the hens' meat. 'And surely,' Alicky had said, 'Jenny herself can feel for a poor dumb beast of a dog that canna see straight.'

Mistress Macintyre had lost her temper altogether on hearing that. She had hoped that Jenny would turn out a beauty and marry into the county, until she saw that the lassie's eyes were going in several directions, although no one could tell which. So, when Alicky drew a parallel between Jenny's difficulties of vision and those of a verminous beardie collie, Mistress Macintyre, the stout, managing body that she was, lost her temper altogether. She had warned Alicky never to dare show his face in her presence again, not even at the sheep gatherings he was accustomed to attend. Thus another neighbour's door was slammed in Alicky's face.

Nor had Alicky any comings or goings, in a social way, with Mackenzie of Strathord. Mackenzie's bonnie wife, that he had married out of a town to the ruin of his digestion and the havoc of his mental peace, *she* had no use for men unless they were young, good-looking, and easy in their talk. The unkind gossips of the countryside, especially those that were plainer of face than bonnie Jean Mackenzie, whispered that she had no more than the one use even for that type of man.

In Lochend Alicky Mag was no longer the

fiddling hero of olden times. Only once that winter had he played at a dance—and that, not in the Assembly Rooms, which had become the Majestic Cinema, but in the Boys' Brigade Hall. The young people stood about smoking cigarettes and calling each other by their Christian names. Alicky played. He played 'Jenny, Catch Your Skirts Up,' and nobody danced. He played the saddest, most sublime of tunes, like angels whispering together. He put his heart and his soul in his playing and somebody laughed. A young girl, powdered, painted, came across the hall. She raised the places where her eyebrows were drawn and opened the scarlet oval which represented her mouth. 'Tell me, old man,' she said, 'can you play jazz?'

Thus, in sick loneliness of heart, Alicky awaited the end of the year, when the Old Year would die in anæsthesia and the New Year get up in the morning with a splitting head. Alicky awaited Hogmanay, the only night when all honest merchandising Scotsmen leave the pedestals of dignity they have so recently attained; when the Provost announces that he too is one of Jock Tamson's bairns and can swallow a dram and tickle a lass as well as any drunken tinker, and turns a deaf ear to his wife whispering 'Geordie, Geordie, keep yersel' in mind o' next year's honours list!'—*Hogmanay*, when a man's a man while he can keep his feet—*Hog-*

manay, when Hugh Maclean and Mackenzie of Strathord and Alicky Mag, the Glendruid puddock, were wont to forgather in the shepherd's cottage of Glendarroch to see the Old Year out, the New Year in. But Hugh Maclean was dead.

All through the later days of December, Alicky haunted the crest of the ridge that formed the march between Glendarroch and Glendruid, hoping to catch sight of little Johnnie Gillies and to receive the invitation that was his by custom. But it seemed that in those same days of late December, little Johnnie Gillies avoided the Glendruid march, for linger as he might in the cold winds and lashing showers of sleet, Alicky never so much as heard an echo of Johnnie's cheery whistle.

The Old Year faded into death in the sunless cavern of Glendruid, and Alicky wished that he might die there too. He would find himself talking to his dogs for company as though they were brother men, and then when they crept on their bellies towards him, licking his hands, he would spurn them with his feet for the savage beasts they were. He was so lonely in the dark, sunless pity of Glendruid while the Old Year dragged its weary limbs to death. It would be easier to tolerate his loneliness in the spring days when the willows by the river-bank would make unto themselves garments of spun gold, when the hill birds that spilt melody on the wind would

join the hoodie crows that flapped like undertakers across the valley in winter, seeking the
carrion dead. In winter it was only the white
hares that gave him friendly company, the small
beasts all white as the winter's snow, that came
gambolling down from the peat hags to listen to
his fiddling while he played.

Now that he was growing old he could not
face the climb to the Sliaghmhor through the
drifted snow. The track that was an old friend
in summer would be death to him at an Old
Year's end. He could not visit the Sliaghmhor
until the spring came, and until then he could
not see Mairi, like forgiveness for sin, steal to
him with bared feet over the sleeping waters of
the loch. He could not hope to feel the fairy
touch of her spring-cold fingers on his sleeve.
He could not find peace again until spring came.
Until then he was alone—haunting the high ridge
between Glendarroch and Glendruid, awaiting
an invitation which never came.

When the dusk of the last evening of the year
changed to the total darkness of its night, Alicky
grew restless in his chair. Never before in his
remembrance had he spent Hogmanay alone.
The lonely darkness oppressed him, making him
afraid. Somehow, through the repellent cold
of the winter's night, he must struggle out,
seeking for friends. Perhaps, even at such a late
hour, little Johnnie Gillies, out of the kindness

of his heart, might have faced the wind sweeping across the cold Glendarroch moors, might have struggled across the moor, his cap drawn down over his face, his coat collar up, to extend a last-minute invitation, a tinker's bidding as it was called, to a neighbour herd who dwelt alone. Alicky left his house on the off-chance of meeting him. He set out into the night with his flask well filled against the cold, and his pipes under his arm. If little Johnnie Gillies were waiting on the crest of the ridge to extend an invitation to the warmth of Glendarroch fireside, it was certain he would inquire whether Alicky had brought the pipes with him. The pipes would be needed to play the Old Year out and the New Year in.

When Alicky left the shelter of his house, the cold gripped his heart at the very door. The Druid river thundered down the glen, sending the spume of its anger scudding over the high parapets of the hump-backed bridge. Wind caught the clouds by the throat, and dashing them against the hills, dissolved their bodies in cold rain. The rain came down Glendruid, the wind behind it, sweeping down Glendruid, merciless and deadly cold, the mournful sough of the wind behind it.

Alicky struggled up the hill to the Glendarroch moor, and there the wind died and the rain ceased, leaving monopoly to cold. Far ahead he could see the star of lamplight shining out in the night from the cottage of Glendarroch, the light that shone out like a star and grew suddenly dim as the clouds of the shadows of men passed before it. Alicky could imagine the warmth and light, the laughter and the conversation, the song and the story, the food and drink, that spun the fine web of companionship within Glendarroch house, and he outside and alone on the cold moor.

Alicky thought that there might be a reason for the absence of an invitation. Perhaps they in Glendarroch cottage took his Hogmanay visit for granted, a matter of old custom, requiring no special formality. At that very moment those within Glendarroch house might be saying to one another, 'Alicky Mag—aye, surely he'll be coming across. He'll be on his way here now. He hasn't missed a Hogmanay here for these twenty years and more. Aye, it wouldn't be Hogmanay at all without the old bodach here. Aye, he's sure to bring his pipes with him. He's played the Old Year out and the New Year in here these twenty years and more. Aye, the old man won't fail us—he'll be on his way here now.'

Alicky comforted himself with thoughts such as these as his feet squelched on the rain-soaked peat, and his dogs, stealing like wraiths at his heels, snarled, baring their fangs at the shadows of stones. He comforted himself with such thoughts until he was within hail of Glendarroch house, at the foot of the track that wound steeply up the brae to the house. There he hesitated and stopped. Perhaps, after all, he was mistaken. Perhaps Mary and Johnnie Gillies had decided together that now Hugh Maclean was dead, there was a grand opportunity of breaking the custom of twenty and more years. They might have decided that the evening would go better without the Glendruid puddock among their guests. Could that be so? Had he not always been the life and soul of their Hogmanay gathering for twenty and more years, leading the fun for them, playing the music for them, piping the Old Year out and the New Year in? Had there not always been a hum of pleased anticipation when, well fortified by the contents of his flask, the door opened and he stepped in amongst them? Had there not always been the same excited question asked, 'Have you your pipes with you the night, Alicky Mag?' Was it possible that now, after so many years, he was not wanted?

Was it possible? The light shone out through the window like a star and shadows of men and women passed before it. A scent of peat smoke came drifting down to the cold moor. Was it possible? The door kept shut. Every moment Alicky expected the door to swing open and the voice of little Johnnie Gillies hail him across the moor, crying, 'Alicky Mag, are ye there? What for are you standing out there in the cold, man? We'll chain your dogs and you'll come in to the fireside!' Little Johnnie Gillies calling to him across the moor, accepting no refusal to come in. But the door kept shut.

Then Alicky thought to himself, 'But how could those that were in the house know that he was out there alone on the moor? He might wait there all night and they would not know he was there. He must give them some means of knowledge that he was out there, awaiting the opening of the door.' He lifted his pipes to his shoulder, gripping the bag beneath his arm. At the first skirl of the drones, the brindled beardie dog strained its throat upwards to the sky, howling like a wolf, and the rain came again in a cold sheet, sweeping across the moor.

Alicky played his favourite march tune—the tune he was wont to play in salute to the mistress of a house at the end of a warm day's clipping in July. He played his favourite march tune— 'The Red and Blue Hackle,' marching backwards and forwards over the rain-soaked moor. He played it as he had never played it before—he played it to its end. Then he waited for the door to open.

He saw the shadows of heads come to the window looking out on the night. So they had heard him play! They would recognise his playing and his favourite tune. It would be only minutes, only seconds now before the door opened and the voice of little Johnnie Gillies would call him in. But the door kept shut.

So that was the way of it! The absence of an invitation was no mere accident. He was to be shut out, ignored. Where the old people had died and the old ways had vanished, he was no longer welcome. He was an unwanted stranger in his own land.

After one last look at the shut door and the shining window, Alicky turned for home, for in future Glendruid his shelter and his home must be, to hide in from the rebuffs of all mankind until the willows should awake and sunshine light the long hill-track to the Sliaghmhor. He struggled back through the wind and slashing rain to his cottage in Glendruid, his dogs snapping like wolves at the shadows of stones. At times he broke into a run on his way home, as though fleeing from shame. For had he not pleaded an entrance to Glendarroch house and been refused? Was that not cause for shame?

In the cottage of Glendruid he found the fire out—the room lonely and still—streaks of damp on the walls where the rain had beaten through. The clock showed the time to be a quarter to twelve. Soon the Old Year would be out and the New Year in. In Glendarroch house they would be looking to the loading of the gun, to fire the shots that would bring the New Year in.

Taking the lamp in his hand Alicky went through to the lumber-room where he had first slept on coming to Glendruid. From the litter of nets and dip-cans he disentangled the old and rusted gun and the box of cartridges which he never used except to scare the hoodie crows from the newly-born lambs. He loaded the gun, pressing back the triggers. Then as midnight crept near he went outside. He listened, counting the seconds, feeling the beating of his own heart. He heard the echo of shots fired in Glendarroch. That would be little Johnnie Gillies firing the Old Year out, the New Year in.

Alicky Mag lifted the old gun to his shoulder and fired in response. He would prove to Glendarroch and the world that there was a shadow of pride left in the last man in Glendruid. Only when he came inside again did Alicky realise that he had gone out meaning to turn the gun upon himself.

VI

THE New Year was no more than ten days of age
when Mr. Blake, the new factor at Dunblair,
drove up Glendruid in his grey ten-horse-power
car to see Alicky Mag. Mr. Blake was a young
and pleasant pink-faced man in brown tweeds.
He was an enthusiast for all things Highland—
the pipes, strathspeys and reels, the Gaelic
language, literature and song, Jacobite relics,
and matured, unblended whisky. He had spent
six summer vacations following the marches of
Prince Charles Edward Stuart and the Marquis
of Montrose. He played the chaunter and the
Celtic harp. He wore a kilt of an ancient varia-
tion of his maternal grandmother's tartan until
he found that the Highland collie of to-day has
no proper respect for bared knees.

Since coming to the Dunblair estate as factor
to the aged Lady Waterton, which was only a
matter of weeks and days, Mr. Blake had looked
forward to meeting the old man called Alicky
Mag, who shepherded Glendruid, and who was
said to be an unrivalled expert on the fiddle and
a fine performer on the pipes. There were far

too few of his kind left in the country. It was a great disappointment to Mr. Blake, therefore, that his first meeting with Alicky Mag was to be the fulfilment of the unpleasant mission of dismissal. For Alicky Mag had got to go and his sheep must go with him.

This was the way of it.—For very many years the Glendruid sheep stock had been in the proprietor's hands. Once the first boom in sheep-farming was spent, no tenant could be found whose fancy was taken by the dark, unchancy glen with its small-sized infertile sheep, with its damning record of bottom prices for wether lambs and cast ewes at Cranok market. Each factor to Lady Waterton left the unpleasant and unprofitable task of the final disposal of the Glendruid sheep stock to his successor. In the estate books the sheep continued at the book value which had been paid the last outgoing and bankrupt tenant some seventy years before.

Now, it was known to each successive factor to the Dunblair estates that, despite the passage of years and the general rise in values, the Glendruid sheep stock if dispersed in the Cranok market would realise less than half its book value, and yet, after repeated advertisement no tenant to take over the stock at valuation could be found. The Glendruid sheep stock continued in the proprietor's hands losing money each year.

It was Mr. Blake's good fortune to conclude

negotiations with an afforestation company, by which the lands of Glendruid and Sliaghmhor were to be acquired for the purpose of planting trees, and the Glendruid sheep stock was to be taken over at valuation on the hill before its final disposal, the loss thus falling on the afforestation company. It was all a matter of strict business carried through in the lawyers' offices in Edinburgh and Lochend. It was a satisfactory piece of business for the Dunblair estates. The book value of the Glendruid sheep stock was saved from severe depreciation. Of course, old Alicky Mag must lose his job. But during the friendly negotiations conducted between the interested parties in lawyers' offices in Edinburgh and Lochend, Alicky Mag was neither thought of nor mentioned. He wasn't a person there at all, merely a debit against wages.

It was Lady Waterton herself, nearing the century of her years, who inquired whether the Glendruid sheep had no shepherd, how long he had been in her service, and whether any suitable provision had been made for his future. Mr. Blake told her what he knew of Alicky Mag and made extracts from the estate books for her information. When she learnt that Alicky had been over fifty years in her service, she insisted that other suitable work be found for him on the estate, and that after his days of work were over he should be found a cottage and a pension.

When Mr. Blake informed Lady Waterton, as he felt bound in duty to do, that she had no legal obligations towards Alicky Mag and that strict economy in the management of her estates was both necessary and urgent, she replied that a fifty-years period in her service imposed an obligation upon her more binding than any law, more urgent than any economy. It might be imperative for the old shepherd to leave Glendruid, but there was no necessity for him to be dismissed her service. She would sooner dispense with her factor than consent to that. So Mr. Blake had departed for Glendruid to break the news of the Glendruid dispersal to Alicky Mag and to give him the offer of the job of shepherd to the Cheviot flock on the Castle park lands.

Mr. Blake had never found any glen so forbidding and depressing as Glendruid. He thought it was like driving into the mouth of hell —so bare were the hills, so sunless the valley, so pitch dark the river. No life was in the glen except a few miserably stunted and lean black-faced sheep, the hoodie crows that flew singly or in pairs from hill to hill, a few old grouse, a plague of mountain hares. The ruins of the clachan, too, were depressing to Mr. Blake, for he dreamt of a repopulated, renovated Highlands, with crowds of comely lads and quiet-eyed lassies weaving tweeds in unison, singing the old Hebridean plaints with the perfection of the Glasgow Orpheus Choir. He tried to express, in the tongue of his maternal grandmother, what he felt. *Tha mi bronach*—no, that wasn't the idiom at all.—*Tha bronach rium*—that sounded better. It might be right or it might be wrong. But in the unmistakable meaning of the tongue of all his other ancestors, he found Glendruid a damned depressing hole. At first sight its shepherd was little better.

Alicky Mag came down from his cottage to meet Mr. Blake at the garden gate, which had fallen off its hinges altogether. It was clear that the old man had been drinking and that he hadn't had a bath for years. And Alicky saw the new factor, who, like all factors, would be out for a reduction of wages and additional trouble.

Mr. Blake was new to country ways. He believed in getting down to business at once. In the country that is rudeness, for there a period of general conversation must precede a bargain. Without any preliminaries, Mr. Blake announced the purpose of his visit, and Alicky Mag, well-primed by his flask from the first moment he had seen a car coming up the glen, gave a flat refusal to quit.

'Ye canna do that,' he said, 'ye canna turn me out of Glendruid, nor the sheep either. The sheep's mine. I know the grannies and the grannies' grannies of every single ewe that's in the stock to-day. I've worked here all the days of my life. The sheep's been here long before either of the two of us were born. You'll have no delivery here, sir.'

Now Mr. Blake had been warned that Alicky Mag, the Glendruid puddock as he was most commonly called, was three parts daft and a quarter sober. He had expected difficulties and objections but not a denial of the rights of private property, something much more binding than the ten commandments. So he said, 'You are taking up a silly attitude, shepherd. You have nothing to do with the land being sold and the sheep dispersed. Both land and sheep are the property of Lady Waterton.'

'And what does Lady Waterton know of the land or of the sheep? She was a grand dancer when she was younger than she is the day, but she has never been in this glen to my knowledge, nor could she be finding her way to the Sliagh-mhor unless Alicky Mag himself was to guide her there. Nor has she ever so much as been to the Cranok sales to see her lambs and her cast ewes sold. What right has Lady Waterton to drive the poor beasts of sheep away from the hills they've been hefted on these hundred years and more?'

Words of argument tumbled over each other on Alicky's tongue, but in his heart was a nameless dread that he was wrong. It might be that he would be thrown on the world that despised

274

him, to learn new ways and to make new friends, and he was too old to do either now, no matter how much he drank. Then, if Glendruid and the Sliaghmhor were to be planted with tall larch and fir, how could he hope to find the winding track to the loch of the Sliaghmhor, and to Mairi coming barefoot and smiling to him over the calm water? He must try and explain to the factor, make a friend of him if a dram could work such magic in emergency, persuade him that this thing could not be done, impress upon him that the right to private property was no more sacrosanct than the holding of a secret dream in the depths of a man's heart. He must give up his attempt to quarrel, and make friends, for he had neither the power nor the will to fight.

So Alicky said, 'Maybe you'll come in and take a bit dram, sir. It will have been a cold run for you up the glen the day, and it looking its worst at this time of year. And if you'll not have a dram, sir, maybe you'll take a bite of dinner to yourself and a warm by the fire. Then we could be talking over these things better than out here in the cold. I've heard it said, too, that you've a liking for old tunes. If you would step in, sir, I could play a tune that was taught me by a shepherd that came over from the Island of Skye. He told me, sir, that when he would be playing that same tune out in his boat on a quiet summer's evening at sea, the dumb seals would be following him, and the salt tears from their eyes running down into the salt sea. And when I will have played you that same tune, sir, you will maybe believe what was told me by that shepherd from the Island of Skye.'

The very mention of anything that was both of the Gael and of Romance was enough to send Mr. Blake tramping throughout a hot August from the Larig Ghru to Derby, or over the steepest mountains betwixt Inverness and Inverlochy. He followed the dwarfed shepherd of Glendruid to his cottage which, by its appearance, seemed to be dwelling-place, store-room and dog-kennel all in one. Mr. Blake said he did not want dinner nor yet a dram, but it would be a real pleasure to him to hear the fiddle tune brought over by the shepherd from the Island of Skye.

Alicky played the old tune as he had never played it before, putting his soul into the melody, so that he was lifted away to where the sea is blood-red in sunset around the jagged hills. Mr. Blake said, 'Play that again, please.' Alicky played the air a second time but without losing his soul. For just as he began his encore he noticed that young Mr. Blake was swaying his body and tapping his fingers on his knee, and neither the swaying nor the tapping had the least resemblance to the rhythm of the tune. Alicky Mag was amazed. The factor had no music in him, yet his eyes were dimmed with tears. Alicky could have played the fine jig tune 'Jenny, Catch Your Skirts Up!' and called it a strathspey. The factor had no notion of music at all, yet his eyes were dimmed with tears.

Mr. Blake said, 'I'd rather hear that than Beethoven's fifth symphony. There's nothing tugs a man's heart like the music of the Gael. Play on, Alicky, I could stay here listening all day.'

Alicky went on playing. He thought that his playing might make the factor change his mind about the sheep delivery. But he found it dull work and difficult, for Mr. Blake took to tapping on the floor with his foot, and the tapping was all out of time. At last Mr. Blake seemed to have enough of it, for he got up, saying, 'When you come down to the Castle to herd the park sheep, I should like you to teach me to play some of these fine old Highland airs.'

Teach him! Alicky could hardly keep the jibes off his lips. *Teach* him! Why, the pink-faced goat would have wept to order if he'd been told 'Jenny, Catch Your Skirts Up' was a lament for the massacre of Glencoe! Teach the tradition passed on by Archie Campbell to a man who couldn't keep time! Yet, if it would save Glendruid and the Sliaghmhor, Alicky would even demean himself to that. He leant forward, holding out his fiddle, saying:

'I'll tell you what I'll do for you, sir. I'll teach you to play my own fiddle in a matter of six weeks, and at the end of that time you'll no' be fit to tell my own playing from *your* own.'— (Alicky thought to himself, 'And, indeed, that's God's truth')—'I'll do that for you on the one condition, sir,' Alicky went on, 'that I'm left to end my days, and that canna be long now for I'm growing old, on the ground that myself and the sheep is tied to. I'll teach you, sir, on the one condition that there's no delivery of the Glendruid sheep this May.'

There, Alicky thought, was a bargain indeed! He would go through the farce of pretending to teach the fiddle to a man who had no more music in him than an untuned set of pipes that had lain in the damp for a twelvemonth, and all he asked in return was to end his days working among the sheep that had been hefted on the Glendruid hills for longer than any living memory.

But Mr. Blake shook his head saying that he was awfully sorry. He was merely an instrument carrying out the orders of others. In this matter he was acting not for himself, who thought Highland music more important than either fir-trees or sheep, but for Lady Waterton, who had sold part of her estates, including Glendruid and the Sliaghmhor, to an afforestation company as the only feasible method of meeting a crushing burden of criminal taxation.

'Then can I no' speak with Lady Waterton?' asked Alicky Mag.

Mr. Blake replied that he thought that impossible. Lady Waterton was a very old lady in delicate health. She was as keen as ever in her mind, but talking business tired and upset her.

'No' as much as it would upset me and my sheep being turned out of Glendruid,' said Alicky Mag.

It seemed as though the arguments and discussion would never come to an end. Alicky related all he had done in the service of the Glendruid sheep—the storms he had faced, his sixteen hours of daily labour all through lambing time—the nights he had lain out in the heather guarding the sheep from sheep-stealers and sheep-worrying foxes or dogs. He pointed out the lowness of his wages, lower than those of any of the neighbouring herds. He told how only in Glendruid, of all the district's glens, was the ewe stock equal in character and numbers to what it had been a score of years before.

'Yes,' Mr. Blake agreed, 'we all know that you are a good, hard-working shepherd, Alicky. We've nothing against you as a shepherd. Your wages might have been raised if you'd ever asked for a rise. But the facts of the case are that the land is sold and that the sheep will be delivered to the afforestation company at the May term. It's very probable that the company will want you kept here until the sheep are finally sold in autumn at the Cranok sales.'

'And you'll no' let me have a word with Lady Waterton?' Alicky pleaded. 'I fiddled at her youngest daughter's wedding at the Castle, and Lady Waterton had me then to speak with her to thank me for my playing. I'm no' saying but that's a long time ago, sir, but Lady Waterton would likely mind of it, for she was a grand dancer in her time—none better in Argyll. You will find a chance for me to speak to Lady Waterton, sir?'

Young Mr. Blake considered the matter in his mind. He knew perfectly well that Lady Waterton could do nothing at all, for the offer for Glendruid and the Sliaghmhor had been made and accepted. Legally, everything was in perfect order. But there was a possibility that Lady Waterton with the prestige of her age and position, her long residence in the Highlands and her sympathetic knowledge of its people, might persuade Alicky Mag to consent with good grace to an inevitable change in his home and way of living. After all, it was Lady Waterton, herself, in the first place, who had raised the question of the future of Alicky Mag. She might even enjoy meeting the fiddler who had played for her dancing in the old Assembly Rooms in Lochend.

Besides, Mr. Blake hoped that once Alicky was smoothed down, the old man would be persuaded to teach him the fiddle. Mr. Blake had a dream of appearing in his maternal grandmother's tartan at the Lochend branch of An Comunn Gaidhealach, where there were no collies to lick bared knees, and there play the haunting melodies of Gaeldom in the interval between the President's address on the decline of the kelp industry of the Western Highlands, and the Committee meeting where the monthly crop of resignations was accepted without regret. So he told Alicky Mag to come down the glen next morning to the Castle, and that if the matter could be adjusted he would arrange for him to meet Lady Waterton there some time between eleven and one o'clock.

Alicky agreed, but no sooner had Mr. Blake driven away than bitter memories of the past, dread panic of the future, returned to trouble the old man's heart. There was no one in the world that would speak for him, except himself, and he himself was growing old.

VII

Lady Waterton was an immensely old lady. She was ninety-five years of age. Like a cricketer approaching the first century of his career, she batted during the nineties with infinite care. She was kept alive by her fears for the future of a multitude of servants when she should die, and it was the ministrations of a multitude of servants that kept her alive. But taxation had made ladyship a burden rather than a privilege in her later years. Her aristocratic generosity was checked at every turn by the advice of her lawyers and the intractability of bankers. There were even suggestions of turning Lady Waterton into a limited liability company—she, Lady Waterton, who had held her liabilities unlimited to all those who lived on her estates and gave her faithful service. Her lawyers would remind her that times were changing. Who changed the times except the men and women who lived in them?

She received Alicky Mag in an immense room with a fire at each end. When Alicky entered he had to look about him for a moment before he saw the old, old lady sitting crouched forward

on a high chair to ease the strain of ninety-five
years upon a kindly heart.

'You *are* Alicky Mag, are you not? The
fiddler? You played at my youngest daughter's
wedding. You were quite a little boy then.'
She spoke with a deep, booming voice that
sounded strangely coming forth from the wizened,
bent body. It sounded to Alicky as though somebody else, quite separate from the body he saw,
were speaking to him.

'Let me see you, Alicky. Come closer, man!
I shan't bite you. Yes, I should have recognised
you at once. You looked so old when you were
a boy. Now that you are old you keep something
of the look of a boy. Sit down and tell me what
you want to see me about.'

She was so old that it was like talking to God.
She was so impersonal—a body wrapped in black
silk and covered in white shawls, so impersonal.
Only her voice lived. Her very eyes—blue and
misty behind glasses—seemed dead. She was so
old that it was like talking to God, and Alicky
could tell her what was in his soul. There was
no need to swagger and boast before her, disguis-
ing from her what he really was. There was no
need for self-defence, no use in lies. One so old
could not be deceived. She was so old that she
must see all, know all, understand all, pity all.
She was so old that it was like talking to God.

She said, 'I understand that you have appealed

283

against the decision to relieve you of a post you have filled faithfully for many years. You understand that you will be pensioned? Even Lloyd George shall not prevent us from doing that! You understand that we do not want to keep you away from shepherding, and that you will get work among the sheep about the Castle parks. What is your complaint, Alicky?'

He told her, knowing that she would understand this was no grumbling of a dismissed servant, but the agony of a soul. He told her how he knew no other home but his cottage in Glendruid, no other companions but the sheep, the hares, the deer that lived there, the trees by the river that grew there, the seasons that passed in their ever-changing glory over the hills there. He told her that he was without human friends —all except the one—Mairi Macgregor of the Sliaghmhor.

Lady Waterton interrupted him, saying, 'Stop! I remember that affair so well. It happened a long time ago. Mairi Macgregor—the dark girl—I always thought she looked so delicate. Yes, I remember her. She married an old man Campbell and left the estate. But she's been dead for years. She died quite young. You are speaking of somebody else?'

'No, your Ladyship. It is indeed that Mairi Macgregor that I am speaking of. Mairi Macgregor—daughter to Duncan Ban—dark Mairi

284

of the Sliaghmhor—she went away as bride with Archie Campbell to a wether grazing in Lochaber. Aye, your Ladyship, she died away yonder—but when she was dead she came back to the Sliaghmhor where she had aye been happy. Aye, your Ladyship, she lives there now. She will be coming to me when I go up yonder to the Sliaghmhor on a quiet evening, when there is nobody about. She will be coming over the loch to speak with me when there is nobody about, your Ladyship. She aye comes to me where the lochside is all white stone and never the weed that grows there, your Ladyship, on the white stone. And—ach—your Ladyship, she will be laying the fingers of her hand, your Ladyship, on the sleeve of my coat, and when she would be doing that, your Ladyship, I am at peace.'

The old lady knew all and pitied all. She did not laugh at Alicky nor call him mad. She said, 'But surely, Alicky, if you leave Glendruid and cannot go to the Sliaghmhor, then Mairi will come to you where you are?'

'She will not, your Ladyship. Never yet have I seen her nor felt her fingers on my sleeve—just *here*, your Ladyship—except in the one place, your Ladyship—where the stone is snow-white on the shore of the loch of the Sliaghmhor. You will understand, your Ladyship, that that was where she lived all the years that she was happy.

She never knew sorrow while she was beside the loch of the Sliaghmhor. But when she left the Sliaghmhor it was nothing but sorrow that she knew. Then why should she be leaving the Sliaghmhor again now for the sake of a daft old bodach like Alicky Mag?—So that is why I am asking you, your Ladyship, to be allowing me to herd the sheep on Glendruid until I am dead and that cannot be long now, your Ladyship, for I am growing old. I will herd them to you, your Ladyship, for no' bigger a wage than will keep me and the dogs in meat. Aye, your Ladyship, Alicky Mag will manage away fine without his dram if you will leave him to finish his days in Glendruid and his evenings on the Sliaghmhor. I will not allow a single lamb to die for want of warm milk or a fire to lay itself by; I will allow no single ewe to die from backing before she be shorn; I will allow no single tup to stray or drown in the back-end, your Ladyship, if you will but leave Alicky Mag to end his days in peace in the country with which he is acquaint. It would not be me, your Ladyship, that would have been asking Mr. Blake, your man of business, to have a word with you, your Ladyship—("Tell her Ladyship," says I to him, says I, "that's it's old Alicky Mag that's asking this one favour of her—Alicky Mag that's played for her on many's the occasion when her Ladyship would be set on dancing")—I would not have been asking Mr. Blake to have a word with you, your Ladyship, if it had not been, your Ladyship, that I know the sheep and that I know the ground, and that I'm aye fit for my job and never off the hill if the sheep be needing me, and no' seeking a big wage at all, your Ladyship, if you'll but let me bide.'

Lady Waterton listened patiently to Alicky's pleading. Then she said, 'If I wanted a man to herd Glendruid, Alicky, I know I could find no better man than you. But if Glendruid and the Sliaghmhor are to be planted, there can be no sheep or shepherd there. I shall do all I can for you, Alicky, but I cannot buy back land that is sold, nor engage a shepherd where there are no sheep. You must make up your mind to the change, Alicky. We shall give you a bonnie flock of Cheviots on the Park lands—I always did so much prefer Cheviots to Blackfaces—and I am sure you will find that dark Mairi will have pity on you. She might not like the Sliaghmhor once it is planted with trees.'

But Alicky could only sit hunched on his chair, muttering, 'You canna understand, your Lady-ship, you canna understand. It's the life of me you're seeking to take from me and me no' dead.' He said aloud, 'I doubt I'm too old now, your Ladyship, to heft on new ground. I would aye be coming back in the spring, like an old ewe, to the hill I knew.

'You'd maybe no' believe me, your Ladyship, when I'm telling you that the very white hares in Glendruid know old Alicky Mag. Aye, when I would be sitting at the door of my house, playing a bit tune to myself on the fiddle, the white hares come bobbing down from the peat hags where they play thegither on the top of the high hills, and they sit up on the green turf by the river-side, their wee paws stretched out to catch the notes of the music as they fall; and the wild geese that's flying North, they will turn back over the hills to hear another tune from old Alicky Mag before they'll be flying away.

'You'll maybe no' believe me, your Ladyship, when I'm telling you I've a name for every single tree by the Druid's banks, and that there's a willow-tree that'll be bowing like a queen with a gold crown on her head to old Alicky Mag himself when he goes out among the sheep on a spring morning.

'As sure as I'm sitting here, your Ladyship, and you can believe it or not, but it's the truth I'm telling to you, your Ladyship, dark Mairi will be up there waiting on me on a summer's evening by the loch of the Sliaghmhor, aye at the same spot where the loch's shore is white as driven snow, and where you won't find anything but clean silver water over the white stone though you were searching a twelvemonth for it. And then dark Mairi, she will come walking in her bare feet over the quiet waters, all in a dress that's white at the top end and blue below— aye, like a white seagull above and the blue sea below, your Ladyship, and aye the quiet laugh on her bonnie face. And when she's come across the loch, your Ladyship—she'll be laying the fingers of her hand on the sleeve of my coat— just *here*—and when she does that, your Ladyship, thon daft old bodach of an Alicky Mag—the Glendruid puddock as some folks call him—he would not change places with a *King*!'

Lady Waterton told Alicky he must go. 'All talk tires me and some talk makes me very sad,' she said. 'Tell me, Alicky,' and she laid her hand withered from age upon his on which the skin had been withered from birth—laying her hand ever so gently upon his—'Tell me,' she said, 'do you ever play "Jenny, Catch Your Skirts Up" now? That *was* a fine tune to dance to!' She said she would do what she could for Alicky, and that Mr. Blake would let him know. Alicky left her, hope high in his heart.

She stayed. She could not move without assistance. She was so old. She would do what she could for Alicky Mag, and there was nothing she could do. It was nearly two thousand years since Christ had died. So much had happened since. Nowadays men were hands, and souls were only talked about on Sundays.

VIII

THE letter from Mr. Blake, the Dunblair man of business, fluttered down upon the floor. It was the first letter Alicky Mag had had for years, and the postman on his motor-cycle had brought it all the way up Glendruid from Lochend, brought it all the way up Glendruid to kill hope.

It had been such a fine morning, too, if a man had but the flicker of a hope in his heart—a mild February day—the hazel catkins yellow by the river's bank—a whaup calling softly over the valley a promise of warm days—the Druid soft and gentle in its flowing—a day of dress rehearsal for spring's splendours. But the warmth of the sun is nothing without hope.

The letter said in writing what Mr. Blake had said verbally before. Glendruid and the Sliagh-mhor had been sold to an Afforestation Company —there would be a delivery of the sheep stock at the May term—there was the offer of a shepherd's job on the Castle policies for Alicky Mag. Lady Waterton regretted that she could do no more. Mr. Blake trusted that Alicky would have the sheep in the best possible order for the delivery.

For, at the May term, the sheep would be gathered in to be sold at valuation, and then in the autumn they would be driven off the hills that were their home, down the glen, never to return. They would drive away the deer from the Sliaghmhor and slaughter all the white hares, so that the trees might grow unharmed. Glendruid and the Sliaghmhor would be hidden from sight in a forest of sighing trees. Lady Waterton regretted . . .

Alicky could not face the sorrow that lay before him. Memories—of a cuckoo calling to summer in the Pot of Glendruid—of duck falling down from the sky to stroke the loch's waters of the Sliaghmhor—of a fairy touch upon his sleeve —they flooded through the channels that fear had carved since childhood in the substance of his brain. He could not face that sorrow without help.

All day he sat as in a trance—the bottle before him. Sometimes he would sink his head upon his hands to sleep, and his dogs would whine about his feet, asking to be fed. All through the fine day he sat with the bottle before him, while outside, the laughing pageantry of spring's dress rehearsal passed unobserved. All day he sat draining his aid away, and by evening it was done. He could not face the coming night without help. Suppose the parade of ghosts should come stealing down Glendruid glen that night and he without help? He could not face the night without help—he must tramp down the glen to Lochend to seek it. He had no money—his wages were done—but Jimmy Mac-Bain, the licensed grocer in Lochend, would surely oblige him when he learnt the need.

Alicky set out for Lochend, lurching down the glen road, his two dogs whining at his heels. It might have been mid-winter or the height of summer's heat. He paid no heed to the costume of the seasons he so loved. His eyes were fixed on the white ribbon of the glen road, his mind was obsessed by the termination of his journey to Lochend. He must have help supposing he died for it.

When he reached Lochend the people were at their doors and windows, walking on the streets, because the February night was mild and fine. They hadn't enjoyed weather like that since September of the previous year. The people saw the dirty old shepherd in his dirty rags of clothes, his two lean and savage dogs—the brindled beardie dog and the old black bitch—padding like wolves at his heels. They saw the old man lurch and mumble to himself—the dirty, drunken little dwarf that he was! Aye—he had aye been the same since ever they could mind of. Aye, he had always been dirty, and drunken, without a civil word to anybody, thinking he could do just what he liked because the County said he was the only fiddler left in Argyll who kept the proper rhythm of a country dance tune. Who wanted to hear country dance tunes nowadays, anyway, except the County and the Girl Guides at the Musical Festival? There was the wireless now, wasn't there?—Aye, there he was going down the street to Jimmy MacBain's, the licensed grocer's. A shame if they gave him anything there. He'd had more than enough already. Aye—there were the bairns running after him—jeering at him. They'd better keep their distance or those wild-looking dogs would turn on them and tear out their throats. Now, where was the daftie bound for now?—Aye, he was nearly in the gutter that time!—Aye, he was going round the doctor's house to the kitchen. Now, what could he be seeking there? Did he hope to get a drink there? If a policeman came along he should be told. A disgrace— that's what it was—a public disgrace!

Alicky Mag stumbled past the green railings, past the meat-safe, to the kitchen where old Bella Pringle had lived until she died. In his ears the jeers of his escort of children were ringing—'Daftie, daftie! Ye're aye daft, are ye? Alicky Mag!'—He must escape from them, past the green railings to the kitchen of old Bella Pringle, where he would be safe. Nobody had ever dared to follow him there. He stumbled into his old sanctuary, and the two new maids there screamed, shouting at him to be gone. He wondered dully why anyone should seem to fear him when he was so afraid himself. Of course, he should have remembered that Bella Pringle had been dead these twenty years. He mumbled what he meant as an explanation and apology, but the maids screamed the more, shouting at him that he would get nothing there, and that if he wouldn't be gone they would phone for a policeman.

The mention of the police frightened Alicky Mag. He started to run. When he came out on to the street, men would have laid hands on him had they not feared his dogs, the brindled beardie dog and the old black bitch. He ran down the street and into a close between grey houses which led down to the sea. He would be safe there—he had always been safe—by the sea. Indeed, the children of Lochend soon tired of chasing him and of throwing stones from a safe distance at his dogs. After a little time only a few, more persistent in their daring or their cruelty, were behind him. Then they too tired of the game and were gone. Alicky was alone with his dogs on the Lochend shore.

On a February evening, none else was there. The white birds wheeled down over the slowly breaking waves as they had done for thousands of years that were gone and would do for thousands of years after a man and his fears had died. That comforted Alicky Mag as he trotted along the foreshore of Lochend, rejected by mankind. The sea and the hills would continue in their glory long after his agony was done. For hours he trotted beside the sea until the sounds and the sights of Lochend were gone, until dusk changed to darkness, until stars shone out in their myriads from a clear sky to prove that eternity was true.

For long Alicky walked by the quiet sea, and then he thought he would go home. He could have gone up over the rumbling shingle and then across the smooth sea turf to the road that runs by the loch to the mouth of Glendruid. But the unconscious memories of his childhood led him back along the shore, up through the close where once upon a time a dead seaman had been found with his pockets full of gold, up between the old grey houses to the High Street of Lochend. From there he would walk out of the town until he was safe again among the Glendruid hills.

The town was sleeping now—the streets so deserted—so quiet. It was dark too—with small pools of light on the pavement beneath the gently swaying lamps. Every now and again a light died in an upstairs window of one of the tall houses. Another day ended—another soul seeking rest. All along the quiet streets was the smell of the sea and the sound of the sea, and the whisper of a wind coming down from the hills.

Now and again footsteps of a man coming home late sounded monstrous in the street. Then a door slammed—close shut until morning. Soon Lochend would be quiet as the air before dawn, until the milk-carts came rattling in from the country over the cobbled streets of the town.

Alicky crept along the streets, keeping close to the concealing shelter of the walls, his dogs padding like unsubstantial shadows at his heels. He wanted now to escape from the town, unseen and unmolested, to feel the scent of the hill-herbs in the wind off the hills. He wanted to be out as quickly as he might without running, on the winding road among the hills. For did not happiness come to him only where streets ended and the hills began?

He wished he had stayed just a little longer by the sea. Then on his way home he would have found the whole town safely sleeping. He had come too early from the sea, for on his way through the lamp-lit High Street of Lochend a man passed him and then turned to stare; a policeman stepped out of a hidden doorway to watch where he might go. They seemed suspicious of a shepherd and his dogs stealing like shadows so late through the streets of a sleeping town.

But nobody was in sight when Alicky was passing the shop window of Jimmy MacBain. He was almost past the window, and then he stopped so suddenly that the beardie collie bumped snarling against his legs. The shop had been closed for hours and the blinds were down, but one corner of a blind had become twisted up and caught so that an angle of the window was exposed. Had it not been that Jimmy MacBain, the principal licensed grocer in Lochend, had recently engaged a new apprentice, Alicky Mag would never have stopped before the window on that February night. But the new apprentice was walking out with a girl who left him only the half of his mind, so that, thinking of other things, he had never noticed the rucking up of the blind and the exposure of the goods within his master's window. As for Jimmy MacBain, if his wife had not been ill and he anxious and hurrying home to her, he too would have paid his usual close attention to the closing of his shop. But the blind was tucked up and a row of whisky bottles exposed to the passer-by, and it was the sight of the bottles long after he had resigned himself to tramping homewards without aid, that made Alicky halt, all of a sudden, before the window of Jimmy MacBain's.

When Alicky saw the bottles, all the flood of bitterness and sorrow returned to his mind. He remembered what had brought him that evening from Glendruid to Lochend, help to dull his misery, help to deaden his fears should the parade of ghosts come stealing through the Druid's glen, help to forget his coming exile from the sleeping loch of the high Sliaghmhor. In his bitterness, his misery, his fear, he decided that whatever the consequences to himself might be, he must have aid to blunt his bitterness, to dull his misery, to deaden fear. And just as though somebody else had taken temporary command of his body and his brain, he felt his right arm raised and the stick it held crash through the plate-glass window of Jimmy MacBain's.

Alicky snatched the bottle that was nearest to him through the broken glass, and clutching it between his unbuttoned jacket and bare skin, ran away down the street that would take him the soonest out of the unfriendly town, and his two dogs padded like shadows at his heels. He heard the shouting of a man behind him, and the sound of an upstairs window in a neighbouring house flung open, but once he was round the corner, the long road to the friendly hills was under his racing feet.

Soon he was on the sea-loch road, and disturbed sea-birds were flying like moths before his face. He could hear the healing sough of the waves and feel the mist of the spray on his seaward cheek. Far out over the loch there must be a boat, for he could hear the faint clocking of rowlocks dying away.

It was all so peaceful on the sea-loch road. Alicky wondered what had come over him all

298

day, that he should have sat so long over the bottle, neglecting the sheep, that he should have set out without money to buy drink in a town, when towns were reserved for those who had money. He wondered what devil had possessed him, willing him to crime for the first time now that he was growing old.

Like pain returning after the effect of an opiate has passed, Alicky remembered it all— the dispersal of his sheep, his eviction from his home, his exile from Mairi and the Sliaghmhor. He hugged the bottle closer to his bare breast, hastening his walk, walking and running in turn until he was on the Glendruid road leading to his home. After all, he could not without help face the misery and fear of a lonely night.

At first he felt safe in his cottage. It was so lonely, all hidden away among the hills, that it seemed a place where the consequences of a crime might be forgotten, the crime itself excused. Once the fire was going and the dogs sleeping at his feet, the glass at his elbow and the fiddle on his knee, he could pass away an hour until sleep came over him. Perhaps when he slept he might dream of finding himself 'an t-each uisge—a handsome youth all in fine raiment, by the loch of the Sliaghmhor. He would settle down cosily by the fire until he grew heavy with sleep. He must get sleep that night and be out at daybreak among the sheep. He could not neglect them, poor beasties, two days in succession. But in the meantime he'd make himself cosy by the fireside, if only for an hour. Was it good whisky he had got from Jimmy MacBain? Of course he would pay Jimmy for the whisky and the window the very next time he had a pound in the house. Likely enough Jimmy would take it all as a joke, another ploy of old Alicky Mag's. Was it good whisky he had bought at Jimmy MacBain's?

The first taste brought Alicky back to reality. It was coloured water in a show bottle, not whisky at all. He had stolen it and broken a window in doing so, not bought it, and a broken plate-glass window would cost more pounds to repair than he was ever likely to have in the house. When people broke windows and stole in the High Streets of towns, then ran away, the police paid them a visit a little later on. The police would come to Glendruid a little later on. It wouldn't take them many minutes in a fast car. They might be coming at any minute. They might be on the road now.

'Wheest, dogs! Can ye no' let a body listen?'

IX

ALICKY sat by his fireside, waiting. Had he been seen? Would they come after him, up the glen, following him like hounds snuffling the bloody trail of a wounded beast? Would they come for him? What would they do with him if they should come? Would they drag him away to asylum or to prison? Would they brand him criminal or mad? Or would they give him another chance? Would they warn him, listen to his promises and explanations and then be friends? Perhaps if they found him playing the bagpipes or the fiddle they might let him be. They might say then, as men had said before, 'Aye, he's daft right enough—a dirty, daft old man—but he's a grand hand at the fiddle and the pipes. Listen to him while he's fit to give us a tune—for he canna last long the way he's going on. Let him alone, there's not many like him left in the countryside.' Yes, it would be better to be playing a tune—*if* they came for him—*when* they came for him. He brought out his pipes and laid them on the table beside him. The police would think more of the bagpipes than of a fiddle—they had a pipe band of their own. He would be playing a grand tune for them—if they came.

Wheest! Was that a sound out there on the road? Hold your noise, dogs, can ye no' let a body listen! Damn the clock, can it no' bide still and let a body listen! Ach! it's nothing at all but the wind in the willows by the river-side. Wheest! What was that again? Would nothing be still that he might listen?

He went to the door, opening it gradually, cautiously lest anyone were there. The night was still—the river rippling gently as in summer —branches of trees sighing—all still—not a sound on the road.

Perhaps, after all, he hadn't been seen in Loch-end. Perhaps, after all, the shouts he had heard there were just the bairns jeering after him again, calling him daftie. If they *were* coming for him they would come for him that night, they would not leave such a fine game over until morning. If daylight dawned and they had not come for him he would be safe. Why was the daylight so long in coming? Why was the night so dark outside?

What if they should come! Would they put hands on him, dragging him away? He could not stand that—to have strong, crushing hands laid upon him. It would be like the horror of school he had so barely missed—running, running, towards the high playground railings, his legs useless as pillows, his heart bursting from fear. Would they lay hands that hurt upon his shrinking flesh, dragging him down the glen road, through the jeering people of Lochend, and each man turning towards his neighbour saying, 'Aye, I knew fine what would be the end of it all. Aye, he's brought it on himself right enough this time. He couldna go on the rate that he was going.' They might take him away and shut him up, and he could not bear to be shut up. He would die, beating against the walls to get air.

Wheest! What was thon? — The brindled beardie dog rose slowly from its place beside the fire, rose very slowly, all its muscles tense, its lips curling upwards and backwards like red india-rubber over its white fangs. Far back in its throat it growled.

Wheest! What was thon? Be quiet, dogs! be quiet, clock! be quiet, *everything!* What was thon?

Alicky heard a car coming up the glen. Peering through the window he saw the searchlight of a car's headlamps sweep round into the glen. They were coming for him sure enough.

Alicky heard the car stop and the sound of men laughing together on the road, yes, laughing. Why should he be so afraid when the men who were coming to take him away were laughing together, treating his theft as a joke? Everything would be all right after all. They would tell him that they would let him be this once if he would promise never to leave Glendruid again so long as he should live. Was not that what he wanted? Was not that all he asked for? To be left quiet and alone until he should die?

Wheest! They were coming up to the house now. Someone had stumbled over the fallen gate. He must play them a tune now, a tune that would make them friendly towards him, clapping him on the back, telling him there wasn't his equal as a piper in the whole of Argyll. He would play them a march, the tune he played to salute the mistress of the house at the end of a hot day's clipping in the month of July. He would play them 'The Red and Blue Hackle.' He reached for his pipes, and before the men were at the door the surge of the melody and the skirling of the drones drowned the dogs' fierce barking.

The door swung open. There was a policeman standing there, no laughter on his face at all. He shouted out, 'Put down those pipes, man, and come quietly or it will be the worse for you!'— and the brindled collie dog flew at his throat.

Alicky rested his pipes on the table. The time for music, for the making of friends, was past. He heard the angry shouts and oaths of men running back down the garden path. He heard that, and the snarling, worrying sound of a dog at grips with its enemy. He heard the car reverse and drive off down the glen, and the beardie dog crept whimpering into the cottage, its head twisted horribly to one side because its right ear had been beaten in by a blow from a heavy boot. And Alicky thought that the men would never dare come for him again. They would surely leave him alone now. There had been enough trouble caused already over an old bodach like himself that never meant anyone harm. Aye, they would leave him alone after this. After a time he would forget about it all, the danger and the deadly fear of it all. It was February now. March—April—and then May—with the lambs on the hills—the cutag in the Pot—the snow gone from the track to the Sliaghmhor. March—April—May—and the touch of spring-cool fingers on his sleeve. Two more months of winter and waiting, and then peace.

Alicky washed the blood from the beardie collie's head, soothing the beast's dumb agony, talking quietly to the dog as though it were a hurt child. Then he took off his clothes to go to bed, for he thought that unless he got some sleep now he would be useless among the sheep in the morning. He fell asleep watching the glow of the dying fire, and when he slept he dreamt of the Sliaghmhor. . . .

Everything happened so quickly that Alicky had no time to think or fear. He awakened to hear the swift rushing of feet all round the house, the door that he never locked burst open, the roar of explosions and the howl of the dogs. Then everything was still.

Alicky peered out over the edge of the box-bed, tapping the floor with his fingers in search of clothes. When he had been a boy he had worn his day shirt during night as Archie Campbell had told him to do, but long ago the last of his shirts had worn into rags and he had never bought new ones. Alicky slept naked, and now the light of lanterns shone in upon his privacy and his nakedness.

The room was bright lit from the light of lanterns, and Alicky saw the police and other men standing at the door. He saw the body of his beardie collie stretched dead before the fire, and the still-twitching body of his old black bitch huddled under the table whither she had fled— poor old bitch that would wag her tail at the sound of any human voice.

Alicky crept out over the edge of his bed, whimpering, 'My God! what have they done to the poor beasts!' and then he saw his old enemy of sheep-gatherings—Jock MacCulloch, head keeper to the Dunblair estates, stepping forward from the group of police and other men — pulling the ends of his huge moustache — peering forward. And Jock MacCulloch said, 'What like mark is thon stamped on the old bodach's back?' But the policeman, without answering Jock MacCulloch, told Alicky to put on his clothes quickly and to come.

Now was the time for Alicky to crack jokes

and put them all in good humour, changing their angry enmity to tolerant contempt. Now was the time to make one of his old jokes about Jock MacCulloch's bush of a moustache—one of the old thin jokes that always raised a laugh among the herds. If only he had had a dram he could have made them laugh and all would have been well. But without a dram he felt so small and so weak, so naked and ashamed, and Jock MacCulloch had asked, 'What like mark is thon on the old bodach's back?' He felt so ashamed pulling on his ragged clothes while a dozen eyes pierced the secrets of his nakedness before they could be hid. He could feel what the men were thinking, 'Well, and is *that* what the puddock looks like without his clothes?'—God in Heaven! would his shaking, fumbling fingers never tie his clothes together? Would he die of fear and shame before he was clad? Ah! now the worst of his shame was over—he was ready to go.

Jock MacCulloch said, 'What's the bodach done with the whisky he stole? I could do with a dram. I could never stand the sight of an object. It puts me off my sleep for weeks. I canna get it out of my mind. Where's the bottle, Alicky Mag?'

Alicky tried to explain that there was none in the house, but what between fear and shame he could not find words to fit his tongue. He mumbled like an imbecile with a cleft palate.

Jock MacCulloch sneered, 'Ach! the bodach's too fou to speak.'

But the police-sergeant stepped forward quickly from the group about the door. 'The old man's going to faint. Here, Alicky boy, take a dram from my flask here. It'll put you right in a second, boy. This has been a gey hard night on you, Alicky Mag.'

The very suspicion of kindness was too much for Alicky. He muttered out blessings on the sergeant, using the old Gaelic words he had heard the *cailleachs* use—*Mhoolie matail—mhoolie matail!* He felt the hot tears racing down his cheeks. He sobbed brokenly like a penitent bairn. He clutched the sergeant's flask and went on drinking so long from it that the men laughed at him.

Aye! That was better! He was safer when men laughed at him. The dram had done him good. He was feeling a man again. He would go quietly with them, giving no trouble at all, making fun. He would go quietly with them to Lochend and in the morning everything would come right. He must not expect too much from life now after this. He would just have to be content with the Cheviot flock in the Castle parks. He would get an old quiet dog that would give nobody any trouble and would do an in-bye herding fine. He wouldn't touch drink except maybe at sheep gatherings and at markets. He would do what he could to teach the fiddle to the factor. He would try to please everybody and give trouble to none. Perhaps no more than twice in the year, on the fine summer days, he would take a day off to make a pilgrimage to the loch of the Sliaghmhor among the newly-planted trees—just once or twice in the year until he should die.

Yes, he would go quietly now. He had never meant to do anything else. He had never thought the beardie collie could be so wild. The beast wasn't used to strangers, seeing so few in the glen. Yes, he would go quietly now and everything would be all right again in the morning. It wasn't so long until summer now— February—March—April—May.

Perhaps they would be gentler with him if they knew he was an educated man. The police-sergeant might not have heard that he was an educated man. So he said to the sergeant in his affected, Englified, high-pitched voice:

'You might not think to look at me that I'm an eddicated man and can speak in the Latin tongue.' The silly, meaningless jangle of Latin words returned to his mind, the only Latin he could ever remember, the only Latin he would never forget—

A, ab, absque, coram, de,
Palam, clam, cum, ex or e,

as they led him away to the waiting car.

X

THEY put Alicky away for they called him mad.
They took away from him his whisky and his
work. They kept him from the sheep he loved.
He was denied the hills and the sea, bird-song
and the changing seasons. They took away his
bagpipes and his fiddle, his means of music, his
keys to the sympathy and companionship of men.
They kept him away from the loch of the
Sliaghmhor where, in the evenings, the duck
stroke the water with the down of their breasts,
where dark Mairi that had died so many years
before would steal quietly to him across the
waters, bringing him peace. They put him
away, and there very shortly he died, proclaiming
to the end that he was an educated man. He
died there, and the unequal struggle was at an
end—the unequal struggle of his soul against the
world, the unequal struggle that began so long
before in a woman's agony of fear on a lonely
winter's night of snow. His struggle was ended,
for say what you will of it, death brings peace.

And now in Glendruid—! Sometimes on a
winter's night a parade of ghosts come stealing

through the Druid's glen. The cry that starts
as a whisper from a slit in the rocks at the head
of the glen, a wind out of nowhere stirring the
tops of the trees new-planted there, sweeping on
through the glen to the arms of the hidden sea.
The sound of the galloping horses—the strange
pipe music—the forgotten Gaelic—the shuffling
of brogued feet on heather and grass—the cries
of the homeless, the crackle of flames and the
Devil that sneers 'Progress' and is gone—all
these were heard in the Glen of the Druid no
more than a year ago.

And in the ruins of the shepherd's cottage in
the glen, the ruins that soon will be hidden from
the moss-covered road by the growing trees, men
have seen a light burning late into the night,
and have heard the strains of an old-fashioned
fiddle playing an old-fashioned tune. Can it be
'Jenny, Catch Your Skirts Up' that is heard?
For the tune that is played is a merry, merry
tune, or so folks say.

Should you ever trace your way by the forgotten track to the Sliaghmhor, you will find the
calm waters of the loch set amongst the concealing trees. You will see the duck stroke the sleeping waters of the loch with the soft down upon
their breasts. You will find the corner of the
shore where the rock is white quartz and where
no water weeds grow. And if it be a summer
evening and you lie among the heather so very

still that the bumble-bees suck honey from the spray you hold, then you may see a tall girl and a dwarf boy running races together by the loch's quiet shore. They run up and down the loch-side, laughing together, and happy together through all eternity—or so folks say.

But who can really say for sure? For when the owls hoot out from the trees that enfold the loch of the Sliaghmhor in a chaplet of evergreen, a trout may rise ever so lazily to the surface of the still waters. You hear the splash and turn to watch the ripples grow, and when you look back on the shore the girl and the boy, the tall dark girl and the squat dwarfed boy, have gone romping and laughing, laughing and romping, away and away. And you have no chance of seeing them again that night—or so folks say.